WHITE HATS

HATS

STORIES OF THE
U.S. NAVY BEFORE
WORLD WAR II

Floyd Beaver

THE GLENCANNON PRESS

MARITIME BOOKS

PALO ALTO
1999

Art Director: S.L. Hecht

Copyright © 1999 by Floyd Beaver
Published by The Glencannon Press
P.O. Box 341, Palo Alto, CA 94302
Tel. 1-800-711-8985

First Edition, first printing.

Library of Congress Cataloging-in-Publication Data

Beaver, Floyd.
   White hats : stories of the U.S. Navy before World War II / Floyd
Beaver.
        p.   cm.
   ISBN 1-889901-11-3 (alk. paper)
   1. United States--History, Naval--Fiction.   2. United States.
Navy--History--Fiction.   3. Sea stories, American.   4 War stories,
American.   I. Title
PS3552.E235W48   1999
813'.54--dc21   98-44140
                                                            CIP

Dedication

To Irons and Mike and Gary and David and Barbara.

By the same author:

The Homeward Bounder and Other Sea Stories

Contents

FOREWORD

For generations of Navy sailors — American and foreign alike — stories often constituted all there was of entertainment and recreation aboard their ships. Away for years at a time and largely apart from normal human contacts even when in home ports, sailors in their isolation prized good stories and became adept in the arts of their telling.

Those arts are much diminished in the modern Navy, I suppose. The introduction of moving pictures — and now television and videos — with their polished technologies and expensive talents have put to rest the simpler stories of the past.

But, although the old story tellers could not compete against the seduction of Hollywood's epic scope, brilliant color, and bosomy heroines for lusty young seamen, the victory of technology has not been entirely a gain. Something of value was lost with the passing of the old spinners of yarns.

There still must be, here and there and now and then, some who remember what such stories — and the men who told them — were like. Some who remember and appreciate the part they played in maintaining that store of common knowledge and shared tradition which lies so solidly at the base of all Navies and of all men who go to sea.

For those old enough to remember, the stories in this book may stir bittersweet memories of what once was. For those not yet that old, they may break new ground in bringing to mind that small subclass of men who, of their own free will, chose to spend their lives in the Navy, set apart as they were from much of that which conventional society considered normal and right for men in the period between the Wars.

As late as 1897 — not all that long before the era in which these stories are set — the United States Supreme Court reflected the popular general view of sailors by ruling that "Seamen are . . . deficient in that full and intelligent responsibility for their acts that is accredited to ordinary adults."

The Court was talking about merchant seamen, but except for a brief hiatus during World War I when sailors of both persuasions were found to be useful after all, the American general public lumped Navy and merchant seamen much alike into one denigrated subclass of society.

There were places in American towns and cities where Navy sailors in uniform were not welcomed, or even admitted. Richard McKenna, writer of the magnificent Navy novel *The Sand Pebbles* and himself a former machinist's mate, cited in a later (nonfiction) book the case of a Chief Petty officer who sued a Newport, Rhode Island, restaurant for denying him admission while in uniform.

Although the infamous signs ordering "Sailors and Dogs, Keep Off the Grass" in Norfolk, Virginia, Canton, China, and other Navy towns were later officially pronounced apocryphal, Navy sailors were familiar with the sentiment and firmly believed the signs existed. They knew all too well that respectable people found Navy sailors unacceptable as companions for their daughters or as guests in their homes. It was easy under those conditions for sailors to accept their linkage with stray dogs and behave accordingly.

With the coming of the Great Depression in the Thirties, the dearth of civilian jobs and the narrowing of the gap between civilian and Navy pay eased this prejudice against sailors somewhat, but acts of discrimination against enlisted sailors persisted until our entry into World War II when fear-based patriotism came again to the defense of lowly white hats.

They were never many in number, the men of the regular U.S. Navy in those years. In 1935 the Navy counted only 82,500 enlisted men. As late as 1937, with the buildup towards World War II already under way, there were still only 100,000 to man the entire Navy and the new ships then beginning to join the Fleet. There were times when even combat ships sailed with no more than seventy-five to eighty percent of their authorized crews on board, making it occasionally impossible for some ships to fire all their guns at the same time.

During the first part of this period the United States enjoyed an uneven but generally good economy in which jobs were plentiful and civilian pay very much greater than that of enlisted Navy sailors. Those men who chose to join or remain in the regular Navy were viewed by their civilian countrymen as somehow deficient in intelligence and lacking in that greatest of American virtues: ambition.

To pass up the comfort and prosperity so readily available on the outside for the deprivations and restrictions of Navy life was seen by many as an affront to common sense.

Nevertheless, some men, of their own choice, spent their lives behind the steel walls of the Navy's ships and the chain link fences of its stations, preferring the camaraderie and familiarity of this life.

For present generations this world of the white hats may seem improbably hard, often profane, cruel and politically incorrect, but it was their world and the one in which they lived and often died.

Told in the first person, the stories which follow are written in a conscious effort to recapture the idiom, rhythm and color of stories their writer heard many years ago in ships of the American and British Navies. They will be best enjoyed if visualized as being told aloud by an old sailor in the midst of a small group of his mates — preferably young and impressionable mates who will be not too demanding of fact nor expectant of literary formality.

All too often, it sometimes seems, the history of any period is told as little more than a cold listing of dates and numbers and great events. It is only when this hard white light of fact is passed through the prism of living memory that the full color of a history is known and its participants come to life.

It is to provide that revealing prism that these stories have been written of the Navy sailors and their ships who were holders of the flame through the lean years, and whose experience and presence served as an invaluable foundation for the great fleets which won World War II for America and what was then called the Free World.

These stories are all fiction, of course. Their events are events which might have happened to any man of those times and places but which, in their details, probably happened to no man. The particular fact that they happened to Navy men is coincidental to their truth as stories of all men who lived in ships.

Now that the ships of that era are gone, and the men who sailed them slipping ever more swiftly away on memory's inexorable ebb, it is hoped that they will be remembered in even so modest a form as this.

Floyd Beaver
Mill Valley, California

LANDING FORCE

Drawn, as they were, from every part of the country, and from families who made their living in every imaginable — and some not imaginable — trade and occupation, Navy sailors had some pretty exotic skills and experience to draw upon when needed. But, I never knew anyone with odder skills than those of Everett Matuszak, nor anyone who drew upon them with greater effect in his running battle with officers.

Well, a guy I knew once who worked on a Clydesdale stud farm might have had an odder job. His stories about how the massive Clydesdale mares were made ready for the stud almost made you sick to your stomach, but I don't think he ever found any real use for that particular art in the Navy. But Matuszak did find a way to use his.

Matuszak's father was a radical union Shop Steward in the big Brown Shoe Company factory in St. Louis. He bred into

1

his son both a distrust for and an emotional reaction to authority which kept the boy in constant trouble with the discipline and regulations of the Navy. And, of all the things which bugged Matuszak, Landing Force was probably first on the list.

"If I had wanted to be a God-damned soldier, I would have joined the God-damned Army," he blurted when told that was his assignment for the next couple of years. Although we might not all have been so profane about it, just about all of us agreed with Matuszak about the charms of duty with the ship's Landing Force.

Once Boot Camp was behind us, most of us never wanted to see a rifle or a bayonet again in our lives. Most of all, and sure as hell, we did not want to be doing any more marching in canvas leggings, and that is what the Landing Force did. They also sometimes jumped out of boats into surf and ran to the tops of some pretty tall and rocky hills.

The Navy, however, as it so often did in matters of white hat preferences saw things differently. Before the War, Navy ships had Landing Forces. Maybe they still do. Ostensibly, they were small units of men put ashore in times of trouble to fight as infantry in the protection of American lives and property in foreign lands. Although given only rudimentary training in landing and infantry tactics, they sometimes did just that in places like China or Latin America.

But, most often, Landing Forces were put ashore to make look-see pidgin in such emergencies as Fourth of July, Navy Day, or American Legion Convention parades whether in foreign lands or not. That is what, in Matuszak's telling words, "frosted our balls."

Since the duty was so detested, it fell, in the natural course of events, to the most junior members of a ship's crew. A bare minimum of senior petty officers ever enjoyed the exercise, and even fewer officers. One of the petty officers who did go, though, was a signalman. There always had to be a signalman, with rolled semaphore flags stuck in his leggings.

Of course, it could be a junior signalman, and that is how Matuszak came to be in our Landing Force. He was the newest rated man on the bridge, second only to me. He had come to us from a destroyer and was not used to all the look-see pidgin that goes on in a major flagship.

Matuszak put in part of an apprenticeship in the shoe factory before joining the Navy. This not only left him something of a hardhead in his relations with authority, it also left him with some skills in regard to shoes which led to one of the few, if petty, triumphs I ever saw a white hat score over an officer. And it was a *Marine* officer, at that.

Cruisers and other major Fleet units then carried Marine Detachments who manned part of the five-inch battery, served as orderlies and handled a lot of the ceremonial ritual of Navy protocol. Their officers sometimes qualified for and stood officer of the deck watches. Captain Earl Malone, commanding officer of our Marine Detachment, was such a watchstander. And that is what led to Matuszak's brush with him.

Malone was a particularly hard-nosed example of a hard-nosed breed. Had an artist wanted to draw an archtypical Marine Officer he would need only photograph Malone and be done with it. He was tall, always impeccably tailored and shod, physically hard as an athlete, and encased in an arrogant military dignity proof against anything I ever saw him meet. Except for what Matuszak did to him. In fact, it was that dense military dignity which was the captain's Achilles heel and which left him vulnerable to Matuszak. A more balanced man would not have been bothered much at all by what Matuszak did.

One of the many oddments of Naval life is the way in which men — especially officers — pick up nicknames. Academy officers are especially vulnerable to the disease. Admiral Stark, Chief of Naval Operations before the War, for instance, answered to the warlike nickname of "Betty" from his Academy days.

I no longer remember Captain Malone's Academy nickname. White Hats seldom learned officers' nicknames in the first place, except by chance. Certainly, they never used them in front of the officers themselves. But I do remember the nickname Captain Malone wore in the Fleet after Matuszak got through with him. If he is still alive, he probably remembers it, too.

We were a cruiser flagship in the old Hawaiian Detachment, which meant we saw more in the way of ceremony and look-see pidgin than an ordinary ship on an ordinary assignment would have done. Our old man — and the admiral, too, for that matter — liked to send his Landing Force ashore for parades and other shows for the locals. I always thought it a truism that the older officers get — and the less likely they would have to march themselves — the more they like to see other men march.

Anyway, we had a more active Landing Force than most ships, but all ships had prescribed training to do. There was even an annual review on Pearl's grassy, tree-bordered parade ground to determine which ship had the best Landing Force.

Usually, Landing Force was just a nuisance, but sometimes it was not pleasant at all. I remember going out to the Army's firing range at Oahu's Barber's Point one time to fire our old Springfield rifles. Although the Springfields were good and extremely accurate guns, they had a recoil like a sledge hammer. Black eyes and split lips were standard for guys coming back from firing practice, but firing at Barber's Point had an additional hazard as well.

The sand there, as it is in much of the Hawaiian Islands, is coral, and coral sand is both hard and sharp. Our uniform of the day at the time was white pants and skivvy shirts, which meant elbows were bare. This was pleasant enough for the hot ride out through Hawaii's mesquite-like algarobe trees on the Coast Artillery's dinky narrow-gauge railroad, but it was not pleasant at all when we flopped down for prone firing and supported our rifles on our elbows in the sand.

Every time we pulled a trigger, our elbows were jolted back an inch or so, leaving just about that much skin ground into the gritty coral sand. A tarp spread on the ground would have solved the whole problem, but that is not the Navy's way. There would be no tarps spread in a fight with a real enemy, you see.

All that was hard enough for Matuszak, but Captain Malone had nothing to do with it. Marine officers did not go ashore with the Landing Force.

Malone had nothing to do with the Navy Day parade we put on in Hilo that year, either. Those of us in the Landing Force had all the fun of marching in the hot Hawaiian sun, while our liberty party was enjoying whatever there was to be enjoyed in Hilo.

We were the only Navy ship present. Ordinarily, it was fun to be alone in an out-island port like that. This was all well before the time of resort hotels and jet airplanes. There might not be much to do, but there were not many sailors trying to do it, either. Hilo was then a small plantation and sugar mill town with not much in the way of bars or other white hat recreation. Plantation owners of the time did not encourage drinking on the part of their workers. There were, as I recall, three or four open-air shacks where *okoolehau*, a hazardous island booze made from sugar cane, and local beer, could be bought, but that was about all. Except for some free-lancing bootleggers.

But, whatever Hilo had, it beat the hell out of walking around under a Springfield rifle with cartridge belt and bayonet scabbard grinding sweat stains into your whites that would be hard to scrub clean later.

Hilo did have two whorehouses, maintained, I suppose, for the Filipino and Japanese field hands working the surrounding plantations, few of whom had women of their own on the island. The houses, low wood frame structures half-buried under trees and other rank tropical growth, were painted the drab green nearly everything else in the Islands was painted then. Oddly, but logically, they were named for the colors of the staggering picket fences in front of them — the Red Fence and the Green Fence. We called them Port and Starboard for the colors of the running lights ships show when underway at night.

It didn't help our mood worth a damn that our parade route passed in front of both houses. It helped even less to have the guys from the liberty party calling out from open windows

5

and doors to give us brief, but exciting, word of what was available and going on inside.

Our officers called for silence in the ranks, but the guys in the whorehouses took the reasonable position that *they* were not in ranks and kept up a running commentary, with some gestures, for as long as we could hear them.

By the time the parade was over and we were back aboard ship and had turned in our gear to the armory, there was not much point in trying to go ashore. We sailed that night without ever learning anything worthwhile about the Port and Starboard whorehouses of Hilo. The guys who learned something about them went to great lengths to tell us what we missed, but that wasn't the same at all.

But Marine Captain Malone had nothing to do with any of that. It was not until after our landing exercise on Kahoolawe that he became involved. And then, only indirectly.

Kahoolawe is a small Hawaiian island lying between the two larger islands of Maui and Lanai. It was uninhabited, except for a few wild goats. The Navy used it for a bombing and shelling range, and for Landing Force exercises. Although not large, it rises more than a thousand feet above the sea. A thousand feet of very hard and sharp and hot bomb and shell fragments and splinters of shattered rock. Anything vegetable on the island had lots of stickers on it. Kahoolawe fell well short of being the lush, picture postcard tropical island.

Our assignment that day was to land on the beach, charge up that God-damned thousand foot hill — and come back down again. It made as much sense as a lot of other stuff we did in the Navy, but not much more.

We didn't have combat fatigues, of course. We did wear the old dishpan steel helmets from the Great War, but our other clothing was skivvy shirts and white pants, with canvas leggings over standard low-cut Navy shoes. None of it offered much in the way of protection from Kahoolawe's hard surfaces.

We wore field packs, empty, thank God, and there were no clips in our cartridge belts, but we carried a canteen of water and our rifles and bayonets. That was plenty to carry up a thousand feet of tropical rockpile. We did not expect it to be much fun.

Another thing which made the exercise interesting was that we did not have special landing craft with nice ramps to let us step off into shallow water. We used our regular motor launches, the same ones that were used for liberty parties and other ship's work. The problem with them for landing over beaches was that they had deep forefeet (lower portion of the boat's stem).

This was made more significant by the fact that coral sand beaches are sometimes remarkably steep-to. Kahoolawe's sure as hell was. When the launch's bow grounded forward, the after part of the boat was still in several feet of water. And, since we went over the side wherever we sat in the boat, some of us, packs, rifles and all, found ourselves gasping and sputtering, over our heads in salt water full of surf-churned sand.

The boat's coxswain could keep it from broaching — swinging broadside onto the beach — only by gunning the engine and throwing full rudder, right and left, to hold his bow against the sand by brute power alone. This meant that those of us in the water had a nice shiny bronze propeller whirling amongst us, threatening to chop us into little pieces.

Anyway, we did get ashore. Those who landed over the bows were wet only waist high or so, but the rest of us were soaked from head to foot. And as we floundered in the dry sand of the beach, and took cover as ordered by our earnest young ensign landing officer, we found ourselves coated with sand.

That was not pleasant, but it didn't hurt much. The sand in our shoes did, though.

In swimming, sloshing and wading through the roiled surf water, we managed to fill our shoes with sharp coral sand. Our shoes were the ordinary low-cut black shoes we wore in the ship. The canvas leggings we laced over them did damned little to keep out the sand.

The result was like walking in loose socks made of emery paper. Our feet, rasped bare and exposed to the soothing effect of salt water on raw meat, led to commentary both loud and profane.

A thousand feet may not sound like much, but when it is damned near straight up and covered with hot rocks and shell fragments — and with your shoes full of coral sand — it is enough.

The ensign would not let us sit down and empty the sand from our shoes. A real enemy would not have let us sit down and empty our shoes, would he? No, we had to "take" the God-damned hill — which no one in his right mind would want anyway.

We got to the top of the God-damned hill, puffing and blowing and pulling at our canteens. The ensign had Matuszak semaphore word of our tremendous victory out to the ship which looked surprisingly small in the distance.

The ensign was good enough to let us rest for a while before starting back down again to where the boat was lying off, waiting for us. The ensign also had sense enough to sit somewhat apart from us in order to have a reason for not hearing some of the things being said about the kind of brains it must take to order something like what we had just done.

Going back down the God-damned hill proved to be almost as painful as coming up it. It was not so much hard physical work, since gravity was on our side going down, but our feet hurt even more. The sand in our shoes had time to bite deep. By the time we were back in the boat and coming alongside the ship's port gangway, we were all pretty well worn down and not thinking all that straight.

That proved to be our undoing. I was the first guy up the gangway. Matuszak was right behind me. We were carrying our rifles *At the Trail* which meant we held them in our right hands at the forward end of the sling, muzzle up and butt aft. It is a handy way of carrying a gun in close quarters, such as on a gangway, but we seldom came aboard under arms.

It is a Navy ritual that men returning to their ships first salute the colors aft, then the officer of the deck. Normally, you do it by stopping and facing aft to hand salute the colors, then turning to face the officer of the deck and render to him his due in the same way.

Tired as I was, and not thinking well at all, I shifted my rifle to my left hand and saluted smartly with the right. And, tired as *they* were, the guys coming up behind me followed my stupid example. At least seven or eight of them did. The rest were smart enough to do the thing right, but they were behind me and I didn't notice what anyone else was doing.

The ship was not anchored. She was simply lying to, dead in the water, waiting to retrieve the boat. Ordinarily, that would have meant the officer of the deck watch would have been on the bridge. But this time, for whatever reason, Marine Captain Earl Malone was on the quarterdeck to receive us, white gloves, regulation telescope and all, pretty and dignified as ever.

And that is how he came to get on Matuszak's shit list. Spit and polish all to hell and gone, and without saying a word, Malone motioned me to stand to one side. I and Matuszak and the next seven or eight guys got the same unspoken but imperious order. We fell in alongside the port catapult silo, standing at parade rest, rifles again in our right hands.

"At attention," Captain Malone snapped at us.

And there we stood, feet bleeding, whites dirty and stiff with dried salt water and caked sand, confused and bewildered, while the entire God-damned Landing Force filed aboard and went below for their showers and clean, dry clothes. Guys going about their business in the ship looked at us and grinned. They didn't know what terrible sin we had committed, but it is a fact of white hat life that seeing someone else punished is funny.

It must have been around one-thirty or two o'clock in the afternoon when we returned aboard. Our ship was waiting for the return of the other boats which had gone in after us. And that God-damned Malone kept us standing at attention the whole time until his watch ended at four o'clock. Most of the time, he completely ignored us, bothering only to snap "You are at attention!" if one of us happened to relax even an inch.

By that time, I figured out what I did wrong. In watching the other guys salute properly as they came aboard, I remembered how I saluted. The proper salute under arms *At the Trail* is to leave the rifle in the right hand and to bring the left

9

smartly across, palm down, at the stacking swivel. It was easy as hell, and we all knew how to do it.

It didn't help at all to realize what was happening was my own damned fault. I stood, soiled and hurting, in front of God and everyone for doing something the rawest boot would know better than to do.

The other guys were not all that happy with me, either. They stood there only because they did what they saw me do. I had been in the Navy longer than any of them. I was supposed to know better, for Christ's sake.

After about thirty or forty minutes the quartermaster of the watch took a telephone call and told Malone that the Armory reported eight rifles missing. Eight happened to be the number of us standing at attention on the quarterdeck. Malone did not grin at us — his God-damned military dignity would not permit that — but his eyes narrowed a bit as he looked at us. The son-of-a-bitch was enjoying himself.

"Tell the Armory the missing rifles are on board," he ordered the quartermaster. "They will be returned shortly."

Given our available options, there was not a hell of a lot we could do. We fell back upon the white hat's ultimate response: when rape is inevitable, relax and enjoy it. When Malone was busy, or when he moved out of earshot, we could even talk out of the sides of our mouths if we were careful.

"You see the shoes that son-of-a-bitch is wearing?" Matuszak said once.

"Yeah. What about them?" Anything Malone wore would naturally be the best, but I saw nothing about his shoes that was any more remarkable than anything else in his uniform. They shined like glass, of course, and they looked to be a little redder than regulation Marine officers' shoes, but I could see nothing else noteworthy about them.

"They're cordovan," Matuszak said.

"What the hell is cordovan?"

"It's the best leather in the world for shoes," Matuszak said. "It comes off the hindquarters of horses."

"That figures," I said bitterly. "Off one horse's ass onto another."

Before Matuszak could reply, Malone's relief reported. And, after the brief exchange which goes with the changing of a watch, Malone came over to us. "You people know what a rifle salute is?" he said.

We all agreed that we did, indeed.

"Very well, then. Fall out and return your weapons to the Armory," Malone ordered. He didn't say another word, and nothing else was ever said about the matter. I think seven of the eight of us accepted the reality of Navy life and forgot all about it — remembering only to salute properly the next time we came aboard under arms.

We all forgot, except that is, for Matuszak. Matuszak did not forget for one God-damned minute. But there was not a hell of a lot he could do about it. Or so I thought.

The Armory gunner's mates had some interesting things to say about the condition of our rifles as we checked them in. Salt water and coral sand are no better for rifles than they are for white hats' shoes. But the guns had not been fired, and cleaning guns was what gunner's mates got paid for.

Some of the guys simply threw away their shoes. Salt water made the leather hard and inflexible, but Matuszak showed us how to save them if we were willing to work a little. He showed us how to soak them in a bucket of fresh water while we showered, and how to knead them with saddle soap. (Don't ask me where he got saddle soap on a Navy cruiser.)

Anyway, while we were squatting on the washroom deck and working with our shoes, I asked Matuszak about cordovan leather again.

"Makes the best God-damned shoes in the world," he said. "You see the ones Malone was wearing?"

"Yeah. "

"You see how they shined? Deep shine, not like that patent leather look you see sometimes. I'd give my right nut for a pair of shoes like that. Only thing is, they can squeak like a son of a bitch if they're not made right."

Mess call sounded then, and we put our shoes to soak in a corner while we had supper. I never gave another thought to what Matuszak said.

White hats are not allowed into the part of the ship where officers live. That is called Officers' Country and we were not to defile it with our presence, unless summoned by an officer. The only exception is that, in extremely heavy weather, we were sometimes allowed to go to and from the bridge through Officers' Country.

An ordinary rainstorm was not enough. It had to be a real bitch kitty, with boarding seas and screaming winds making passage of the weather decks not only uncomfortable, but literally dangerous.

We ran into weather like that one time about six hundred miles northeast of Pearl. That part of the Pacific is usually well-behaved, but it wasn't, then. We lost all four of our catapult airplanes, for example, and suffered a good deal of other damage. It was so bad, in fact, that we were allowed to pass through Officers' Country to and from our bridge watches.

The long passageways of Officers' Country were strangely quiet. Closed doors lined either side, much like the doors in a good hotel. For light, there was only the dim blue glow of standing lights. The storm sounds of wind and sea were muted. Only the thrashing about of the ship reminded me of the violence going on outside. I had to put out a hand sometimes to balance myself against the motion.

But the strangest thing I remember in Officers' Country was the shoes. Beside all the doors, pairs of shoes rested against the bulkheads. It was spooky in a way; as though invisible sentries were standing there and all you could see of them was their shoes. I even saw Captain Malone's cordovan shoes which so impressed Matuszak. I learned later that officers left their shoes out for their stewards to shine. I mentioned this to Matuszak, and he said "Yeah, I saw that, too."

As I mentioned before, we were a major flagship. In the course of time and Navy practice, our admiral was relieved by another one. It happened in Pearl, and it happened with all the ritual and ceremony to be expected of such a great event. The entire Pacific Fleet was based in Pearl by that time, and we had admirals in great abundance, all zealous in their determination to be honored according to their ranks.

For us on the signal bridge, it meant a hell of a lot of look-see pidgin, but we were decently isolated from all the hoopla on the quarterdeck. Mostly, we simply had to report the approach of senior officers so that they might be rendered the proper honors as they came on board.

The Navy's schedule of honors was rigid. Sideboys, in the appropriate numbers, greeted boarding officers at the gangway. The band sounded Ruffles and Flourishes. The ship's crew, in spotless whites, manned the rails or stood at formal Quarters. Sometimes gun salutes were fired.

The Guard was paraded, too, of course. The Guard was the ship's Marine Detachment, under Marine Captain Earl Malone. It promised to be a busy day for Captain Malone, and one of which he could be expected to take full advantage. An officer could be in the Corps for a lot of years before he got another such chance to show off his military talents before so many senior officers, and senior officers determine promotions.

We knew all this was coming for some time, of course. The Navy was not likely to approach anything so important as a change of command ceremony without providing time for proper preparation. And, although I didn't know it at the time, one of the people making his preparations was Matuszak.

This particular change of command happened in 1940 or 1941. It was not long before the War, and the Navy did cut back a little bit in the observation. We did not wear dress whites, for instance. And the officers, although they did wear their swords, wore ordinary whites with white shoes. The Marines wore khaki, which meant Captain Malone would be wearing his cordovan shoes, along with starched khakis and a spiffy Sam Browne belt which looked like it was made from the same leather as his shoes.

I happened to go ashore with Matuszak not long before the big show, but I paid little attention when he stopped for a minute in a shoe repair shop on Fort Street not far off Hotel. He came out with a small package which he stuck inside the waistband of his pants, and we went on with our liberty.

Several times, after we returned to the ship, I saw Matuszak working with a small bit of folded leather. "What the hell are you doing?" I asked him once.

"Just fooling around," he said. "My dad showed me how to do something one time. I'm just seeing if I remember how to do it."

For those of us who had been in the Navy for a while, there was not much new or different about the day's ceremony. The ship was scoured and polished to glistening perfection. Our newest colors were flying, and the crew itself was spotless in new whites and shining shoes. Everything was set, but Malone went over his Marines until the very last minute, then dashed to his quarters to get into his best uniform.

I noticed Matuszak watching Malone with more than usual interest, but we were all busy that morning and I paid little attention to the fact. We were at Pearl's Ten-Ten Dock, and admirals were coming at us from all directions. There were even some Army generals as guests.

Everything went smoothly for the main part of the operation. When our new admiral came to inspect the Guard, I saw Matuszak slip out onto the little platform we had aft of the signal flag bags. He was as close there as he could get to the quarterdeck and, since the signalmen's part in the ceremony was largely over, I joined him.

I have always been curious about the purely military part of Navy life, the saluting and the posturing and the wearing of funny hats. From where we looked down on the quarterdeck, for instance we could see the fancy embroidery on top of Captain Malone's cap. I never understood how all that could make a man fight better.

While I was pondering that, Matuszak suddenly dug his elbow into my side and pointed. "It's working," he gloated. "Hot damn. Look at the son-of-a-bitch."

"What the hell are you talking about?"

"Malone," Matuszak said. "Look at his face. Red as a spanked baby's ass."

The Guard had opened ranks by that time, and Malone was escorting our brand-new three-star admiral in his ritual

14

inspection of the Guard. He walked at rigid attention and kept the prescribed distance from the Admiral. But Matuszak was right: Malone's face and the back of his neck were bright red under the shadow of his cap. Even from the signal bridge, we saw that.

"Listen!" Matuszak hissed.

"To what . . . ?" I started to say, but Matuszak shushed me.

Then I heard Captain Malone's shoes. They were squeaking with every step he took — loud squeaks. I could hear them all the way up on the bridge. I saw the admiral turn and look at Malone questioningly. Then I saw other officers on the quarterdeck fight back grins. Even the Marines in ranks struggled to hide their smiles. Everyone on deck, except for Malone and the admiral, wore expressions of stifled laughter.

I wondered why it was so funny. The only explanation I've come up with is that this was By-The-Book Captain Malone and his shoes were squeaking on a quarterdeck full of flag officers. If Malone were anyone else, it would have been no big deal.

Malone was obviously mortified. He looked like he wished a hole would open up and swallow him and his shoes. And Matuszak was elated.

The only time I ever saw Matuszak — or any other man for that matter — happier than he was that morning was one time when I was with him on the bridge. We overheard the admiral address Captain Malone as "Squeaky."

WHITE HATS

Punchy O'Rourke

Boxing used to be a big deal in the Navy. Organized tournaments determined ship, division, type, force and, finally, Fleet championships for all the weights every year. Sometimes, in fact, the Navy produced some pretty fair pros. World Heavyweight Champion Sailor Jack Sharkey was probably the most famous, but there were a lot of others, too.

Punchy O'Rourke, for instance. Punchy was at one time middleweight champion of the whole damned Navy. That was in the late twenties and early thirties. He got out of the Navy then and turned pro. Punchy never won a belt, but he was good enough to make a lot of money — all of which, thanks to crooked managers and promoters, and his own foolishness, got away from him in one way or another until he wound up, in the late thirties, broken both financially and physically.

When, as the Navy began gearing up for World War II, some former sailors were let back in, Punchy jumped at the chance, glad to get his feet under a Navy mess table again and his ass in a clean dry Navy bunk every night. He came aboard our ship one day in nineteen-thirty-eight, as part of a draft of other old guys who were in the Navy before.

We called them Metal Men — silver in their hair, gold in their teeth, and lead in their ass. Some of them were not worth the powder to blow them to hell, but others pulled their own weight after a little catching up. Some of them brought back special skills they learned in the civilian world which made them useful in the ships.

That was true of Punchy. We had a couple of guys on board at the time who were pretty good boxers. Jimmy Brower, a young signalman second, for instance, took the Scouting Force Championship that year, in the middleweight division, by a knockout. He came damned close to taking the Battle Force guy, too, for the Fleet championship. That was as close as our ship ever came to a Fleet championship.

It was close enough, in fact, to make our skipper start thinking about the next year. Our skipper was a boxing nut. He was himself a lightweight champion as a midshipman. He saw a lot of value in boxing for sailors, and when he found out Punchy, a former contender, was on board, wheels began turning in his brain.

Navy boxers were amateurs. He figured, I suppose, that if an old pro like Punchy trained our guys and gave them the benefit of his experience, that might be all it would take to make them winners.

The problem was Punchy didn't want to do it.

I don't know how old Punchy was then. Around thirty-five, I guess, but he looked a lot older. His nose had stopped too many gloves. Old scar tissue swelled his frontal bone and slitted his eyes. His ears were mangled wads of gristle on either side of his head, and he moved awkwardly. Sometimes he lurched while walking as though the ship were rolling, even when it was moored in still water. He looked like what he was — an old pug.

Even worse, his brain was scrambled. That's why we called him — cruelly, but accurately — Punchy. He was punchy as hell, in fact. We had to warn him before we struck the bells, for instance. Otherwise, he would drop into a fighting crouch and lash out with either hand at whatever or whoever was close. Some of the guys would deliberately not tell him, just to see the show. That was mean, and the chief raised hell.

Punchy's speech was often slurred, too. Especially when he was tired or under stress. I used to feel sorry for the poor guy.

He wasn't much good on the bridge, to tell the truth. We used him most of the time for the donkey work of hoisting flags or recording messages somebody else received. He did that reasonably well. And he kept his cleaning station up. That's about all that was expected of a white hat, then.

Maybe all that was why Punchy did not want to train our boxers. He still had the wit to realize what had happened to him and he didn't want to be responsible for getting anybody else into the condition he suffered.

Still, skippers of Navy ships have a way of getting what they want. I don't know if our skipper ever spoke directly to Punchy or not, but our division officer and signal officer sure as hell did. Punchy was so low on the bridge totem pole that they couldn't do much in the usual way of punitive assignments to bring him around, but they tried. There were always things which could be found wrong at inspections, and his name could always lead the list for working parties. Stuff like that.

Even more effective pressure came from the boxers themselves and the other guys in the crew, signal bridge and ship's company alike. Navy sailors did not get one hell of a lot in the way of gratification in those days. The chance of getting a Fleet Champion in the ship was too good to miss. It would make them all feel better if that happened, I suppose; anyway it would be a break in the God-damned boredom. And all that stood in the way, they soon came to feel, was Punchy's stubbornness.

"For Christ's sake, Punchy," Jimmy Brower said one day. "Give us a break. All we're asking is for you to tell us how to do it. Is that too much to ask?"

"You want to be like me?" Punchy growled without looking up from the halyard he was splicing.

19

"What's that got to do with anything?" Brower said.

Punchy put down his halyard. He looked at Brower. "I wasn't always like I am now," he said.

"Like what?"

"Like, *punchy*," Punchy said. "Like ducking when somebody strikes the bells. Like not being able to semaphore anymore. Or read code. Or falling on my face sometimes. Or looking into the mirror when I shave and wondering who in the hell that is looking back at me."

Brower could not understand what Punchy was saying. He saw no connection between what Punchy said and himself. Brower was young. He had not had his brain scrambled. Yet.

"All I know, Punchy," Brower said bitterly, "is that you could help your shipmates and you damned well won't do it. That's chickenshit, Punchy."

"I ain't going to help you dumb bastards screw yourselves up," Punchy said.

"Whether we screw ourselves up or not is our business, Punchy. Whether you help us or not, we're going to box. Whether you help us or not, it's going to happen."

"Sorry," Punchy said sullenly.

Brower tried a different tack. "Maybe, if you would help us, Punchy, we wouldn't get hurt so much," he said. "Maybe, if you showed us how to protect ourselves and everything, we wouldn't get hit so much. Or so hard."

But Punchy would not budge. He just kept punching the splice in the braided cotton signal halyard he was working on.

The rest of us were just about as hard on Punchy. Guys in other parts of the ship jumped on him for not helping. Even the God-damned black gang got in on it. Things were not all that pleasant on board for Punchy during that time. Most guys would have nothing to do with him. Nobody went ashore with him or drank beer with him. Guys, when they gathered about the bridge coffee pot for their never-ending off-watch bull sessions, ignored him.

That kind of treatment is rough on anybody. It was especially rough on an old guy like Punchy who had just about hit bottom before getting back into the Navy. Punchy was even married once, but the wife he even yet loved with a bleak hopelessness had long since left him, taking with her the son Punchy would never see again. It must have hurt like hell to have his new-found shipmates turn on him that way.

Getting back into the Navy was like a second-chance homecoming for Punchy. He had not been so happy for a long time. Now, that all blew up in his face and he was again as lonely as ever he had been as a scarred club fighter in tank towns and big city prelims, all over the country.

I felt pretty sure Punchy would weaken under the pressure at some point, but he made a stubborn resistance. Once you understood his position you even saw something good about what he tried to do. At least I did. I was signalman first then. As it happened, Jimmy Brower and Punchy were both in my watch. Brower and I talked about Punchy sometimes when Punchy was where he couldn't hear.

"He's doing it for your own damned good," I said to Brower one time. "Punchy knows what he's talking about. You don't."

"I'm no God-damned baby," Brower blurted back at me. "I don't need no old punch-drunk has-been son-of-a-bitch telling me anything 'for my own good', for Christ's sake."

"Okay, okay, Brower. Forget I said anything."

The one who broke Punchy down finally, I think, was Kathy. Kathy was Brower's girlfriend. She was a nice kid, pretty in a dark-haired kind of way. I used to wonder how a girl like her ever got mixed up with a smart-ass like Brower in the first place, but she did. She was in love with him. After that, you don't need to know anything else. There's no explaining girls in love with sailors. Later, I came to know she wasn't the sweet little thing she pretended to be, but I didn't know that then.

Our chief used to have the whole liberty section out to his house about once a month for beer and hot dogs. Most chiefs wouldn't be found dead doing anything like that. Bad for discipline, I suppose. In fact, I don't think our own chief thought much of the idea. It was his wife's doing, I found out later.

21

Not many sailors — even chiefs — were married in those days. But ours was. His wife was a round little woman of quick wit, ready tongue and ample opinion. We used to joke on the bridge — when the chief wasn't there — about how she jerked around her big-bellied husband. It was the chief's wife who had us all out to their little rented house in San Pedro.

Her name was Flo. In her own words, the Good Lord "had not blessed their union with children." She clearly meant to fix that by mothering the whole damned signal gang. She was especially attentive to the young guys. She joked about it by pretending to protect them from the evil influence of us older guys. She was nice to all of us, though.

Except for the chief, nobody on our bridge was married. But anybody who had a girlfriend was welcome to bring her along. That's how I came to meet Kathy, Brower's girl. And that's how Kathy came to meet Punchy.

Neither the Chief nor any of the rest of us would have invited Punchy to the monthly parties, but Flo would not hear of his being left out. She had heard us talking about him. She knew how we felt about his refusing to help the ship's boxers. Knowing Flo as I did, I suspect that's what made her so determined that Punchy be invited. She was always on the side of the underdog in anything.

Anyway, Punchy came to one of the parties. We all tried to be nice to him out of consideration for Flo, but it wasn't easy. It wasn't even easy for Punchy who was not punchy enough to think anything had changed in how we thought about him.

The only one who seemed genuinely attentive to Punchy was, oddly, Kathy. Being of devious mind — and some experience with women and their ways — I got a fresh beer and sidled over close enough to hear what they said.

Sure enough, Kathy got around — smoothly and oh, so sweetly — to the subject of boxing. I am not sure Punchy realized what she was doing, but she was sure as hell doing it. She was working him over. Good.

"Jimmy tells me you are a boxer, Mr. O'Rourke," Kathy said, handing Punchy a hot dog he was too bashful to get for himself.

I think Punchy may have recognized method in Kathy's words. "Used to be," he said carefully.

"Jimmy said you were very good," Kathy went on. "Fleet champion three years, he said."

"Yeah," Punchy said. I think by that time he had a pretty good idea of what was coming, but he was so starved for attention of any kind that he didn't put up much of a defense.

"Then you went out of the Navy and fought outside for a long time."

"Quite a while."

"You must know an awful lot about boxing, Mr. O'Rourke," Kathy said innocently.

Punchy squinched up his hard-used and ill-mended face into what he probably thought was a smile. "I've forgot a lot, too," he said.

"Jimmy thinks the world of you, Mr. O'Rourke," Kathy said.

"Don't call me Mister," Punchy said then without rancor. "I'm Punchy. That's what they call me on the ship."

"Jimmy thinks he could learn a lot from you . . . Punchy," Kathy said. She had trouble even saying the word.

By that time Punchy was clearly uncomfortable. "Can I get you something?" he said. "Hot dog? Beer?"

Kathy smiled sweetly and shook her head. "No. Thank you, Punchy. I'm not hungry. But thank you for asking. It is sweet of you to ask." She was laying it on pretty thick.

The thought occurred to me that maybe Brower had put her up to it and I looked around to see where he was. He was playing horseshoes at a pitch the chief had set up in his backyard. If he knew what Kathy was doing he didn't show any sign of it. I decided she was doing it on her own.

"Jimmy loves boxing, Punchy," Kathy went on. "It's his whole life I think, sometimes."

"He's pretty good, for an amateur," Punchy grudgingly admitted. "Green, but pretty good."

Kathy studied Punchy for a moment without speaking. Then she said, "Why don't you help him, Punchy? He would love it if you would."

I didn't have to listen any longer. Punchy's goose was well-cooked. It didn't happen right then, or even very soon, but it happened. Punchy agreed to help train the ship's boxers.

The skipper permitted the setting up of speed bags and a big body bag he bought out of ship's service funds. Mats were laid out so the guys could skip rope without marring the decks, and we got used to seeing guys doing laps, shuffling along sometimes with their shoulders hunched and shadow boxing as they went.

All of this had gone on before, of course. But it took on a new earnestness after Punchy took over. He was excused most of his watches for the purpose of training the boxers. The boxers were excused most of their watches, too, for that matter. It meant more watches for the rest of us, but we didn't care. We could see the difference Punchy made. We began to feel the ship really might take a Fleet championship.

The biggest change came about on the bridge. No longer the pariah he once was, Punchy became the hero of us all. He was included in everything we did, and everyone was ready to standby for him if he wanted to go ashore. (Which he almost never did.) Except for with Brower.

Brower forgot all the bad things he once thought about Punchy. He insisted the old fighter go ashore with him. Brower basked in the reflected glory of his relationship with Punchy. Kathy was always with them when they were ashore. Kathy continued to butter Punchy up.

That is when I first became uneasy about what was developing. Kathy laid it on pretty thick. Even Brower took notice. It didn't take much brains to see that Punchy responded. He had been lonely too long not to react strongly when shown even a little bit of affection or appreciation. Especially by a pretty young girl, and Kathy sometimes showed more than a little bit of both affection and appreciation.

She may not have realized what she was doing. She may even have been sincere in seeming to like Punchy — although I never thought she was. I never thought she was doing anything other than jerking Punchy around to get what she wanted for Brower.

Whatever, Punchy soon began to show unmistakable signs of more than a little interest in Kathy. He then was well short of forty years old, and Kathy probably about twenty. Guys older than that have made damned fools of themselves over young women.

I didn't see a hell of a lot I could do about it. Except for Brower's occasional suspicions everyone else seemed happy with the way things were going. Even the skipper stopped by for training sessions sometimes, deferring always to Punchy's opinions. That was heady stuff. What was happening was so damned pleasing for Brower he wasn't about to say anything to Punchy which might change things. I suspect he felt he could always get another girlfriend. He wasn't likely to get another Punchy in his corner.

At any rate, that is the way things went right through the early stages of that year's tournament. All of our boxers did fairly well. Brower was brilliant. He won bout after bout, right up to the Scouting Force finals and Punchy didn't think he would have much trouble there, either. Kathy jumped up and down and hugged Punchy the night Brower knocked out the Battle Force champion, a classy fighter off the *New Mexico*, for the Fleet title.

We all jumped up and down ourselves and yelled at the top of our lungs. Everyone was pounding each other on the back. Even the officers, from their properly reserved section, forgot their dignity for a while.

Punchy was at ringside, of course. So was Kathy. Punchy took care of that. Anyway, when Brower's glove was raised over the fallen *New Mexico* sailor, Kathy threw her arms around Punchy and hugged him tight. She kissed his scarred and misshapen face, happy tears streaming down her face.

I doubt that anyone else noticed. I probably would not have noticed myself, had I not been looking for it. But, all of a sudden, Punchy hugged Kathy back as though he meant it. His battered old mouth found her fresh young one and, for a little while, they kissed in a way to make Brower very unhappy as he looked down upon them from the ring.

He had hardly worked up a sweat in the bout and his beaming face was unmarked as he sought Kathy's eyes and her always adoring appreciation of what he had done. That made the sudden darkening of his face as he saw Punchy and Kathy all the more striking.

For her part, Kathy drew back from Punchy, her face a curious mix of surprise and shock and something more troubling that was neither. She seemed confused and turned back to Brower, smiling up to him and clasping her hands over her head in the fighter's traditional gesture of triumph.

After a moment or two of seeming indecision, Punchy took up bucket and towels and all the other fighter's gear and left for the locker room without looking back. God knows what his thoughts were. Maybe he remembered all the times when the cheers were for him, in a hundred fights or more. Maybe he just wanted to get away from everything his life had become.

I did not see Punchy again that night. I learned later that he went to a ginmill on The Pike and drank himself silly. Because he was out of uniform, as well as being drunk, the Shore Patrol returned him to the ship under arrest. Until that time I never saw Punchy take more than a beer or two at a time, but he sure as hell did that night.

Even worse, drunk as he was, he decked a couple of Shore Patrolmen and, in general, raised holy hell. Nevertheless, the skipper gave him a slap on the wrist at Mast the next day and sent him back to training the ship's boxers.

Brower's big win had come in a shoreside arena. The procession back to the Pico Street Fleet Landing and return to the ship was triumphant. It was only a few blocks. Brower paraded in the lead, already showered and in dress blues. Kathy clung to his arm and looked adoringly up at him with laughing eyes full of promise. The rest of us, a crowd of two or three hundred from the ship along with the usual hangers-on, sang and shouted our way, completely closing streets as we passed.

There was always a good contingent of Shore Patrol at the Pico Street landing, including some officers. But they were tolerant of us and waved our liberty boats in ahead of others to take us back to our ship. I didn't see what happened to Kathy in all the hubbub, but she wasn't allowed on the ship in any event. I didn't see Punchy there, either. I remember hoping, even then, that they would not do anything foolish. I needn't have worried, Punchy was drinking himself blotto at the time.

Our normal mooring was Buoy George inside the inner breakwater at Long Beach, a brief three-minute ride from the landing, and we arrived back at the ship still in a state of noisy celebration which was not dampened entirely even by the Navy's sober rituals for coming on board.

The living compartments throughout the ship rocked with the glad talking and laughing of what had happened. Brower, of course, was the hero of the time. He held court in the signalmens' compartment, reenacting the fight with gestures and happy descriptions. No one seemed to notice that Punchy was not there at all.

That put an end to it for the time being. The skipper was happy that he had his Fleet Champion at last. The crew counted their winnings and bragged in the bars of "their" great achievement. Brower himself soon came to believe all the crap being thrown around and announced that he was getting out of the Navy and turning pro. He had less than a year to go on his hitch. Some pro fight manager already had contacted him.

Kathy jumped up and down at that news, too. She was getting good at jumping up and down. I was pretty cynical about Kathy by that time. I suspected she was already counting the diamonds and fur coats which would come when Brower started pulling down some big purses. I also noticed she wasn't as attentive to Punchy as she used to be, either. My guess was she thought Brower wouldn't be needing Punchy so much when he turned pro and could get himself a real manager and trainer.

In fact, about the only one who was not jumping up and down at the thought of Brower's turning pro was Punchy. The Skipper didn't like the thought of losing his Fleet Champion, but he was big about it and would take whatever credit he could for having developed such a fighter on his ship. Besides, he probably figured that, for as long as he had Punchy on board, he could bring along other boxers better than the other ships could since they did not have such expert help. That is pretty much the way the guys in the crew felt, too.

Personally, I didn't much give a damn what Brower did. He was never a very good signalman in the first place. He would never have made second class if he weren't a boxer. After he won the championship, he was worse than ever.

Except for me, Punchy was about the only one in the ship who did not join the parade. "What's the matter, Punch," Brower crowed one day. "Don't you think I'm good enough? That ain't what that son-of-a-bitch off the *New Mexico* is saying."

Punchy looked at Brower.

"Any third rate club fighter will knock your head off inside of three rounds," Punchy said quietly.

"What did you say?" Brower said.

"I said, any third rate club fighter will knock your head off inside of three rounds," Punchy said again.

Brower laughed uneasily and glanced at those of us lounging around the pyrotechnic locker the signalmen used for their coffee gear. We had two heavy wooden benches on the bridge which were most often used by the admiral's staff officers underway. We moved them back of the flagbags for watching the movies. In port we kept them by the coffee gear to make a nice place to shoot the breeze.

Things got a little tight there for a minute. None of us knew what to make of Punchy's truculence. He was always an easygoing guy on the bridge. Confused sometimes, but easygoing. Brower seemed as puzzled as any of us. In the end, he tried to make a joke of it. "Hey, that's funny, Punch," he laughed. "Guess you didn't train me good enough. That it?"

"I got the mid," was all Punchy said. "I'm going down and get some sack time."

I never heard anything more on the subject, but nobody forgot what Punchy said. Guys talk in a ship. It wasn't long before everybody in the ship knew what Punchy said about Brower's chances as a pro. Brower sure as hell did. He tried to pump me about it sometimes. He knew I was as good a friend as Punchy had in the ship.

"What the hell does the old son-of-a-bitch mean?" Brower demanded one night.

I confessed ignorance and tried to let it go but Brower would not be put off. "No, God-damn it, I mean it," he said. "I beat the best in the whole God-damned United States Navy. That ought to mean something, for Christ's sake."

"I told you, Brower," I said. "I don't know diddly about boxing. You got a question, you ask Punchy." I could not resist the dig I took then. "You want to find out what he thinks, maybe Kathy can find out for you."

I thought for a minute Brower was going to take a poke at me, his face got so dark. But he didn't.

I think Brower knew it was Kathy who got Punchy to train him in the first place, but he wouldn't admit it. I remembered his face the way it was the night he beat the battleship guy and looked down from the ring to see Punchy and Kathy kissing.

"Go to hell," Brower said as though he meant it. He stomped off the bridge then.

Punchy wasn't there when this exchange took place, but a half dozen other guys were. That was enough to get the word spread through the ship. It wasn't long until everyone in the ship knew Brower was nervous.

I don't know if Punchy saw Kathy during that time. I know he stopped going ashore with Brower. Or with anybody else, for that matter. He stopped hanging around the boxing team, too. I could see the whole damned thing firing up again.

It was the scuttlebutt running through the ship, though, which brought things to a head. Brower could not stand hearing what the guys were saying. He could stand even less what he *didn't* hear when conversations stopped short as he came upon them.

Finally, in what looked like a deliberate confrontation, Brower challenged Punchy. "I been hearing what you're saying about me, Punchy," he said. "You got anything to say about me, you say it to me. Okay?"

Punchy hesitated only a minute before he said, "I got nothing to say to you, Brower."

"That ain't what I been hearing."

"Maybe you been listening too good."

"Maybe. Maybe not." Brower hesitated. "You been talking to Kathy, Punchy?"

"No." Punchy said, shortly.

"I say you have." Brower said. But when Punchy failed to answer, Brower let it pass. He changed the subject, abruptly. "Pat Murphy offered to manage me," he said smugly. "You think a guy like Murphy would sign me if he thought I couldn't hack it?"

"Pat Murphy's a crook," Punchy said flatly. "He'll suck you dry for whatever your Navy title's worth then dump you like a hot rock."

"Like he did you, Punchy?" Brower smirked.

Punchy hesitated before he replied. "Yes, like he did me, Jimmy," he said.

"And you're still sore about it."

"Maybe," Punchy said. "But I fought for him a long time. I made a lot of money for him, you don't figure to do that."

Brower's face darkened. "You keep saying that, Punchy. You don't think I can cut it with the pros."

"You can't," Punchy said. "Oh, Murphy can probably get you some prelim shots and maybe a club bout now and then, but you get close to the big time and you'll wind up flat on your ass, your face flattened and your brain scrambled, like me."

"That ain't what Murphy says," Brower grinned. "Murphy thinks I got a shot at the title someday."

"Murphy's full of shit," Punchy said.

"Kathy thinks I can make it," Brower said, then shrewdly added, watching Punchy's face for reaction, "Kathy and me are getting married soon as I get out of the Navy."

Punchy again hesitated, long enough for it to be noticed, before he replied. "What does Kathy know about fighting?" he said. Then, after a longer pause, "And what does Kathy know about being married to a stumble-bum pug, living in cheap hotels, never knowing from one day to the next when

30

the next concussion will make her a widow or — worse — will leave her hooked to a punch-drunk stumble-bum?"

"Yeah?"

"Yeah," Punchy said. Then, more earnestly, "If you loved her, Brower, you wouldn't put Kathy through that. You wouldn't put anyone you loved through that."

I think Brower sensed then that he had touched upon a vulnerability in Punchy. I think he knew then that Punchy loved Kathy.

Brower grinned and turned away, but Punchy caught at his arm. "Don't do it, Brower," Punchy said. "For Christ's sake, don't do it."

"What's it to you, Punchy?" Brower grinned again. "What do you care what I do?"

"Nothing," Punchy said, his voice empty of feeling at last. "I don't like to see anybody do what I done, I guess. I just don't like seeing you take Kathy down with you."

"What's Kathy to you?"

"Nothing," Punchy said dully. "Nothing, I guess."

"Okay, then," Brown said, darkly. "Let's keep it that way. Okay, Punchy?"

Punchy had a funny way of squinching up his face when he tried to think. "How about a deal, Brower?" he said. "You think you're good enough for the pros. Okay? How about if I can take you — old, out of shape and bunged up as I am — how about if I can take you, you forget about the pros. Okay?"

"What the hell are you saying?"

"I'm saying that I'll take you on. Regulation ring. Ten rounds. Six ounce gloves. Ten point must system. You win, I train you for the pros. I win, you forget it. Deal?"

Three or four of us were standing by the coffee pot while all that was going on. All of us dropped our jaws. But none of us dropped our jaws as far as Brower.

"You will train me for the pros?" he said, as though finding it hard to believe. Hell, with Punchy in his corner, he couldn't miss. I don't think it ever occurred to him that Punchy might win.

"If you can take me, yes," Punchy said.

Brower's face shined. "Why, hell, yes," he said.

Anyway, that's how it came about. Punchy didn't even bother to train. A few days later he got the use of a Los Angeles gym, and half the crew, it seemed, rode the big red Pacific Electric train into town for the fight. Kathy was there, too.

If you've ever seen a fighters' gym, you know what that one was like. Rough, unpainted pine floors. Hooded bulbs hanging from a shadowed ceiling. Unwashed windows blurring dingy daylight. Showers stinking of sweat and liniment and mildew from somewhere in the back. Speed bags and body bags wherever they would fit. And, down the middle, three roped-in rings with thin canvas over wood floors.

It was Pat Murphy's gym, I found out later. He was there, of course, along with a mixed bag of fighters and ex-fighters and hangers-on of one kind and another. Some of the pugs were working out. Two were sparring in the middle ring, but everything stopped as our crowd came in and found places to stand. There were no chairs or benches for so many people.

"What's up, Punchy?" Murphy asked from around a very large and well-chewed cigar. "You said on the phone you wanted to borrow a ring."

"Yeah," Punchy said. "Me and Brower are going to spar around a little bit. Okay? We won't be long."

"Sure. Sure, Punchy," Murphy said. "But you didn't say it was going to be you. You remember what the doc said?"

"Yeah. But we're just going to spar a little bit. I ain't going to get hit."

Brower already was pulling his blouse over his head and holding out his hands for the taping. His mind was busy with thoughts of glory and money. I don't think he heard what Murphy said. I don't think Kathy heard, either. She stood beside Brower and paid attention to nothing else. I don't think she even said hello to Punchy.

"You sure you know what you're doing, Punchy?" Murphy said. And, when Punchy nodded after pulling off his own jumper, Murphy shrugged and said. "Okay. It's your funeral."

That had an ominous ring. I began to wonder what it was the doc said. In all the time Punchy was in our ship, he never mentioned anything about a doc saying anything. Not to me, he didn't.

But it was too late then. Both men had their hands taped. They didn't bother with jock straps. They would fight in their blue bell-bottoms and white Navy skivvy shirts. A brief run-through of rules, and the fight began. Murphy served as referee. What looked like an old-time club fighter kept the time and rang the bell.

I suppose it was a fair fight. Brower was younger and stronger and faster than Punchy, but Punchy had a lot of moxie in his head — if he could only remember it. The big thing he had to remember was to end the fight fast before Brower's youth wore him down.

In the first round, Punchy stood for the most part flatfooted and waited for Brower to come to him, saving his strength. Brower, for his part, paraded his young body and played to the crowd, dropping his hands to his sides from time to time and winking to Kathy where she stood at ringside.

Near the end of that round, Brower struck with a flurry of blows, all of which Punchy blocked or slipped. The crowd screamed, but I thought I saw the beginning of doubt in Brower's face. He tried to hit Punchy, but he missed.

I watched Kathy. Her face was bright as she yelled for Brower. I didn't find even a trace of concern for Punchy. The rest of the crowd from the ship was clearly in Brower's corner, as well.

Brower did not bother to sit down between rounds. He jigged in his corner and grinned down to Kathy. Punchy, even though he did virtually nothing in the first round was breathing heavily. The flesh of his upper body sagged and bulged with his lack of condition.

In the second round Brower struck with a series of vicious combinations, some of which scored past Punchy's slowed reactions. Emboldened, Brower tried again and Punchy stopped him cold with a straight right which made him wobble-legged for a moment.

This became the pattern of the fight. Punchy took more, but lighter, blows in order to deliver fewer but heavier ones. Still, his age hurt Punchy. He could not keep up for long even those restrained tactics. His breath came in gasps, and his face and body grew flushed and swollen from the power of Brower's blows. Old scar tissue split and tore, spattering the white skivvy shirts of both men with red in the hard glare of ring lights. Still, Punchy hung on.

Slowly, during that round, the crowd came to sense, I think, that something other than the fight itself was on the line. More of them came to pull for Punchy. Punchy's dogged and increasingly desperate struggle was beginning to impress them all with respect and a perhaps reluctant admiration for the old fighter. They watched in unnatural silence. Only Kathy continued cheering Brower. I saw Punchy once look at her with bleared eyes, but there was no way to know what he thought.

From the start of round three, Punchy held on. He smothered Brower's blows with his arms or deflected them with his gloves. But, increasingly, some of them got through and Punchy had to hang on. That was when he fell back on all the tricks, dirty and otherwise, he learned in his hard years as a fighter. He hit low, hard enough to bring a grimace to Brower's face. He backhanded. He pushed the laces of his gloves across Brower's eyes. He pounded Brower's kidneys.

But even that was not enough. Midway through the third round Brower measured Punchy and hit him with left, right, and left again before Punchy fell out of range to the ring floor.

It was over. I felt a little sick in my stomach at seeing Brower hurry from the ring and take Kathy in his arms. Neither of them looked back to where Punchy lay prone and bloody under the white glare of the ring lights. The crowd again found its voice and pressed about Brower and Kathy, laughing and shouting their excitement and release of tension as Brower's gloves were pulled off and the tape cut from his hands.

From Punchy's corner I climbed into the ring to where Murphy leaned over him and took out his mouthpiece. There was no doctor there, but our ship's doctor told me later it would have made no difference.

"The doc told him not to fight again," Pat Murphy said with a tenderness rare in so rough a man. "The doc told him not to fight again. Why did he do it?"

As I looked at Kathy clinging to Brower as she was and still not knowing, or even caring, that Punchy was hurt, I thought I knew. Punchy was not the first, nor will he likely be the last, sailor to make a fool of himself for love of a woman.

We did get Punchy on his feet and back to the ship. But that night, at chow, he complained of a headache. He died before we got him to sick bay. Brower had not yet returned to the ship when it happened. He was probably somewhere on the beach with Kathy.

WHITE HATS

DC

It used to be that after a Navy sailor was missing for thirty days he was officially declared a deserter and, in keeping with a tradition as old as Navies themselves, the man's property was branded with the letters "DC" and auctioned off to his former shipmates. The money went to support the ship's various morale and recreational activities.

It was not a commonplace ritual. In nearly thirty years of Navy life I saw it only once. And, in that case, the sailor was the last man in the Navy I thought likely to desert. But he was a friend, and I bid on one of his handkerchiefs. I never used it. I wanted it, I suppose, as something to remember him by. I still have it.

The Navy probably has a more complicated method of doing it now, but in 1939 replacing crew members in a ship, especially on such a remote station as ours at the time, was handled in a notably direct way. When a ship found itself short a man of some particular rate, other ships in the area were required to give up whatever they might have in the way of surplus hands in the field needed. That is how we came to get Schnozz as a replacement for Bill Harden, a well-liked signal striker whose enlistment ran out. We got Schnozz from the *Northampton*, a Fifth Division cruiser. I don't even remember his real name.

Although the system had the undoubted advantage of simplicity, it had one serious flaw in that ships required to give up a man were unlikely to give up their best. On the contrary, the very worst available was most likely to pack his seabag and lay up to the quarterdeck.

That is why we didn't expect to get much in the way of excellence out of Schnozz. If Schnozz wasn't the worst the *Northampton* had to offer, he was very close. Just adequate as a signalman, he was marginal as a sailor. Part of a forlorn subclass of men who were foisted off by first one ship then another, they were accepted only in the sure faith that they could be sent on to the next ship or station requesting a replacement.

During the Depression years it was hard to get into the Navy. Without jobs on the outside, thousands of men wanted in. And those who were in stayed in, creating few openings. That made it a mystery to us how a man like Schnozz got into the Navy in the first place.

I think we all concluded he probably was a "Judge recruit." In those days, when a man got into trouble with the law as a civilian, sometimes a judge gave him the option of jail or the Navy. Judges seemed to have influence with recruiters that way and got men into the Navy who would never make it on their own. The Navy, in the interests of public relations, liked to pretend this never happened, but it did. Sometimes.

I was then in a heavy cruiser stationed in Pearl Harbor as part of a cruiser-destroyer force intended to counter Japan's growing belligerence in the Pacific. The problem, so far as Schnozz was concerned, was that our ship was the Force Flagship and the admiral expected a certain smartness of appearance and manner in the men on his Flag bridge. Unfortunately, Schnozz offered little in the way of either smartness or manner.

It wasn't that he wasn't intelligent, although the Flag chief signalman did sometimes question even that. It was more that he was clumsy and inept in manual things, and he moved in such a way, and wore his whites in such a way, that he seemed slow and dirty even when he moved readily and wore a fresh uniform.

The very fact of his nickname — Schnozz — stemmed from his enormous beak of a nose. "The only man in the whole God-damned Navy who can smoke a cigar in the shower," the chief liked to say. The fact that Schnozz was short and thin almost to the point of emaciation made his nose seem even larger than it was. His nickname was ordained from the first time we laid eyes on him.

A lot has been written over the years about the warm bonds which grow between shipmates, but the fact is that sailors, like anyone else, can be pretty damned cruel, too. Especially in the case of misfits.

Schnozz almost immediately took on the role of signal bridge scapegoat. Signalmen were seldom called upon for working parties in those days, but when we were, Schnozz's name was always at the top of the list. Any dirty or unpleasant job was his in what became an accepted matter of course.

As do all the excluded of the world, Schnozz hungered for acceptance. He knew how the rest of us felt about him — he would have had to be a fool not to know that — and he would do anything to win our approval. He was always good for loans we never repaid, or for standing by on watches we did not want for no better reason than that we wanted to sleep in. He even accepted the cruel insult of his nickname as an affordable price for what he took to be our acceptance. He was so starved for acceptance, that he laughed at the meanest of the tricks we pulled on him almost as much as we did. Had we been decent enough to think about it, we would have been ashamed of ourselves.

I came, in time, to like Schnozz, although, to tell the truth, I did wish he had been put in someone else's watch. Flag Bridge signaling is not relaxing, conducted as it is with the direct supervision of an ambitious flag lieutenant and under the very nose of the admiral himself. Mistakes were not tolerated, and, in the press of drills or actual maneuvers, mistakes were hellishly easy to make — with sometimes disastrous results. I did not enjoy any more than anyone else being laid out for some stupid thing Schnozz did.

The duties of a signal striker are not demanding in any ordinary sense. "Striker" is the Navy's word for a man learning a rate. Men "strike" for signalman or radioman or quartermaster or whatever. Mostly, strikers do the idiot work of cleaning and running coffee gear and the like of juniors everywhere. Still, they are on the bridge, and the whole elaborate edifice is built upon a base of what strikers do.

Schnozz had one saving grace as a signalman: he was one hell of a hoister. And he could stow flags faster and more surely than anyone else on the bridge.

These two things are more important than they may seem. In hoisting flags, it is all too easy to snatch the hoist from the hands of the man bending it onto its downhaul — in which case the flags fly out in the wind of the ship's speed in an unreadable twist of colors. Everything then comes to an embarrassing halt while any flying signals are cancelled and the errant hoist recovered. All under the burning eyes of the admiral. I never saw Schnozz jerk a hoist out of a man's hands.

Then, no matter how quickly or smoothly a hoist goes to the yardarm, no new signal can be made until the flags are again on deck and stowed again in their bags, each in its proper place. Nothing is more certain to create chaos on a signal bridge than for someone to try to make up a hoist from a mass of colored cloth sometimes piled knee-deep about his legs. Schnozz sorted out and stowed flags faster than anyone I ever saw.

Thus, Schnozz found his productive niche in our little world. In the words of a classic sailor expression, he "pulled his weight" on the bridge. After a time he was even accepted, to a certain extent, but never as an equal. Schnozz was always an outsider, hovering on the fringe of crap game kibitzers or standing decently in the background of coffee pot bull sessions. Sometimes he would offer awkward attempts to participate, but was usually ignored or put down with such profane contempt that he eventually held his silence and participated as a listener only, happy to be granted even that modest measure of acceptance from us, his betters.

Most of us, I think, let this become the norm so far as Schnozz was concerned, but Joe Cook didn't. Joe was a kind of *de facto* gang boss over our signal bridge. He was only signalman second and in charge of the starboard side of the bridge during drills, but he threw his weight around with a will which well exceeded any formal authority he had.

As often happens within groups of men, Joe, with an innate talent for leadership, seemed to intimidate those over him and cow those under him. The Navy's slow promotions of that time worsened the situation in that men of such natural leadership abilities found themselves sometimes serving under men of clearly lesser powers who enjoyed the privileges of rank only because they were in the Navy many years and were promoted during more generous times.

Men like Joe did not suffer this injustice with much composure. It embittered them and caused them to act with even greater arrogance than they might otherwise. It led them, even more than most of us, to seek out scapegoats and use the weaknesses of others to prop up their own self-promotion. To that end, Schnozz was perfect for Joe.

Not very tall, but well-muscled and handsome in a scarred-face kind of way, Joe Cook was a model, though not a very admirable one, for the younger men on the bridge. He drank more and whored more and cursed more profanely than anyone else. Even more effective with the younger men was the way in which he created an air of rebellion against authority, although he was careful never to step over the bounds of what was accepted. For young guys whose every aspect of life was subject to sometimes stern and arbitrary authority, this was heady stuff.

In Schnozz's case, Joe Cook became the leader of the signal gang's calculated oppression of the gawky misfit. The others — especially the younger ones — seemed to compete for Joe's favor by devising ever new and more demeaning acts against Schnozz. To their own discredit, the senior petty officers on the bridge did nothing to make life easier for Schnozz. Even the chief stood apart in tacit recognition of the morale benefits gained for the gang as a whole by having Schnozz's status as scapegoat maintained. Things were never so bad for them that they could not look at Schnozz and realize things could be worse — they could be Schnozz.

Such matters, of course, were beneath the notice of the ship's officers or the flag lieutenant. As for the admiral, the thought of his intervention was ludicrous.

Oddly, Schnozz never seemed to resent his treatment. So far as we knew, he was a product of the Depression whose pre-Navy life, like that of most of us, was precarious at best. At least in the Navy he had as much to eat as anybody else and his bed was as clean and dry. His persecution, I suppose, seemed little enough price to pay for that kind of certainty.

Things might well have gone on like that indefinitely had not something happened to change the whole situation.

It was at Christmas. Navy enlisted men of that time were essentially homeless, cut off from the more normal world of families and permanent friends for sometimes years at a time. Almost none were married. The longer they were in the Navy the more rootless they became as previous families and friends were lost to the mists of absence and forgetfulness. As for all homeless, the Holidays had a greater sentimental value than they do for more normal people.

Sailors suffered an almost mawkish reaction to Christmas, for instance. Ships' chaplains, although frequently stiffed in their good works by cynical sailors during the rest of the year, never had problems arranging Christmas parties for children from local orphanages or setting up other wholesome activities as the sailors sought ever more hungrily, at Christmas, for their romanticized memories of what holidays once were.

Ships then usually were kept in port during the Holidays more than at other times and, when in port, the signal bridge became a kind of private club for the signal gang, subject only to the work of the watch. Officers seldom came there and other enlisted men never did. Since we were at Pearl, and our home port remained Long Beach, California, leave was out of the question. The men were left largely to their own resources. The signal gang gathered about the coffee gear set up on the pyrotechnics locker on the starboard side forward for long and often sentimental sessions of remembering family and friends from a steadily receding world whose imagined warmth and perfection increased with every passing year.

Joe Cook, of course, dominated these bull sessions as he did everything else on the bridge. He was from somewhere on the East Coast and boasted endlessly of a childhood and early life which held the rest of us enthralled by the wonderful things he told us of his growing up. Few of the rest of us had much in the way of pleasure to recall at all. Whether any of what Joe said was true or not, we did not know nor much care. We liked to hear that *someone* had such Holidays.

Maybe it was this even greater than usual deference Joe Cook found on our part as we listened to his stories which softened his attitude towards Schnozz. "How about you, Schnozz? Your folks ever do much for Christmas?" Joe asked once. He looked to the rest of us as though saying: "Watch this, guys. This ought to be good."

Schnozz, for his part, was suspicious of this invitation to take part. He half expected, I suppose, that Joe's asking him in was leading to nothing more than another way to put him down. He remained still. Had there been dirt on the bridge, he would have dug his toe into it.

"Aw, come on, Schnozz," Joe Cook persisted, "Tell us what Christmas was like when you were a kid. We want to know, don't we, guys?"

Taking their cue from Joe, the others urged Schnozz on. "Come on, Schnozz," they laughed. "Tell us, Schnozz." They were as certain as Schnozz that Joe was merely setting Schnozz up for still another cruel trick, but they didn't want to miss it. "Come on, Schnozz," they cried. "Tell us."

Schnozz would not be moved. He actually blushed at being the center of attention, but he would not tell anything of his own Christmases as a boy. Finally, we gave up and left him alone.

Joe Cook had stumbled upon something, though, which he did not want to give up. Two days later, he returned to the subject. "Come on, Schnozz, for Christ's sake," he pleaded. "Your folks must have done something when you were a kid."

The rest of us joined in and, this time, Schnozz did talk. He wasn't nearly as inarticulate as we had thought. Given the seemingly sincere interest we showed — not least Joe Cook — he began to talk.

Quietly and hesitantly at first, Schnozz told us about a Christmas one time with his family. His father was a judge. A God-damned *judge*! Not a few Navy men of the time knew judges. Usually in the capacity of defendants before the bar of what to us seemed a pretty damned cold justice, sometimes. But certainly none of us knew anyone who was related to a judge. Especially not the son of a judge. I doubt any of us ever considered the fact that judges might even have sons. We looked at our little shipmate with the big nose with a new respect.

Schnozz never told us exactly where he had come from, but I got the impression it was somewhere in the Middle West. Maybe a small town in Iowa or Ohio. Anyway, he said there were lots of trees and green lawns in his home town, with flower beds behind white fences. Schnozz told us his own house was big and white with black shutters and four round columns flanking the front door. At Christmas time there was always a big holly wreath on the door itself and the colored glow of Christmas lights through the front windows.

By that time, Schnozz had us all by the short hairs. Even Joe Cook was only nominally suspicious and prodded Schnozz on with grudgingly respectful questions. None of us had ever been inside such a house as Schnozz described, much less lived in one. It was all new and fascinating.

"Your old man's a judge and you lived in a house like that?" Joe Cook said. "How come you ain't no God-damned officer? What the hell you doing in a white hat?"

Instantly timorous and made fearful by the bluntness of Joe's doubt, Schnozz's old deference came back. He looked from one to another of us as though pleading for help. His air was so abject I felt sorry for him. "Hell, Joe," I said, laughing. "You know Schnozz can't march worth a damn. Officers have to march better than we do, for Christ's sake." That was the truth, too. Along with all his other shortcomings, Schnozz *couldn't* march in time with music, or even keep in step with the other men. How he ever got through Boot Camp, I don't know.

Joe Cook didn't say anything else, and the others laughed along with me at the mere thought of someone like Schnozz being an officer. Hell, he didn't even look like an officer.

Heartened, Schnozz went on. We all wanted to hear more about his house and family. "Mom's name is Emily," Schnozz said. "Dad always wanted to buy her a fur coat, but she wouldn't let him. Her coat did have a fur collar, though." His voice became suddenly quieter. "I remember how soft and warm it was against my face when she kissed me good-bye," Schnozz said. "And it smelled nice."

Even Joe Cook was moved by what seemed the bared emotion in Schnozz's voice. The rest of us were completely enthralled that one of us had such a home and family.

"Aunt Minnie lived with us," Schnozz went on. "She was Mom's sister, and she could cook like anything. Especially cookies. I remember how they tasted while they were still warm from the oven."

We all smiled at the thought of fresh cookies like that, even though few of us ever knew the experience in real life. But Schnozz's voice made it seem like we had.

"Anything I couldn't get out of Dad or Mom I could always get out of Aunt Minnie.' Schnozz went on. "Mom always said Aunt Minnie spoiled me rotten. Dad was always telling Mom she was going to have to speak to her sister. She wasn't doing me any good letting me have my own way all the time.

"I remember one Christmas," Schnozz said. "We were going to the Country Club dance, and Polly Benedick — she lived next door to us, and I knew her just about my whole life then — got me appointed to the dance committee. Polly was always trying to get me 'out of my shell', as she put it."

"Hell, you must have been just a kid," Joe Cook said. "How come a kid gets on a dance committee?"

Our rapt attention gave Schnozz an assurance we never saw in him before. He answered Joe firmly. "They wanted some kids on the committee so the young people would feel part of the goings on." He paused and looked directly at Joe as though challenging him. "I wasn't chairman or anything. I was just on the committee. Polly did most of the work, anyway."

"Go on, Schnozz," we prodded. We were getting impatient with Joe and his doubting interruptions.

"Well, Dad got all upset when it was time to go. He didn't like dances. He only went to please Mom and Aunt Minnie, he said. He especially didn't like getting into his old tux. Dad always said the worst thing about being a judge was that he had to wear a tux sometimes. He had gained a little weight, and it wasn't very comfortable, I guess."

We all grinned at the thought of getting into a tuxedo as a problem. Hell, most of us didn't even know what the hell a tux *was*, for Christ's sake. "Go on, Schnozz," I said.

"Well, that night was especially bad because something white got spilled on Dad's silk hat," Schnozz said. "He hadn't worn it since last year's dance, and he didn't want to wear it that night, but Mom and Aunt Minnie made him wear it. They took a damp towel and got the worst of the white stuff off, and we all went to the dance."

"Did you wear a — what did you call it — a tux, Schnozz?" someone asked.

"No. I didn't even have one. Not yet. Dad said he would get me one when I went away to college, but —"

"You went to college, Schnozz?" I blurted. That was too much to swallow all in one bite.

This time, Schnozz did hesitate. "No," he stammered. "No, not then, but Dad was fixing to get me into his old school. He said he would get me a tux when I got accepted. I was still in high school when all this happened."

I don't remember now how long Schnozz went on like that. We were still grouped around him, hanging on every detail of a life such as none of us had ever known. Instinctively, we knew we would probably never know such a life.

The most surprising thing, though, was the change in Schnozz. He had the mid watch that night and when he stood to go below for some sleep, he did so with an assurance none of us ever saw in him before. The open respect with which we listened to him jacked him up, I suppose, and lent him a self-confidence which allowed him to face down even Joe Cook. "I got the mid," he said. "I gotta go down and get some sleep."

From that time on, Schnozz enjoyed not only an equal status among the rest of us, but a damned sight higher status than most of us. For my part, I was glad to see him come into his own. The rest of us felt the same way, I think. Except for Joe Cook.

I guess Joe could not accept Schnozz's rise in the eyes of his shipmates without seeing in it an at least implicit lowering of his own status. He never openly challenged Schnozz after that first night, but he lurked on the outskirts of the group which formed around Schnozz as he talked. He wouldn't say anything but his face was dark, and he didn't laugh along with Schnozz the way the rest of us did.

Actually, Schnozz didn't talk very often. He told us stories of his old life only every three or four months. Later, we learned there was a reason for that, but we saw nothing remarkable about it at the time. In fact, he never volunteered anything. He talked only after we pressed him, and not always then.

Usually, it was only after he was well into some account of the wonderful life he had at home that he relaxed and spoke with much animation at all. He seemed to need the nourishment he took from our respectful attention. And, to us who never knew such things, they were adventures.

One time he told us how he and Polly Benedick put together a stage show. "I couldn't sing or dance," Schnozz said, grinning self-consciously, "but, as Dad always said, I was loud. Noise, Dad said, could make up for a lot."

Other times he told us about school pep rallies and stuff like that. Schnozz always, he said, had trouble with girls. There were always girls in his stories. But his wise old judge of a father helped him over the humps. His Dad knew just about everything there was to know about girls. Come to that, his Dad knew just about everything about everything. But Schnozz made him seem like a great old guy. After a while, it got so we felt like we knew the old judge, Schnozz described him so well and lovingly.

All of that must have been in the last months of 1940 and the early part of 1941. Our ships' peacetime gray was already painted over to wartime black, and we steamed without lights while at sea. War was closing in on us, but no one realized it at the time. We continued in our usual way, seldom bothered by much outside our routine watches and drills.

Schnozz became a respected member of the signal bridge by that time and, as a result, became a damned good signalman, although still awkward in some things. We all came to like him, I think. All except Joe Cook, that is.

Joe was morose and even more resentful of his failure to be promoted than before. Even after he was finally promoted to first class, sometime in June of 1941, his attitude remained sour. I guess he was used to being a jerk and just couldn't break the habit. He tried some of his old tricks on Schnozz a few times, but none of us supported him and Schnozz himself did not submit so tamely as he did before.

Joe took to going ashore alone. We saw him sometimes, slumped over a back street bar, drinking in sullen silence, against the pain he must have felt at the loss of Schnozz as a whipping boy and the way that Schnozz, rather than Joe, was the bridge hero. Joe couldn't match, with his stories of growing up, the wonderful things Schnozz told us about his former life. Even the nickname — Schnozz — no longer was said with any animus, but became the expression of warm affection a nickname ought to be.

I remember, one time, seeing Joe standing by himself in the sidewalk line for the New Congress Rooms. He pretended he didn't see me, but it was Joe all right. And all by himself.

Another time I saw him sitting alone in the darkness of the Beretania movie theater. Certainly, the gods fell when a sailor like Joe Cook found himself going to movies alone. This time, too, Joe pretended not to see me, but it was him, all right, even though he denied it when I asked him about the picture the next day on the ship.

Joe seldom talked with anyone anymore, but I don't think many of us much gave a damn. Schnozz, by that time, fit into the signal gang and the bridge became a happy place for all of us. Except for Joe. That is the way things were for several months.

That is why it was so surprising when Joe returned to the ship one night and came to the bridge, all smiles, for a cup of coffee before turning in. I had the watch that night, and there were the usual hangers-on around the coffee pot. I remember feeling a twinge of caution at Joe's manner.

"Where's Schnozz?" Joe said, just a bit too casually.

"He's got the mid," I said. "He turned in a while ago."

"Well, it can wait, I guess," Joe said. "I just wanted to ask him something." He seemed greatly pleased with himself.

Joe finished his coffee and went below, leaving me strangely uneasy in the night. Blinker drills were over, and there was no traffic between ships or with the signal tower in the Yard. The warm Hawaiian night, made to seem even warmer by the smoke of burning cane fields in Aiea, was the same as always, but I felt a chill sense of something changed. And not for the better.

I was not long left in doubt. The very next day, Joe, with a flair uncommon in him of late, invited the whole liberty section to go ashore to celebrate his birthday. "Take in a movie," he said. "Get something to eat and have a few drinks at Wo Fat's. Maybe play a little clutch-butt with the bar hops."

I think we were all a little dubious about Joe's new-found generosity, but nobody was going to let a little doubt stand in the way of a free run ashore. Signalmen were given then what was called Watchstanders' Liberty which meant we could leave the ship at one o'clock. Lesser types had to wait until four or five. Anyway, at around two, we were all on the quarterdeck, liberty cards in hand. Schnozz was changed out of my watch by then, but was still in my liberty section. He was there with us.

There was a new Clark Gable movie in Honolulu at that time. At the Waikiki Theater on Kapiolani. I think we all expected that to be the movie Joe asked us to see with him. But it wasn't.

There was also a movie theater on Beretania Street in Honolulu. Britain, especially Britain's Navy, played a big part in Hawaiian history. Beretania was a common proper noun in Hawaii. It was as close as the islanders could come to pronouncing Brittania. Anyway, the theater on Beretania was where Joe wanted to take us.

None of us knew what picture was playing. Certainly not Schnozz. He came along readily as Joe led us up the curving street. It was only when he saw the marquee sign that he stopped. A new Andy Hardy picture was playing.

Joe watched Schnozz closely all this time. "What's the matter, Schnozz? You don't like Andy Hardy pictures?"

Schnozz stood as though stricken. All the assurance and self-confidence he gained in recent months seemed to fall away, leaving him alone and staring at Joe as though acknowledging a fatal blow.

"What's wrong, Schnozz?" I asked. "You all right?"

"Yeah, Schnozz," Joe said, his voice ugly. "Ain't you feeling so good?"

Schnozz then looked at each of us in turn. I have never, either before or since, seen such an expression of despair in a human face. "I — I just thought of something," he blurted. "I got to go. I got to do something on the ship." He turned and ran almost as though in panic away from us. Joe caught at his arm, but he tore himself away.

The rest of us were puzzled at what happened. "What the hell's going on?" we demanded of Joe. "What's wrong with Schnozz?"

Joe grinned evilly. Cold satisfaction glittered in his eyes. "You guys been believing all the crap that little son-of-a-bitch's been feeding you, ain't you? Well, I ain't."

"What the hell are you talking about?" I said.

"All that talk about his old man being a judge, and belonging to a country club and going to college and everything."

"So what?"

"So, there ain't none of it true, you silly bastards. Every bit of it come out of Andy Hardy movies, for Christ's sake. He didn't even have sense enough to change the God-damned names. Emily and Aunt Minnie and Polly Benedick. The big-nosed little son-of-a-bitch ain't any better than the rest of us. Probably not as good. You seen how he run away."

Joe went on a good deal longer, but I didn't stick around to hear the rest of it. The others did, though. They gathered around him, buttering him up just the way they did before Schnozz came along. I felt sick to my stomach and went back to the ship.

I waited up for Schnozz that night, but he never came back. I never saw him again. They found his whites down by the docks. We knew they were his because sailors' names were stenciled in all their clothes. The only way he could get off the island was by stowing-away in a foreign-flag merchant ship. In that case he would have thrown away his dog tags and changed his name.

Anyway, thirty days later, Schnozz was declared a deserter. That's when I bought the handkerchief.

THE SHIPS DO SAIL

I had not read Melville's *Billy Budd* when Eddie Helwig first joined our ship but, when I later came to read the famous story, the comparison between Melville's improbably good young sailor and Helwig was inescapable.

If you remember the story, Billy Budd was a young merchant seaman pressed into the crew of a British warship where his purity of character and beauty of soul made him a favorite of everyone on board, including his officers. But it was that same purity of character and soul which led him into a conflict of tragic consequence, in a Navy and in a world in which there sometimes seemed little room for goodness.

Helwig's problems turned out to be, if not quite so fatal as those of Billy Budd, almost as tragic. Certainly they left me with regrets I have yet to lose, and memories still troubling in dark nights when sleep is slow to come.

Our ship, a heavy cruiser flagship, was in California's Mare Island Navy Yard for overhaul. Yard time for a Navy ship is a dour time at best. Yard workers clamber about in their muddy work shoes to make a Godawful mess of the decks. Air hoses and electrical cables lead everywhere in black tangles to trip people and leave their own filthy tracks on scrubbed teak. The engines are shut down, of course. Even the auxiliaries are idle, causing the ship to lie as though dead without that eternal hum, buzz and throb of pumps, blowers and dynamos which become so much a part of sailors' lives they are no longer heard.

Yard time is when as many sailors as possible are given their leaves, as well, so as not to lose valuable training time. Half-empty compartments and subdued mess tables add to the overall sense of gloom. Often we did not even have heat in the ship. That was when Helwig joined us.

We had been in the Yard for more than two months with almost a month more before the job would be done. That, to a very large extent, was the source of Helwig's problems — and the very real effects they had on us all.

Except for when we were in our home port we stayed in no one place more than two or three days and had little chance to meet local people, other than bartenders, cab drivers, cocktail waitresses and the like. If a sailor got along with his shipmates he had few problems and, certainly, Helwig had little trouble in that regard.

Never late for his watch, always clean and cheerful, and forever ready to help out in difficult moments, Helwig was as near perfect a shipmate as a sailor could expect. Already a signalman third class, he was no more than twenty years old. And those were calendar years. In knowledge of the world, he was much younger and naive to the point of vulnerability in what was, in fact, a rough world peopled by men many times his superior in both experience and dissipation.

He neither smoked nor drank nor, to my knowledge, cursed and blasphemed the way most of us did. In the coarse language of our old Chief on the bridge, "Helwig wouldn't say shit if he had his mouth full."

On top of all that, Helwig was a recruiting officer's dream in appearance and bearing. Blonde, perfectly proportioned, and almost too handsome, he achieved this state of near perfection with so little apparent effort, or even of awareness of it, that he stirred no resentment in us. Most of us, in fact, were protective of him and tried to steer him clear of the worst of the ways in which we lived.

In the matter of girls, for instance, we kept him out of the clutches of the B-girls who then worked the bars of California's sailor towns. B-girls made their precarious livings by getting sailors to buy them glasses of colored water for which the sailors were charged champagne prices. The girls got a cut of the proceeds. It was commonly believed they added to their incomes by a little prostitution on the side.

Anyway, we kept Helwig away from them and, certainly we did not take him with us to the whorehouses where disease and dissolution lay so readily at hand.

I never learned if Helwig had "a girl back home," but if he didn't, he should have. Without ever saying so, I think all of us on the bridge joined in an unspoken conspiracy to save him for that girl, whoever and wherever she might be.

We realized, of course, that if Helwig stayed in the Navy he would, in time, become like us, but we didn't want that to happen before it had to. And none of us, I think, wanted to be responsible when it did happen. Certainly I didn't.

The oddest thing about all this though, was the effect it had upon the rest of us. It sounds strange, but Helwig changed *us* during the brief time he was with us. Without our realizing the fact, we cussed less and talked less about the anatomical details of women and their various uses. Some of us even drank less in Georgia Street's gin mills and called less at the whorehouses in Virginia Street. God knows what would have happened if Helwig had been among us longer than he was. We might even have become more like the Navy liked to think we were — going to church and reading good books and never drinking or using bad words.

Anyway, because we were so long in the Yard, we came to know people on the beach. Vallejo, then, was a small town in which virtually everyone lived off the Navy in one way or another. Built on steep hills across the narrow Napa River from Mare Island Navy Yard, Vallejo's streets met at rigid right angles in a grid which made no allowance whatever for grades. It was not an easy town for walkers. One block of Capitol Street, in fact, was a flight of stairs, it was so steep.

Vallejo looked more like an East Coast mill town than anyplace else I saw in California. Its houses were dingy wood frame structures with high pitched roofs and thin windows, sitting in unkempt yards dug into the sides of hills. Saint Vincent Ferrer's square red brick church tower atop one of the hills, along with the Casa Vallejo Hotel's tall vertical sign, dominated what skyline the town had.

North-and-south streets were named for California's Counties. East-and-west streets were named for States of the Union. Georgia Street, the lower reaches of it, anyway, was Vallejo's sailor street. Bars, tattoo parlors, gin mills, credit jewelers, all the gimcrackery an ingenious society could devise for separating sailors from their money, while, at the same time, keeping them safely isolated from the more respectable parts of town, made lower Georgia Street a loud, noisome and stench-ridden ghetto holding out every form of debauchery known to man — while working hard on any not yet discovered.

Georgia Street ended at the river where small ferries, little larger than water taxis and all named for birds, hauled sailors back and forth between town and Navy Yard. Georgia Street was the first land sailors touched upon coming ashore — and often the last, as well, if Virginia Street be excepted.

Virginia Street paralleled Georgia Street one block to the north. Virginia Street was the street of Vallejo's whorehouses; rundown Victorians with stained glass panels to either side of their front doors. Their windows rattled as sailors went by even when there was no wind. The rattling was that of the girls inside knocking their knuckles against the glass to attract trade. Unlike Georgia Street's garish neon and naked bulbs, Virginia Street was poorly-lighted and crowded with shadows. Figures, both moving and still, were seen through torn curtains at dimly-lighted windows. Raucous recorded music blared forth from opened doors as sailors came and went.

We never took Helwig to see any of that. Most often he stayed on board or went to Rodman Center, the Navy's big recreation complex in the Yard where all kinds of wholesome — and deadly boring — stuff was available. Movies, bowling alley, ping-pong, all of it free or at very little cost. Most of us old guys wouldn't be caught dead there — except for when it was close to payday and we were broke and couldn't afford to go ashore for the more manly stuff in Georgia and Virginia Streets.

Anyway, I met a girl on the beach. Her name was Helen something. She worked in a Vallejo store. We got along from the start. She must have been thirty-three or -four at the time. She was not beautiful, or even pretty, but I was old enough to know looks are a damned poor measure of a woman. She was a lot of fun, in bed and out. We both knew the ship one day would sail and that we stood little chance ever of seeing each other again. We told each other that was all right.

One big part of Helen's attractiveness for me was that I could talk with her about the damnedest things sometimes. She never laughed at me the way some women will. She was smart, too. She had one hell of a lot more answers than I did. Sometimes I got to thinking maybe we might even . . . But sanity prevailed and we enjoyed what we had while we had it, remembering all the time that someday, ships do sail.

I told Helen one time about Helwig. About how damned *good* he was and everything. I told her how the guys on the ship all liked him, and how we wanted to keep him from going the way we had. As long as we could, anyway. I even told her how he was affecting the rest of us in our behavior.

"What that kid needs is a good girl to take care of him," Helen laughed. "Before the other kind get their hooks into him." Helen talked like a sailor sometimes.

"You got any ideas?" I asked.

"Maybe. I got a niece. Seventeen. Nice kid. Still in school, but old enough to get into trouble easy." Helen turned serious. "I don't want anything to happen to her, Sailor. You got that?"

"I got it," I said. "But anybody gets in trouble, more than likely it'll be Helwig. That kid knows nothing from nothing." I paused and looked at her directly. "I don't want nothing happening to Helwig, either."

Helen looked at me shrewdly. "Yeah?"

"Yeah."

"Well, you want me to fix him up with my niece or not?"

Even then, I was a little reluctant to start something I might not be able to stop. Helwig wouldn't be the first sailor to let his gonads run away with him. And he was so damned naive he was easy picking for a girl. And he was so damned serious. It would be easy for a guy like Helwig to forget that someday, ships do sail. That's when sailors get in trouble — when they forget ships do sail. But, hell, he had to learn some time.

"Okay," I said at last. "How we going to do it?"

"Best way is to double date a few times. Find out if they go for each other. After that, they're on their own," Helen said. "You got the duty tomorrow night?"

"No." Duty for signalmen was light while ships are in for Yard. There's a telephone line ashore, and few other ships to signal in any case. There wasn't a hell of a lot for us to do.

"How about wonder boy?"

"I'll get him off."

Cheap hotel rooms in those days did not have bedside telephones. Helen threw on a robe and went down the hall. I used the time to go to the head. I was a little dubious about what I was doing. Helwig had not asked me to stick my big nose into his life. I had seen enough young sailors get in over their heads to know it can happen even to the savviest guys. And Helwig was not the savviest guy. Not in that sense, he wasn't.

Anyway, Helen came back and said everything was set. We'd go to a movie the next night and have a coke afterwards. Play it by ear after that.

But the whole damned thing almost blew up in my face before it started. Helwig did not want to go. Like a lot of young guys are, he was literally afraid of girls — while, at the same time, fatally drawn to them by the crotch drive we all have when we are young. "Hell, kid," I said. "I promised. I told the girl you'd be there, for Christ's sake. You're making me look like a damned fool."

Of course, Helwig wouldn't do anything like that to a shipmate. The date was on.

Helen's niece was a cute and perky blonde kid in saddle shoes, bobby socks and a soft sweater with definite points of interest. She was small and as pretty as Helwig was handsome, but with none of his shyness whatsoever. They would have made the damnedest Norman Rockwell painting you ever saw. She, the high school cheerleader and he, the football hero.

Poor Helwig didn't stand a chance in hell from the first time he saw her. I smelled trouble coming — but it looked like the kind of trouble that would be a lot of fun for Helwig. I hoped so, anyway.

It was winter. Helwig's blues set off his blonde good looks with dramatic effect upon the girl. Penny was her name, short for Penelope. Her old man was a machinist in the Yard.

The sight of sailors fell well short of being a novelty in Vallejo, of course. Penny had seen sailors from the time she was old enough to remember anything, but she had never talked with one. Helwig, in addition to everything else, had the appeal of the forbidden for her. She dimpled and smiled at him in a way which made me feel, all of a sudden, like an old man.

That Penny had never talked to a sailor may sound strange, but it wasn't all that unusual. As did most Vallejo families, Penny's protected their daughters from sailors as much as they could. The families knew damned well that ships do sail. But all this, I suspect, made sailors that much more interesting to Vallejo girls. It added the implied lure of danger, I suppose. Especially for girls with any spirit at all, and Penny had spirit sticking out all over her.

As for Helwig, that night he sat most of the time with what looked like a severe case of sunburn. Every time Penny spoke or even looked at him, he blushed red. But, oddly, after a first few awkward moments, he found himself able to talk and laugh as though they had known each other for a long time. He kept on blushing, but he was having himself one hell of a time. So was Penny.

It was fun just to watch them together, and to remember what it was like all those years ago when I was something like Helwig. I was never *that* good, of course, but I was one hell of a lot better than I got to be later. Helen squeezed my hand and looked at me as though she knew what I remembered. That was another good thing about her. It was not always comfortable, but she always seemed to know what I was thinking before I did. Maybe she was being reminded of things, too.

After that night, we double-dated as often as we could. We knew the ship would sail in a couple of weeks. Helwig was terrified at the thought and hungered every waking moment to be with Penny. I suspect he dreamed a good bit about her at night as well. Actually, I never had so much fun in my life as I did then. We didn't do a damned thing except go to movies and roller skating and high school basketball games and stuff like that. The guys on the ship got to teasing me about it. I didn't give a damn. I was having a good time. So was Helwig.

It was Helen who finally put the brakes on. We were walking along that street which was a flight of stairs. There was a half moon out. From the top of the steps we could see San Pablo Bay and the marshlands beyond Mare Island to the west, shining, all dim and mysterious in the moonlight. It was our favorite place for talking together — Helen and I, Helwig and Penny.

Usually, Helen and I lagged back so Helwig and Penny could have a little privacy. That was about the only privacy they ever got. I didn't know yet why Penny could not invite Helwig to her house or go on dates with him unless Helen was with her. "Those two are getting into some pretty deep stuff," Helen said. "Somebody's likely to get something caught in the wringer, things keep on going like they are."

To tell the truth, I was thinking pretty much the same thing. Helwig showed all the classic signs of being in love. And with none of the experience we older guys had, he was in way over his head. In a moment of confidence one night on the bridge he even talked with me about how a man could get out of the Navy before his time was up.

I laughed, trying to make a joke of it. "We'll be sailing in a couple of weeks, that'll throw a little water on the fire, Kid. Take a nice cold shower. You'll feel better in the morning."

But things had already gone too far for jokes. Helwig glared at me. "You wouldn't understand," he gritted. "Penny's different from the girls you guys know. We're going to get married."

The way he said it made me believe Helwig understood a good deal more about me and the other old guys than I thought he did. All of a sudden, I felt kind of dirty.

"Married?" I said, surprised. I didn't think things had gone that far. Or that he could be so God-damned stupid, either. "Have you told the Navy about this, Kid?"

Signalmen third in those days made sixty dollars a month, less hospital fees. The Navy, in its well-justified wisdom did not approve marriage for lower-rated men like Helwig.

It did not approve of marriage for more senior petty officers either, for that matter. I know I sure as hell did not like having married men on any bridge of mine. They were forever asking favors and making excuses. We called them brown-baggers. Fortunately, there were not many of them in the Navy at that time. Navy pay was not conducive to happy marriages. Neither was shoving off for God-forsaken places all around the world on little or no notice, for God knew how long a time.

"I don't have to tell the God-damned Navy anything," Helwig blurted. "In a couple of years I'll be out, and the Navy can go pound sand up its ass."

That slowed me down. It was the first time I ever heard Helwig cuss. I could see he was mad and it wouldn't do much good to push him while he was feeling like that. I decided to give him a little letting alone. Maybe it would all go away.

It was Helen who cleared things up. I met her that night on the beach and told her what Helwig said. "Oh, for Christ's sake," she said. "I was afraid of something like that."

"So was I," I said. "But what the hell can we do?"

She drank her beer. "First thing's to keep the little bastard on the ship. Don't let him come ashore. Can you do that?"

"Not forever," I said. "Not unless he goofs off. And Helwig does not goof off."

Helen thought about that for a minute. She sipped again from her beer. "Well, they're not getting married," she said coldly. "What we got to do is keep them from doing something stupid until they realize it."

Something in the way Helen said Helwig and Penny would not get married stuck in my craw. "What the hell you mean, they're not getting married? What the hell's wrong with Helwig? He's not good enough for her, maybe?"

Helen looked at me patiently, as though trying to explain something to a child. A very dumb child. "For one thing, the Navy won't let him," she said. "For another thing, Penny's family won't let her. Especially, her father won't let her."

That puzzled me. "What's that supposed to mean?" I knew Penny's father had learned his trade as a machinist's mate in the Navy. Why would he oppose a sailor?

"Her dad's already giving me a bad time for getting Penny to go out with the kid in the first place."

"Okay, let's try it again. What's wrong with Helwig?"

"One, he's a sailor," Helen said. "Two — and a damned sight more important — he's a sailor with a right arm rate."

Right here, I better explain. Some people now — even some sailors now — do not remember that until not long after the end of World War II, some Navy Petty Officers wore their rating badges on their right arms and others wore theirs on their left arms. Rating badges are those inverted chevrons Navy petty officers wear on their uniforms, with a specialty mark in the notch of the chevrons and a spread eagle perched on top of it all. The eagle is why sailors, with characteristic irreverence, spoke of their rating badges as their "crows."

The difference was that right arm rates were those specialties peculiar to the Navy. Boatswains mates, gunners, quartermasters, fire controlmen, and signalmen all were right arm rates. Everyone else was a left arm rate. Machinists, electricians, and carpenters, for instance, were left arm rates. They could leave the Navy and get good jobs in the Yard or in private industry. Hell, the Navy made that a big part of its recruiting pitch: Join the Navy, learn a trade. The sailors' own explanation was: "If what you know is not worth a damn on the outside, you're a right arm rate."

That is what Helen meant by what she said. Helwig was a right arm rate. Penny's old man was a left arm rate, a machinist's mate who got out and got a good job in the Yard. When the ships sailed, guys like Penny's old man stayed right there in Vallejo, drawing down good money and building up a nice fat pension. Home every night and respectable as hell.

"You're not serious?" I said.

"I don't have to be serious," Helen said. "Penny's old man is serious enough for all of us. He's not about to let Penny marry a right arm rate and spend the rest of her life chasing from one crummy Navy port to another all over the world."

Well, that didn't leave me one hell of a lot to say. I didn't want Helwig getting married either, but it grated a little to have him put down just because he was a right arm rate. Hell, I was a right arm rate, too.

Anyway, I took Helen home a good deal earlier than she wanted and went back to the ship, after a stop or two in Georgia Street. Georgia Street drinks were not the strongest drinks in the world, but enough of them, taken close together, could put a man on his ass. In short, I got myself so God-damned drunk I couldn't see straight, and thereby added my bit to the reputation of right arm rates, I guess.

Sleeping compartments in the old cruisers were not palatial. Paired sets of six three-deep bunks were mounted on stanchions with racks for our wash buckets at the ends. A lot of us did our own laundry in those days. At sea we even took our baths in buckets. Stainless steel lockers, big enough to hold our clothes, but no bigger, were jammed in wherever they would fit. The lockers were not big enough to hold our pea coats, the short, cold weather overcoats. Those were kept in a special compartment somewhere else in the ship.

But, at least, we had bunks and did not have to live out of our seabags. In the old battleships sailors still slept in hammocks and kept everything they owned in canvas sea bags where what you wanted was always at the bottom of the God-damned things and had to be mined for.

Drunk as I was, I still felt, as I always felt upon returning to a ship, a sense of coming home. No matter how stormy the weather outside, or how degenerate the last run ashore, ships' living compartments were always, after Taps, warm and quiet and filled with the comforting scents and sounds of sleeping men. Officers almost never came there, and when they did they took off their caps. Sailors in their bunks were safe.

I suppose it is not all that strange that I should feel so at such times, since I remembered no other home or anything like so much security. As a boy, my homes had been orphanages, poor and dirty places from which I fled into the Navy at the first chance I got for its promise of better chow and a clean dry place to sleep, if nothing else.

I went to Helwig's bunk. I sometimes go through a maudlin stage in my drunks. Maybe that was all it was that night, but I wanted to clear away the hard feelings which came between Helwig and me before I went ashore that day. I liked the guy and I guess I felt guilty for getting him mixed up with Penny in the first place.

Because they were in a good part of the compartment, the bunks above and below Helwig's, and the two to either side had guys sleeping in them. I didn't want anybody else to hear what I meant to say to Helwig. There was already enough talk going around about how we spent so much time together. In my boozy confusion, I finally said nothing and crapped out in my own rack. Whatever I meant to say could wait.

I wonder now, though, if maybe things might have worked out differently had I spoken to Helwig that night. First of all, I was drunk enough probably to tell the truth. In the second place, hard feelings just get harder if they're left untended. We mustered on station the next morning and Helwig wouldn't speak to me.

I learned later he called Penny from the dock the night before. We didn't have phones in the ships then for white hats, but some officers of the deck would let us call from a pay phone ashore.

Helwig had not talked with Penny, but he did talk with her old man. The old man told Helwig what he could do with his right arm rate. He told Helwig never to call Penny again. Most of all, Helwig was never ever to see her again. Best thing,

Penny's old man said, was for Helwig to keep his ass on the ship until it sailed.

I don't know why Helwig blamed me for all that, but he sure as hell did. And, after me, he blamed Helen. He was in one foul son-of-a-bitching mood. The fact that none of us ever saw him like that before made the effect all the more telling.

Some of the guys tried to kid Helwig out of his mood, but that didn't work worth a damn. A couple of them even got themselves invited back to the fantail. The fantail was the aftermost part of the main deck. It couldn't be seen by quarterdeck officers. It was where guys went to settle things in what we called knuckle discussions. Helwig was the last guy in the world I expected to see on the fantail, but he sure as hell meant it when he asked those two guys to meet him there.

I saw to it that Helwig did not go ashore that night. Or for the next two nights as well, but after that I couldn't hold him aboard any longer without a better reason.

I told Helen what had happened, though, and asked her to keep Penny away from Helwig. We were only a week from sailing by that time. If we could keep a lid on things for that long, maybe it would all blow over.

It might have worked, too, if I kept Helwig on board. But he went to the chief, and I had to let him off the ship. He wouldn't let me go with him.

The worst thing I feared was that he would get into it with Penny's old man. That could mean cops and jails. It could also mean doctors and hospitals. I had never met him, but Helen had told me Penny's old man was a mean son-of-a-bitch.

Then I feared Helwig would simply shove off, with or without Penny. If he did run, it meant AWOL at best, desertion at worst. Either way, his Navy life would be screwed up.

Signalmen got what was called Watchstander's Liberty in those days. We could leave the ship at one o'clock. Regular liberty did not start until four or five o'clock. Helwig went ashore the minute he could, but I didn't find out he was gone until evening chow. He didn't show up at the mess table. One of the guys said he saw Helwig go ashore.

"He had a face like a God-damned thunderstorm," the guy said.

I wasn't supposed to have liberty that night, but I talked to the chief and explained the problem. He even suggested I take some of the other guys with me to head Helwig off before he did something really dumb and got his ass caught in a crack he couldn't get it out of.

I put the other guys to a sweep of Georgia Street bars. I didn't much think Helwig would be there, but you never knew with young guys in girl trouble.

I felt pretty sure Helwig would try to see Penny, but I didn't know where she lived. I called Helen for the address.

"What for?" Helen asked, immediately suspicious. "Why do you want Penny's address?"

"Helwig's ashore," I said. "I don't know where to look for him. I thought he might try to find Penny."

That was another good thing about Helen. You didn't have to explain things to her. She hesitated, but only for a moment. "Okay, Sailor," she said. "But you are not to go up to the door, you hear? You'll get your own dumb head blown off."

But she gave me the address. It was out on Ohio Street. I didn't go up to the door, but I walked past the house a few times, hoping Penny would come out, so I could try talking some sense into her.

When Penny didn't show, I went to the top of the flight of stairs where Helwig and I so often talked with our girls and sat to wait. I could see Penny's house from where I sat. I thought Helwig might show up. But he didn't.

As it happened, I never did see Helwig. But as I was walking down the hill, I saw Penny. She was walking home from school with four or five other girls, laughing and horsing around as though nothing in the world was wrong. She stopped short when she saw me. The other girls giggled and stared at me.

"Have you seen Helwig?" I asked Penny.

"Why?" Penny laughed, playing to her friends. "Why do you want to know?"

"He's ashore," I said. "I thought he might try to see you."

"Why on earth would he want to see me?" Penny laughed again, looking to her friends.

I guess something in my face finally got Penny's attention. She motioned for her friends to move on.

"I can't see Eddie anymore," she said when we were alone. "Daddy won't let me. Helen told him about Eddie. I — I have to go now."

She didn't look all that broken up about it but there was no use in my trying to change that. Helwig had been dumped. That might not have mattered much to most guys, but I knew damned well it would matter to Helwig.

We never saw Helwig again. The guy I sent to the bus station said no one there saw anyone who looked like him. He probably hitchhiked out of town. God knows where he wound up. After a while we didn't speak of him anymore. In a way, it was a relief. Guys like Helwig can make a signal bridge an uncomfortable place.

OFFICERS AND MEN

I t always bugged the hell out of me that newspaper casualty lists spoke of "officers" and "men" when telling how many died in a battle or some accidental disaster, preserving even in death the sacred distinction between white hats and their betters, like maybe one was deader than the other.

It is a time-honored practice, of course. One of my great-grandfathers, for example, as an old man, wrote a memoir of his experiences with the Army in its bloody campaign against the Seminole Indians in Florida. No one in our family paid any attention to it, but I read that tattered old book for hours on end, completely caught up in his descriptions of a world long gone and utterly alien from my own Middle Western boyhood.

The old man, at the time of his writing, still had a vigorous mind and colorful memory — and was much talented in the way of story telling. His memory may have been too colorful, but I remember still some of the stories he told, and how they made my hair stand on end.

In one, for instance, he wrote of an isolated garrison which was overrun somewhere near the Everglades and wiped out by what he called the "hostiles." The relief party, when it arrived, could do no more than bury the mutilated dead. Since it was a small force and exposed to danger itself, it did so hurriedly and in mass graves — one for enlisted men and one for officers. Even in death the separation was maintained. But that was a long time ago, and I was silly enough to think things might have changed by the middle of the twentieth century.

My grandfather never questioned or condemned the fact, but the gruesome irony of the old story stayed with me for years. So many years, in fact, that it was still alive — and stirred to new life — by something which happened to me in the Navy shortly before World War II.

I was a young signalman in one of the heavy cruisers then operating out of Pearl Harbor as an intended deterrent to an already menacing Japanese Navy. As a second cruise white hat, I had long since come to an accommodation with the separate worlds in which officers and enlisted men lived, but what happened brought new life to some old doubts.

As they did for most young sailors, the privileges of rank galled me as much as they did anyone. Some guys never adjusted to the reality, in fact, and left the Navy as quickly as possible. Those of us who stayed on came to accept the reality of the gap between officers and men as a somewhat silly and inexplicable rule in a game we agreed to play. As the old chiefs were forever telling us: "You wasn't drafted."

But it never occurred to me that the distinction between officers and men might still, even at this late date, extend into death and beyond, as happened to the poor soldiers in my great-grandfather's story of the Seminole wars in Florida.

We were firing a practice out of Pearl. The cruisers' eight-inch firing range was in rough and windy Alenuihaha Channel between the islands of Hawaii and Maui. The northeast trades in those latitudes are apt to be boisterous even if unimpeded. Compressed as they are between Maui's ten thousand foot Haleakala on one side and even higher Mauna

Kea on Hawaii on the other they become wild indeed and kick up a bitch of a sea.

The cruisers themselves, six hundred feet long and sixty or so in the beam, could handle the conditions with some comfort, but the target-towing tugs and motor launches used by the ships' target repair parties suffered badly at times.

Sometimes the ships, after bashing their brains out in a long day of firing would duck into the lee of Hawaii's twin mountains of Mauna Kea and Mauna Loa to ride at peaceful anchor through the night in some isolated cove on the Kona Coast. Things were not yet so tense that we could not find such pleasant respites and that is what we intended on this night.

Weather in the Hawaiian Islands seldom presented serious problems in the way of seakeeping, but hurricanes occasionally strayed up from the deeper tropics and lashed the islands with great winds, enormous seas, and sluicing downpours worthy of oceans anywhere.

We had warning of the approach of this storm by standard weather broadcasts. Since early morning the sea heaved in long telltale swells. We even saw, from shortly after noon, an ominous blue-black buildup of cloud in the southeast, but, safe in our big strong ship, we had little cause for concern. It meant an uncomfortable staying at sea for the night rather than the idyllic anchorage we hoped for, but life, even in the Navy, is full of disappointments.

Although the approaching storm offered little in the way of real hazard to ships at sea, it meant danger indeed to airplanes in flight among tall island mountains.

Heavy cruisers in those days carried four airplanes. They were small steel-tube-and-canvas biplanes which we fired off catapults and recovered from the sea alongside. With their large central pontoons and smaller wing tip floats, they could land in rough seas in the small slick of comparatively smooth water created by the ship's skidding stern as she turned.

When we stayed out for several days, unless too far away, we sometimes sent one of these planes to Pearl for a mail run. The plane, on its return, rendezvoused with us at our planned night anchorage. In addition to taking our outgoing mail, it brought back the incoming letters which are supposed to be so precious to us poor lonesome white hats.

Mail call sounded sometime after noon, and those who had outgoing letters hurried them to the post office where they were bagged and taken up to the plane which was being prepared.

The catapults, one to a side, were on a level with the signal bridge. When trained out for launching they held the planes very close to where we stood our watches. Even though the engines were of modest power compared with those of carrier planes, they thundered with deafening effect as they revved up to maximum revolutions only a few feet away from our buffeted ears. Power for the catapults came from cordite charges which exploded with reports as loud as five-inch guns.

When, at last, all was ready and the plane's engine turning over at full power, the pilot sat erect with his head against a special rest and his rear seat man leaned forward with his head between his knees against the shock of firing.

The silence following a launch was intense. The little plane dipped slightly off the end of the catapult, then climbed away, its sound fading quickly, and the rest of us to got on with our business in blessed silence.

I don't think any of us had much thought of danger on this day. The sky already was growing dark with the approaching storm, but we thought little of it. Pearl was only two or three hours away for even so slow a plane as ours. Maui, in fact, was near enough to be visible at the time we launched, a dim and fading darkness in the growing murk of the storm. The higher reaches of Haleakala already were lost in cloud.

Our plane was fitted with only primitive navigational gear, but it did have radio. If worst came to worst, it could come down to sea level and follow along the coast of an island to find some sheltered cove in which to land and spend an uncomfortable, but survivable, night riding to its own small but adequate anchor, letting us know by radio where it was.

We continued our firing exercises until the seas became too rough for the motor launch carrying the target repair party.

We hurried to hoist in our boats and to lash things down for what promised to be a rough night.

There was always a signalman in any small boat which left the ship. I usually liked the assignment for the break in routine it offered. But I was glad I was not out in a motor launch that day. The weather deteriorated rapidly, both in strength of wind and loss of visibility in rain which beat at us in seemingly solid sheets. It was hard to recover our launch without smashing it against the side of the ship.

I think it was then that I first came to worry about our plane. In such rain it would be impossible to follow any shoreline, no matter how low it flew. But Pearl was well to the north of us, and the wind, growing ever stronger, was out of the southeast. The plane might well arrive in Pearl before being overtaken by the full force of the storm.

Its presumed course was to skirt a long ridge stretching down to the southwest from Maui's Haleakala to end in the sea at Cape Hanamanioa. Passing then inside the small island of Kahoolawe, it would fly over the low pineapple island of Lanai and continue on in a straight shot for Pearl.

I gave the plane no further thought as we busied ourselves preparing the ship for the coming stormy night. Everything loose was lashed down and course was set to allow us to fall off before the wind without risk of fetching up on an island somewhere. We did not have radar then.

By evening chow — supper in the Navy — we steamed in full darkness of mingled wind and rain. Our rigging, signal halyards and the various braces and stays howled as though in terror of the violence of a wind so quickly built against us. At our reduced speed — we were making turns enough for bare steerageway — the ship had not yet suffered any damage, but she rolled heavily and sleep came hard that night.

The most vulnerable to the storm were our three remaining airplanes. Two of the three were struck below and secured in their hangars. They suffered no damage — although the hangar doors were bashed in before the night was through — but the third, left on a catapult, was lost over the side around about midnight, despite all the extra lashings we put on it.

I had the four-to-eight watch the next morning. Although light should have come early in that latitude and in that time of the year, darkness held until well past seven. Even then it surrendered only to a dirty gray of slashing rain and windblown spray.

One measure of the violence of the storm was that we were allowed to go through Officers' Country to reach the signal bridge. Things had to be pretty rough before we were allowed to defile those holy precincts with our presence. But the final stage of the climb took us across the open communications deck, exposed to the full power of the storm. This was the site of the radio shack. On impulse, I opened the dogged door and asked if there was any word from the mail plane.

The wind snatched the heavy door from my hands, creating its own minor storm inside. Amid flying paper, upset coffee cups, and the kind of language usually reserved for something serious, I was told to "shut that God-damned door!"

Once on the signal bridge, though, I used the telephone to check what was, by that time, a real sense of something bad going on. "No," the radioman answered, "we haven't heard a word."

Nor did we ever hear a word. Pearl reported our plane never reached there. Mail for us was collected from the base post office and taken to the seaplane base on Ford Island, but our plane never collected it.

Clearly, the plane was down somewhere. Its fuel would have been exhausted long before. Either it was overwhelmed by the storm and driven into the sea, or so blinded that it flew into a mountain. Given the plane's presumed course and the southeast wind direction, Maui's Haleakala was the most likely mountain.

But until the storm spent itself there was nothing we could do except alert Pearl so that any other airplanes or ships in the area might watch for the lost airplane.

It was a long twenty-four hours until we could launch aircraft for a proper search. Rough seas and high winds were no deterrent, but limited visibility was. It would do no good to launch aircraft if their crews could not see.

One of the Navy's most endearing traits, from our point of view, was that no effort was ever spared in searching out and helping any of its people who might be lost. Both of our remaining planes were readied, and the best of our lookouts selected to be rear seat men. That is how I came to be in the back seat of one of the search planes.

Signalmen were generally conceded to be the best of the ship's lookouts. They were trained to be so. And the Chief Signalman, when asked, named me and Joe Carter as having the best eyes on the bridge.

I had flown several times as rear seat man. In those days a lot of fighter, torpedo, and utility plane pilots were enlisted men. Dungaree pilots, we called them. Our pilots knew my ambition to become a pilot and sometimes let me go along if the mission were not a serious one. Sometimes they even let me take the controls.

When the sky did reopen, I found myself in the back seat of an airplane being fired over a sea still lumpy from the storm just past. The sky, too, remained restless and ragged with torn clouds and hurrying scud.

The most sensible route for us to take was what was presumed to be the lost plane's course. That, and somewhat to the right of it. Since the storm came from the southeast, it was logical to think the lost plane might have drifted off to the northwest of its planned course.

Maui's Haleakala therefore remained the most likely place to look. And Haleakala's most likely spot would be somewhere on the long spur leading down to the southwest from its barren crater summit. Although trending lower and lower to its end in the sea, the ridge remained high enough throughout its length to trap a blind-flying airplane in heavy rain.

For several hours we flew along Maui's precipitous southern coast without seeing anything but the island's lush green wall of cliffs which gushed hundreds of waterfalls, large and small, from the recent storm.

Ensign Hance flew the plane in which I rode. Ensign Blackwood the other. It was agreed between the two, after a time, that Blackwood would fly on along the track to Pearl, but that we, Ensign Hance and I, would continue on our search of Maui.

There was always a chance the lost airplane was simply overwhelmed in the storm and went down in the sea. In that case, we might never find trace of it, but I felt certain we would find it on Maui.

The problem was that the high cliffs along which we flew were engulfed in a dense green growth of tangled shrubs, ferns, and moss, all dripping wet and impenetrable to sight.

Had the lost airplane flown straight into the near vertical cliffs there would have been no time to cut switches. There most likely was a sizable fire from ruptured fuel tanks. The heavy rains of the storm were enough to wash away all but the most indelible signs, even of a fire. But that is what I watched for — a charred place in the dripping green wall of cliffs.

And that, in the end, is what we found. It was at about two thousand feet up on twenty-six hundred foot Puu Mahoe, a prominent peak almost straight inland from Kanaloa Point. Had the plane been no more than five or six hundred feet higher, or only a few hundred yards farther to the east, it would have cleared the land and brought us our mail.

All that was visible was heat-shriveled foliage and tangled bits of what once might have been an airplane. I called my pilot's attention to the place, and he circled low over it. Once suspected, it was easy to see. We had found our lost airplane. There was no sign of surviving life.

We returned at once to the ship which was steaming to meet us. I stood astride my pilot's cockpit to hook on the crane hook, and we were hoisted in. I felt drained of strength. Because of my interest in aviation, I knew Roger Bailey, rear seat man in the lost airplane. To a lesser extent, I knew Mister Wilken, the pilot, as well. Now they were dead. There was no question of that.

By late afternoon the ship reached the Maui coast off Kanaloa Point. A party to recover the two bodies of our shipmates was organized under the command of Ensign Hance. As a fellow aviator, it was felt he was most appropriate. But Harry Wright, a veteran chief boatswain's mate was in effective charge. Landing a boat through the heavy surf was a chancy operation at best and one best left to a seaman, as Wright certainly was.

The plane's wreckage was pinned against a virtually vertical cliff, kept from tumbling farther down only by the dense growth in which it was embedded. I saw it through the ship's forty-five power long glass. It would take little to send it tumbling down. I shuddered at the sight, imagining the two dead bodies sure to be there.

Since a signalman had to go in the boat, and since I saw the site, if only from the air, I volunteered.

There were corpsmen, too, to ready the bodies for removal and treat any injuries to the rescuers. There was also a cook, with food and water supplies in case we might be on shore past mealtimes. After that, there were ten or twelve white hats to handle the donkey work.

For gear, we had shrouds and wire stretchers for the two dead bodies, all the half-inch manila line we could carry, a first aid kit, and hand axes and other small tools and tackles. Although the crash site was two or three miles inland, and some two thousand feet high, the job appeared to be a straightforward piece of hard work requiring little more than muscle and engineering genius.

The landing, of course, was the first problem. Surf never appears so fearsome from seaward as it is. But the leftover rough water from the recent storm and the runoff of heavy rain left the inshore water brown with mud and littered with the shattered wreckage of trees and other debris.

A small inlet just west of Kanaloa Point offered what seemed the best chance for us to get ashore, and Chief Wright swung us about and backed onto the beach through a smoking surf which, the nearer we came, became impressive indeed, both for its size and its endless crashing roar. Mister Hance sensibly left the job to the chief

We came in the motor whaleboat as the most seaworthy of the small craft we carried. It was double-ended, descended from the long line of boats used by whalers for catching and killing their great prey in the open sea. Even so, in such surf as we found that day no boat was likely to survive for long.

The chief took the helm himself and controlled the throttle with a series of simple signals he arranged with the motor man. Normally engine orders are given in Navy small boats by bells, but neither bells nor human voice could be heard over the watery tumult which broke over and around our struggling boat that day.

With bow to sea, the drill was to run in reverse up the backside of each cresting breaker. Then, as the sea collapsed from beneath the plunging boat, to use only enough forward power to hold its bow up to the next advancing sea, then to reverse again as each succeeding wave came upon us.

This worked well enough — for a time. But there came a point when the vertical component of the seas became too much. Water plunged down over the boat's bows before they rose, leaving the boat heavy and unable to rise against the next great tumbling wall of water. Water sloshed about to the height of the thwarts, soon becoming high enough to drown the little engine. Then the boat fell off, helpless, before the breakers.

We were, by that time, close in and took the sand with a jolting shock strong enough to throw most of us right out of the boat. Even those who remained on board were caught up in a thrashing maelstrom of water, men, bits of gear, and fragments of the shattered boat. The water was turgid, as well, with coral sand churned up from the beach and runoff wreckage from the shore.

Each man struggled ashore as best he could, clambering free of the sea's clutching and sucking grasp until collapsing onto dry ground. The boat itself ended — what was left of it — upside down, rocking crazily in a surge of shallow water.

Fortunately, both corpsmen survived relatively unharmed. As much could not be said for the rest of us. The corpsmen were kept busy with sprains, scrapes, cuts, and even some broken bones. They managed to save the boat's first aid kit, but all our food and water was lost.

At first, we thought no one was lost entirely, but a head count found two missing. One of them was Mister Hance. We found his cap, half-buried in the sand, but we never saw either him or the other man, a seaman I did not know, again.

All this time, the ship was riding offshore, serene and untroubled in deeper water. We knew we were watched all the way in, and that our wreck was seen through telescopes. But the chief had me stand on a nearby crag of black lava and semaphore a report on our condition. With Mister Hance gone, the chief was in command in name as well as in fact.

Since I was the only one surviving who saw the crash site, he depended heavily upon me to find it. Using Puu Mahoe as my guide, I thought I could find the lost airplane, although we saw nothing at all of it from where we were.

The ship flashed Morse orders for us to proceed with recovery of the bodies and to return to where we were. Another boat would be sent once the surf subsided. None of us knew when that would be, and there was nowhere a sign of other human presence, then or ever, on the storm ravaged shore.

We salvaged what we could of our gear and set out. I led the way, with the chief immediately behind me, and the others strung out in single file after him. At first, the going was not too hard, but as we neared the steep rising of the mountain it became more so. The foliage was dense tropical grass which tore at our legs and concealed pitfalls which we found by the simple but reliable process of falling into them.

As we came upon the steep lava bones of the mountain itself, the grass gave way to tangled ferns and shrubs and dripping moss which not only hindered our climbing but made our footing both hard to find and unreliable when we did find it. What normally might be soil over the rock was little more than a frosting of rotted vegetation and fallen branches. Sometimes seemingly substantial shrubs pulled right away in our hands, soggy root ball and all.

Our rate of passage fell from slow to very slow. Complaints became both heartfelt and profane. Our numbers were so depleted by casualties that there was only myself, the chief, one of the corpsmen — the other was left with the injured on the beach — and four deck white hats I didn't know.

Sailor muscles are not used to that kind of work, and the tearing of thorns and itching sweat in the wounds from our wreck in the surf became a torment. Progress was measured in yards, then feet and, sometimes, inches. We seldom saw more than a few feet ahead of us. From time to time I had to climb into the branches of low shrubs to see Puu Mahoe at all.

Still, two thousand feet is not forever, and near four o'clock that afternoon we came upon the wrecked airplane, the blackened lumps of its two crewmen still in their seats in those twisted remains of the plane which didn't burn.

Obviously, the airplane flew straight into the cliff. The pilot's only warning would have been a momentary greater darkening of the darkness into which he flew — then the hard compressing of the airplane around him, and the flash of burning gasoline he probably never felt. The rear seat man was crushed upon him, and both pressed close upon the burned out engine.

It was eerie. All was still but for the fluttering about of a small, brightly colored bird. The chief had us take whatever rest we could on the sheer cliff. Our only holds were on the charred vegetation of small trees and shrubs around the airplane.

The plane's impact made a small hole in the all-surrounding vegetation, and its burning a slightly larger one of charred and shriveled leaves and trunks.

"Think you can reach the ship, Flags?" the chief asked when he caught his breath a bit.

It would be a long shot. The ship, riding on the brown storm-roiled sea looked like a child's toy. My semaphore flags which I carried stuffed into the tops of my leggings would not likely be seen even through the big forty-five power long glass in either bridge wing. But the white canvas shrouds we brought along for the dead bodies of the airplane's crew just might.

I opened them both out, using some of the seamen to help me spread them over surrounding shrubs. We would be unable to send or to receive specific messages, but the ship would at least know that we reached the crash site, for whatever good that would do. It was as much as we could do at the moment.

After the brief rest, the corpsman busied himself with retrieving the bodies from the wreckage of the airplane. We all helped as best we could, being gentle and respectfully quiet as we handled what remained of our shipmates.

Rigor mortis had come and gone, so the job was not so physically hard as it might have been, but, emotionally, it was terrible to look upon the burned and mutilated corpses. We tried to work without using our eyes and got the burned bodies into their shrouds quickly. I would remember the ordeal for a long time.

But, far sooner than I feared, we had both bodies enshrouded and lashed into the wire stretchers. At least the horrible masks of their burned faces were no longer seen. That was a relief.

The time by then was late afternoon. The sun was already behind the crest of Puu Homae from where we were, and I felt a chill bite in the shade.

It would be a near thing, our getting back to comparatively level ground before darkness caught us. The chief got us underway at once.

The only way we could do it at all was to lash lines around the two bodies and let them down, hand over hand. Two men anchored each body, lowering it slowly, while two others guided it through the tangled cliffside growth from below for so far as the lines reached.

The bodies then were wedged into whatever would hold them on the near vertical slope, and we let ourselves down and took a new purchase. The process was repeated for what seemed an endless number of times. But, in the end, we reached ground level enough for us to carry the two stretchers in a more conventional way, with two men at each of their rounded corners.

Progress then was much more rapid, but, even so, darkness caught us long before we reached the beach where those injured in the wreck of our boat waited. We had no food, of course — that was all lost in the surf. Nor did we have blankets or warm clothes of any kind.

And it came on to rain. There was nothing for it but for us to huddle in the iffy shelter of trees. Trees in this part of the trek were much larger and provided more protection than anything higher on the cliff, but they still fell far short of comfort.

Through gaps in the trees we sometimes saw the ship's nervous plodding offshore, concerned but unable to help. We imagined the warm mess halls and hot showers and warm dry bunks lying empty below decks while we shivered in our wet clothes and hungered in the dark night.

Only the corpses did not complain. They lay out in the rain, wrapped in their soiled shrouds. Finally, the corpsman moved them into the most protected place, even though it meant he moved out into the rain.

The night seemed never to end. We sat, sodden and wakeful, under our dripping trees and waited for the light. Dawn, when it came, found us stiff, sore, and hungry. We avoided looking at the shrouded corpses as much as possible. The sight of men already dead was too strong a reminder that someday we, too, would be dead.

With the coming of light, we again made our stumbling way to the beach, through tall grass which was as tenaciously entangling as it was before — and we were not nearly so fresh. In an hour or two we were again on the beach and exposed to view from the ship. A signal searchlight asked for our condition and the state of the surf.

That helped. With my semaphore flags, and the ship's searchlights, we became again part of the living world. But we were still hungry, and the surf, although down a little from what it was the day before, remained dangerously high.

"Tell them it's too high right now," the chief said. "But it's lower than it was yesterday. Ask for water and something to eat. They can float it in to us from outside the breakers."

In the end, that was what was done. The ship's pulling lifeboat approached as near as it could, keeping care to stay outside the breakers, and floated in a packet of supplies for us, using an ingenious and hastily improvised arrangement of hinged flaps on a heavy wooden cask. It used the waves' own power to bring it to where we waded out and got it.

After that, it was but a matter of waiting for the surf to diminish enough for a boat to be brought through it.

Until that time, we handled both shrouded bodies without distinction. In fact, so disorganized was our descent off the cliff and the struggling passage of the foothills, none of us knew which was officer and which was man. Both were dead, and thus equal in value so far as we were concerned.

Both lay together in identical white shrouds, muddied by that time and stained green from being dragged, skidded and lowered through the dripping cliffside foliage. During the whole time of their recovery and removal we treated them as interchangeable units of the Navy whole with no regard for individual rank or privilege.

But, sometime that morning, I saw the chief and the two corpsmen open one of the shrouds and look inside. After that, we knew which was Mister Holmes and which was Bailey. There were scraps of unburned cloth under the belts, you see. Khaki meant officer; dungaree, white hat.

When I questioned why it was necessary to do that, the chief said he had to do it so he would know to which side of the ship to bring each dead body when we returned on board.

I had forgotten that Navy officers come aboard ships from the starboard side, white hats from the port.

Anyway, that is when I recalled my grandfather's story of the Army's separate mass graves for officers and men. Things hadn't changed one hell of a lot, I guess.

WHITE HATS

THE DOG

I have no idea where the term came from, but before World War II, if a white hat drank more, whored more or raised more hell on the beach than anyone else, he was called a *dog*. On all those counts, and a few more as well, Axel Swenson rated the title as much as anyone.

He rated the title so much, in fact, we added the article "the" to it as though there was only one dog in the whole ship. The ironic thing is that all the trouble he caused in the ship came after he got religion and stopped being a dog.

The Dog was not a mean drunk. Even when he fought in street and barroom brawls, he did so with a kind of enjoyment which left even those he fought against with no bad feelings toward him. He was as happy with one whore as another so he seldom got caught in that common trap for sailors. In his own mind, I suspect, he was just having a good time.

Back on the ship, once past his inevitable hangover, he was a model seaman. Always on time for his watch and ever ready to standby for anyone who wanted to go ashore, he was what every sailor hoped for in a shipmate. Had it not been for the Shore Patrol reports which followed him after almost every liberty, The Dog would have been a good petty officer.

But there were the Shore Patrol reports, and The Dog, although the best signalman on board, remained a second cruise seaman first. Even when promoted, he was quickly busted back to seaman for some God-awful stunt pulled on liberty. Once he was busted all the way back to seaman second. Only some pretty tall talking by Harry Lyons, our chief signalman, kept him from being kicked out of the Navy altogether.

I think we all expected that, sooner or later, The Dog would be kicked out. But, until then, we continued to like him and to take a perverse pleasure in his antics. We nursed him through his hangovers and laughed with him over his problems with the Shore Patrol.

The Navy's Shore Patrol in those days was a special party of men sent ashore from ships in liberty ports to help local police control sailors.

The Navy was different in that regard from the Army. The Army had Military Policemen, trained specialists who did nothing else. They were professional policemen, so far as soldiers were concerned. The Navy assigned ordinary sailors to the job, men with little or no training in police work. About the only thing distinguishing Shore Patrol sailors was the fact that most of them were right arm rates.

Boatswain's mates, gunner's mates, fire controlmen, quartermasters and signalmen wore their rating badges on their right arms. Everyone else wore his rate on his left arm. For military purposes, right arm rates took precedence and, as a result, were stuck more often with assignments like Shore Patrol, Landing Force and other unpleasant duties.

As a signalman, I got stuck with it a good deal. Especially so because I was often in trouble with the chief.

I don't remember what I did to win the chief's favor that time, but he grinned with some satisfaction as he told me off to draw my leggings, belt, club and the black brassard with yellow SP — all the stuff that marks a Shore Patrolman — and to get my ass down to the quarterdeck. That's how I came to be ashore the night The Dog got religion.

We were in a heavy cruiser at the time. In Panama. The officer of the deck lined us up for inspection on the quarterdeck and gave us special instructions because it was Panama. Sailors then rated liberty ports according to their possibilities for doing things that would bug the Shore Patrol. Panama was very near the top of the list.

Lying between North and South America as it did, Panama had all the vice and filth of both continents to draw upon. As the crossroads of a large part of the world's maritime traffic, it also held an avid and knowledgeable clientele to challenge the ingenuity of as decadent a lot of vultures as ever preyed on innocent sailors, merchant and Navy alike. Some officers of the deck even issued extra condoms in ports like Panama. Sailors said of Panama dives that you had to piss in spurts to keep the clap bugs from swimming upstream.

It promised to be an interesting night. The fact that I saw The Dog lined up with the liberty party did damned little to ease my concern. The Dog could make an evening interesting for the Shore Patrol in any port, let alone one like Panama.

The Dog was a good-looking sailor, tall and blonde and forever smiling — when he wasn't laughing outright. He saw me lined up with the Shore Patrol detail on the quarter deck and gave me a happy thumbs up signal. I knew, right then and there, I was in for an active night, but there was not a hell of a lot I could do about it.

Actually, though, nothing much happened. Not at first, anyway. We checked in at the local police station and got our area assignments and squared things away with the Panamanian cops. The Panamanian cops, in fact, were better than most in that regard. They were willing to leave Navy sailors to us, except in things like murder, arson and so on. Some liberty port cops liked to handle Navy sailors in their own not-always-gentle ways and were jealous of the privilege.

Most of the night we simply strolled, in pairs, along the crummy streets outside the crummy bars and whorehouses. Sometimes we went inside, but no more than necessary.

For the minor stuff — hat on the back of the head and the like — we simply lifted the guy's liberty card and let him go on his way. When he got back to the ship he would have to explain why he didn't have a liberty card. We seldom took guys into custody. Doing that involved work, and we didn't like work any more than anyone else.

We always patrolled in pairs. That night I drew Johnny Rogers, a gunner's mate, for a partner. Rogers was not a bad guy — for a gunner's mate, second — and we took things as easy as we could. We caught a couple of guys with hats on the back of their heads and chicken stuff like that, but nothing serious.

Usually, there was not much trouble until late in the night when the guys had time to tank up enough to get nasty. The bad time came after midnight. In most ports we braced ourselves for the bars and whorehouses closing times when sailors piled out into the streets and were not ready to call it a night. That is when fights started and we had our hands full trying to get the silly bastards back to the ship before they got themselves in real trouble.

Actually, that was less of a problem in Panama than in most ports because Panama bars and whorehouses didn't close.

Anyway, I spent half the night keeping an eye out for The Dog. Not actually looking for him, maybe, but keeping him prudently in mind. It was not natural for him to go all night without getting his tit caught in a wringer somewhere, as white hats put it in their often graphic way.

Twice, I saw him in bars, but he was doing nothing other than drink. His face was red, though, and his neckerchief was skewed around over a shoulder. Another time, I saw him lurching into the door of a particularly raunchy whorehouse where little boys stood outside selling *exhibishes* for two bits.

Exhibishes were an offered service in which rights to a hole were sold. Customers could look through that hole and watch what was going on on the other side of the wall. There some of the most God-awful scenes of debauchery depraved minds could dream up took place.

The Dog good naturedly pushed the kids aside and went inside the house. I didn't much think a guy like him would limit himself to just watching. Not when something more active was there for the buying.

I didn't see him for an hour or two. It must have been well on to midnight. The streets ran wall-to-wall with sailors, soldiers, merchant seamen and locals, yelling and singing and raising hell however they could in the dimly lighted night. Music and women's screams and the occasional crash and tinkle of broken glass spilled out of the never-closing doors. The Shore Patrol began earning its money. That is when I was sure I would see The Dog, but I didn't.

Later, in the way one discordant sound will make itself heard over a general din, I became aware of the booming of a Salvation Army drum, along with cornets and trumpets and thin voices singing hymns.

I have always been impressed by the way in which even the roughest men usually cut slack for the Salvation Army. The worst of them would, for the most part, steer clear of the little uniformed groups. If they had money, they would drop some into the waiting tambourine and they were hard on anyone who did not show the Army what they thought a proper deference.

That is why I was not surprised to see a dozen or so sailors standing in a respectful semicircle, hats in hand, to hear the sacred music. Hell, even Rogers and I stopped to listen for a while. But I *was* surprised when I saw The Dog there. The Dog we knew was not big on church music.

The little band played at the foot of one of those tall straight, white-trunked palm trees you see in Panama. I didn't see The Dog at first because of all the others standing about. But when the music stopped and a plump little man with red cheeks began preaching about the goodness of God, everyone else moved on. Everyone but The Dog.

The Dog was on his knees, tears streaming down his whiskey-blurred face and his whites all wet and soiled from one of the sudden tropical showers so frequent in Panama. He held his hat squashed between his hands at chest level and looked up with an expression of exaltation in his face.

I don't remember what the preacher said, but it had The Dog by the short hairs. The other Salvation Army people crowded around the kneeling sailor. You could see their joy in having made so open a convert, and one who, from his appearance, was so in need of salvation. The Dog beamed up at them and spread his arms wide to accept their blessing.

It was the damnedest thing I ever saw. I half moved to get closer, but a riot broke out just then in the next block and I ran with Rogers to do what we could.

I was still on duty ashore when The Dog returned to the ship. It was far earlier than he usually came back. Guys in the compartment told me later that he came down the ladder as though something were after him, turned on the lights and shouted "Hallelujah!" and "Praise the Lord!" and other crap like that until everyone was awake and yelling for him to shut up and turn in. We were getting underway for Long Beach the next morning, and some of the guys had just come off watch. They wanted their sleep.

Normally, there was little resentment. The Dog always did something outrageous like that, and we laughed it off with him. But that time, he was serious. That night marked the end of The Dog as we knew and loved him.

He slammed open his locker and pulled out every pack of cigarettes he owned. We had opening ports in our sleeping compartments and when moored in the tropics, kept them open for whatever air we could get. Air-conditioning in Navy ships was not known then, not even as a word. The Dog threw his cigarettes out a port and harangued his sleepy shipmates to throw theirs away, too, damning tobacco through it all for the devil's tool it undoubtedly is.

Well, the guys didn't put up with that very long. They told The Dog what he could do with his "Hallelujahs" and "Praise-the-Lords." They also told him if he was going to throw away good smokes, throw some their way.

I never knew him to go ashore after that, except for church if we happened to be in port on a Sunday. He not only stopped smoking, he badgered us all to do the same. He wouldn't even give out cigars when he was promoted, as he soon was, given his new habits.

Promotions were announced every three months in those days. It was the custom for guys who got promoted to pass out cigars, the way new fathers do in celebrating their babies. The Dog passed out geedunks instead. Geedunks were candy or ice cream from the ship's soda fountain. He said he didn't want to contribute to our delinquency and the risking of our immortal souls by giving us cigars.

All of this might have been all right, I suppose, had The Dog kept his new-found sanctity to himself. I knew guys before in the Navy who got religion. Usually, all you had to do was wait them out for a while and they would slip back into a more natural form of Navy life. Or they left at the end of their enlistments and we were free of them and their embarrassing reminders of our own sinfulness.

But The Dog wouldn't do that. He was near the end of his second hitch, but he didn't leave the Navy. Instead, he reenlisted when we got to Long Beach. That meant he was going to be around for another four years. He saw it as his duty, he said, to do what he could to save our souls from the eternal damnation we were courting with our evil ways. He was even beginning to talk like a preacher. He thought he could do more good in the Navy than among the less benighted souls in the civilian world, I suppose.

Well, that might have been true, but it is also true that it gets damned tiresome. The Dog was not popular on the bridge anymore. As often happens, sanctity slipped into sanctimony, and he became a distinct pain in the ass who upset the whole bridge with his zeal. Finally, the chief told him to knock it off. If The Dog wanted to play preacher, he could damned well change his rate and go work for the chaplain.

I didn't think then the chief gave a damn one way or the other about what The Dog was doing. He just didn't want his smooth-running bridge disturbed. I found out later I was wrong.

Anyway, slowed down on the signal bridge as he was, The Dog took to holding prayer meetings in Battle Station Two —

BatTwo in the Navy's shorthand. BatTwo was an emergency ship control station at the base of the mainmast aft. It was, in fact, a small bridge with a wheel and engine room telegraphs, flagbags for signal flags and some signal searchlights, all protected by painted canvas covers most of the time.

It was meant for use if the ship's regular bridge was put out of action in battle, but it proved perfect for The Dog's purposes. It was aft, for one thing, and raised above the main deck level. It could not be seen from the quarterdeck and officers seldom came there except for drills.

I guess there's nothing so outlandish that someone can't be roped in for it. The Dog never got many to join in his devotions, but he always had somebody there. Most were young guys, homesick for the certainties of their former lives and not yet hardened to Navy ways. I don't think The Dog ever had more than eight or nine in his congregation. Most times it was more like three or four, but that didn't slow him down.

One of The Dog's most faithful followers, though, was not young at all. He was a storekeeper third who already was showing signs of slipping his hawser. He was around forty years old at the time. He could still do whatever it is storekeepers third do, but he tended to skid off to one side or the other when you talked to him. In a later slang, he would have been described as not having both oars in the water.

Storekeepers did not stand watches, so that guy made every one of The Dog's meetings and responded with such noise and enthusiasm that he became a mainstay in the operation. Tragically, he proved instrumental in what was the most bizarre thing I ever saw.

BatTwo was just forward of Number Three Turret with its big eight-inchers. The only thing farther aft was the open sweep of the ship's fantail, the aftermost end of the maindeck. The Chiefs' Quarters were just below that deck. Sometimes, in good weather, the chiefs brought up chairs and sat with their coffee cups to take the evening breeze.

They were close enough to hear everything going on in BatTwo, but they never did anything to put an end to it. In fact, I had a clear impression they enjoyed it. Especially the singing. They probably could not make out the words when The Dog was preaching, but they heard the singing.

In those days, even at sea, after the day's exercises were done, we throttled back and lolled through the night at little more than enough speed to keep steerageway. This not only saved fuel, it made for restful evenings and quiet nights for us.

I still remember those times when The Dog was holding one of his prayer meetings and we heard the singing of the old songs we all knew as little boys in homes then becoming more and more forgotten: The Old Rugged Cross, The Little Brown Church, Amazing Grace, Let Us Gather by the River.

The Dog had a good, though untrained, singing voice. There were times on the bridge, especially in the stillness of sunset, when I blinked tears from my eyes hearing those old songs. My mother sang them a long time ago.

Nor was I alone. Guys came up to the weather decks after evening chow and stood in silence to listen. We were not allowed to sit down on the white teak decks unless we took off our shoes — our rubber heels left black marks on the scrubbed wood. I don't think the guys cared, one way or another, about God, but the singing was nice.

At any rate, that's how things worked themselves out after the chief chased The Dog and his Bible off the bridge. The suggestion that he work with the chaplain didn't pan out at all. Our chaplain at the time was a Roman Catholic and not overly receptive to The Dog's freewheeling fundamentalist version of God and His worship. The Dog, for his part, could not bring himself to accept the agency of a pope and the rigmarole of Catholic ritual. He was forced back upon the support of his own small congregation.

This worked well enough before Leonard Sanders came into the ship and it probably would have worked afterwards, as well, if Sanders had the good sense to keep his mouth shut. But Sanders was not that smart.

Sanders was a small, dark-faced signalman second who came to us as a replacement for Dennis Harper. Harper's enlistment expired and he left the Navy. There was always a feeling-out process when new men came into a ship.

Sometimes this took a good deal of time while old hands and newcomer found their ways to working and living arrangements. But it didn't take long at all for us to peg Sanders as a nasty little son-of-a-bitch who was likely to cause trouble.

As are many physically small men, he was pugnacious and quick to take offense. That is a bad combination in quarters as close as those of a Navy warship. It did not take long for the first sparks to fly.

But, after a couple of trips to the fantail, Sanders fitted himself into our way of doing things and calmed down. The fantail was the after end of our maindeck. It could not be seen from most parts of the ship and became the court where disagreements between sailors were settled in what we called knuckle discussions. Most ships, in those days, had a place like that. Sanders quickly learned that, when it came to fighting, he was not far from the bottom of our little pecking order. He became much more agreeable after that.

It did not take him long to learn, either, about The Dog's recent rebirth as a Christian. Whatever else you could say about The Dog, he was serious about his new-found faith. He was no slouch with his fists, but since his conversion, he *wouldn't* fight. The Bible said he should turn his other cheek, and he tried his damnedest to do that but when the chief was not on the bridge Sanders baited The Dog mercilessly.

I remember one time The Dog was laying out the story of Noah and the Ark for a couple of strikers by the signalmen's coffee pot, forward on the starboard side of the bridge, where they were out of the way of the watch. We were allowed to hang out there even at sea so long as we did not interfere with the watch.

It was in the quiet of the second dog watch. The chief was below for his supper. Sanders laughed his nasty little laugh and sneered at The Dog's earnest discussion of Noah's story. "Any one who'd believe that crap is dumber than whale shit, and whale shit's on the bottom of the ocean," he said.

I saw The Dog flush red in his face and shake his ever-present Bible in Sanders' face. "Don't — don't you blaspheme in the face of the Lord," he yelled loud enough to be heard on the Nav Bridge on the next deck above. We were underway at the time, and the Navigation Bridge was where the officer of the deck held his watch. The captain was likely there, as well, since that was his station at sea.

"Keep it down, Dog," I warned him. "The old man hears you, you'll have your ass in a sling." Unnecessary noise was not tolerated worth a damn on Navy bridges of the time.

"Well, tell him to stop blaspheming the Word of God, then," The Dog said tightly, never taking his eyes from Sanders.

Sanders sneered. "Word of God, hell. You know how many languages that damned book has been passed through?" Sanders must have gone to school somewhere.

"I don't care," The Dog said stubbornly.

"You really think Old Noah got two of every animal in the world in that bucket of his?" Sanders laughed. "How about polar bears and kangaroos and stuff the people in the world then never heard of?"

"It says here he did," The Dog said. "And everybody and everything he didn't get in the Ark died."

"How about the God-damned fish? Did they drown? And the whales and seals?"

The Dog had no ready answer for any of that.

"And the God-damned water," Sanders pressed. "Where did all the water go, for Christ's sake? If the whole-God damned world was flooded to the mountain tops, where did the water go after the flood?"

"It says right here in —"

"And, when the flood was over, what did Noah and all those animals eat? You ever see a country that's been flooded? Nothing but mud for miles and miles. Nothing will grow for months." Sanders went on. "What did Noah and his crowd eat during all that time? You ever think about that?"

I don't know where that would have ended. The Dog was mad as hell. He couldn't match Sanders' mocking questions except by quoting the Bible, and Sanders mocked the Bible itself. Fortunately, the chief's cap appeared at the head of the ladder from below and everything subsided.

But Sanders planted doubts The Dog could not shake. He could not bring himself to doubt the holy word of God as expressed in the Bible — still where *had* all that water gone at the end of the flood? He had never thought of that.

And Sanders planted doubts in the rest of us. Most of us had less than high school educations. We did not know how to defend the Bible in terms of symbolism or allegory or metaphor. Hell, we didn't even know what those words meant.

No man can spend much time at sea without sometimes being afraid. Even in modern ships the banshee shrieking of winds and the shuddering shock of seas against a hull can be unnerving. Steel can be torn and rivets popped and men washed over the side. Fear is the darkness against which men pit the light of their invented gods.

The big thing that was wrong with Sanders' disturbing arguments was that he never offered anything to replace the faith he destroyed in us.

The conflict between the factions on the bridge became real and deepened with each passing day. Guys snapped at each other and took sides in bitter arguments on things not connected at all with the Bible. Our bridge, which before was one of the most pleasant duties I ever knew in the Navy, became a place of suspicion and ill-feeling.

Of the two groups, the one siding with The Dog was probably the luckier. It had at least the certainty of its faith upon which to rely. Those in the other camp had nothing with which to replace the trust in God which Sanders, with his questions, took from them. I suspect we in that group were scared. If The Dog was right, we were in deep trouble.

It didn't help that the chief came down on The Dog's side. He couldn't answer Sander's questions any better than the rest of us, but he didn't see the fact as a problem. As a kid he was told there was a God. That was good enough for him.

Chief petty officers in those days had a good deal of power over white hats and the doubters on the bridge found themselves assigned all the dirty jobs on the ship. We got all the working parties and what we called the "shit details."

One of the things he did was to assign doubters the job of "decorating for divine services" and running up the Church Pennant. Deck Divisions set out chairs and benches for church services on deck, but it was the signalmen's job to take an armful of signal flags and drape them about the area in the ship where the chaplain heard Mass. During services we had to dip the Flag and run up the Church Pennant, symbolizing, I suppose, the subservience even of the Navy to God.

The Church Pennant was a white pennant with a blue cross. The Navy made much of the fact that the Church Pennant was the only thing ever hoisted above the American flag. Anyway, the chief saw to it that we doubters on the bridge got the chore of rigging for church and handling the pennant business. I suppose the chief wanted to rub our noses in it.

That was petty, of course, but we showed the old bastard we could be just as petty. One time we hung up the flags so they spelled b-u-1-1-s-h-i-t in an arcing screen behind the chaplain as he preached.

Fortunately, no one noticed. A lot of Navy guys couldn't read the flags anyway. They were seen as no more than colorful decorations rigged in the honor of God, I guess, but it gave us a precedent for spelling out all kinds of interesting messages for future services.

Sooner or later, of course, we would have been caught in our blasphemy. And, given the ardor of the establishment Navy in regard to religion, our punishment would, in all likelihood, have been unpleasant.

Anyway, it was in this rancorous atmosphere that the bizarre tragedy I mentioned took place. The Dog's most faithful disciple, the old feebleminded storekeeper, took a dog wrench and crushed Sanders' head with it. The Dog had preached a pretty heated sermon, I heard later, about the duty of God's servants to destroy the forces of evil. The old guy considered himself a servant of God, I suppose, and The Dog had lambasted Sanders as a force of evil. I guess the old storekeeper saw it as his clear duty to kill the son-of-a-bitch.

That, too, has always seemed to me the history of religions: if somebody doesn't agree with you about God, kill the ignorant son-of-a-bitch.

I don't know if Sanders actually died or not. They took him off the ship to a hospital on the beach and we never saw him again.

They took the old storekeeper away, too. We didn't know whatever became of him either. He probably wound up in a mental hospital somewhere.

The only one who remained on board was The Dog, but something was taken out of him by what happened.

It was he who set the storekeeper against sinners, but it never occurred to him that the weak-minded old guy would actually do what he did. At least, that is what he tried to tell us, but I was never really quite sure about that. I sometimes suspected The Dog had known perfectly well what he was doing — and that he planned the whole thing.

He did try after a while to resume his ministry to us, his sinning shipmates, but his heart was not in it anymore. He never again spoke with the same surety of faith. Many years later, when both of us had moved on to other ships, I heard that he had given up entirely and gone back to his old ways.

I was sorry to hear that. I guess he never figured out where all that water went after the Flood.

THE ALLOTMENT

Navy sailors who had dependents could, with their commanding officers' permission, make allotments from their pay so that the money was sent directly to those dependents. The sailors never saw it. It was like the withholding system the country later used for paying income taxes. The Navy did a lot of stuff like that for sailors, although they seldom appreciated it.

I always thought it was a lot of crap. It might be all right for the support of a guy's old mother or something like that, but some guys married broads on the beach and made out allotments to them so they could shack up with other guys. Sometimes even with soldiers.

I swore then I'd never make out an allotment to anybody. I would spend my own God-damned money.

One thing the Navy did that I thought was nice was to return the bodies of dead sailors to their homes. The Navy not only returned the dead bodies, it provided an escort as well.

One time in the late thirties I drew escort duty for the body of one of our guys who was killed on the ship. He was a signalman. George Martin was his name. He fell from the port semaphore platform one day. It was not a long fall, and one not likely to be fatal, but it was.

Semaphore was the system of signaling we used in which a man held small flags in his hands and moved them in ways to indicate letters of the alphabet. It was faster than flashing lights and more flexible than code flags. When it could be used at all, it was the system of choice. I understand that now it is no longer even taught in the Navy.

The first requirement for semaphore, of course, was that the man doing the signaling must be visible from the ship being signaled. This was made possible by the erection of semaphore platforms on either side of the signal bridge which extended out over the sides of the ship. They were small, no more than two or three feet square, with two inverted metal arches set at right angles to each other. The arches were meant to serve as braces for a man's legs as he balanced himself to signal, but they came little higher than the knees. I never understood why they weren't at least waist high. At that height they wouldn't be in the way and, who knows, they might have prevented poor George's dying the way he did.

These precarious perches were not so bad when at anchor or alongside a pier. But things became less restful when the ship was underway in rough seas, with forty knots or so of wind tearing at a man's body and the ship reeling and staggering like a wild thing. At times like that semaphore platforms were not for the faint of heart.

As it happened the ship *was* quiet when George fell. As a flagship, we rated a buoy inside the inner breakwater at Long Beach. Water doesn't get much flatter, but that is where he fell.

In semaphore, one man calls out the words to be signaled and another man does the actual signaling. I was reading off a message for George to send and had just turned away to log the fact of its completion when I heard his body hit the bridge deck.

I did not see how it happened. He must have slipped in disentangling his legs from the platform leg braces. When I turned around he was lying on the deck, the bright red and yellow flags still in his hands. His head was twisted awkwardly to one side.

His neck obviously was broken. We had sense enough not to move him. We simply stood about him, staring dumbly like cows and other herd animals will do sometimes when one of their number is struck down. First a hospital corpsman and then the ship's doctor arrived. The doctor pronounced George dead on the spot, and some of us carried him below in a Stokes stretcher.

As with everything else, the Navy has procedures which must be followed in the event of a man's death. If a sailor thinks he can escape the reach of Navy Regulations simply by dying, he is sadly mistaken. The captain and his executive officer, the Medical Department, the supply officer and the chief master-at-arms all have clearly defined roles.

The only ones with no formal responsibilities are the dead man's messmates. Except for the sobering reminder of the nearness and the unpredictability of death, they are left to get on with the business of the ship. The Watch, Quarter and Station Bill is adjusted to ensure coverage of duty assignments, and everything continues as before.

If the dead man has no known family or has made no other arrangements, his belongings are auctioned off to the crew and the proceeds go to support the ship's various recreational and other services for the crew. The amounts are not likely to be large. Sailors' belongings in the pre-War Navy were apt to be both few and of little value. In George's case, they were his hammock and a seabag of well-worn uniforms.

Aside from toothbrushes, shaving gear and the like, there was nothing else, except for a small novelty carving of a peach seed. These little carvings were once common in some parts of the country. They depicted a monkey curled within the arc of its own tail. For me, they always bore a vague resemblance to the intricate carvings Chinese sometimes do in jade or ivory. My dad carved me one once, but I lost it somewhere. I always wanted to get another one. It was the only memory I had of my dad.

As the chief master-at-arms, in the presence of witnesses, inventoried the contents of George's locker, I asked if I might have the little monkey. After a cursory glance to confirm the thing's lack of value, the chief tossed it to me. That may be why I drew the duty of escorting George's body back to his last home of record. I sure as hell did not want the job, and was never so glad to get back to a ship as I was when it was over.

An escort is provided only when one is requested by the dead man's next of kin or family. The fact that I was assigned as escort was the first indication any of us ever had that George had next of kin or family. He never received mail that any of us remembered. Not even at Christmas time. He was always a loner, anyway, given to sour moods and surly responses. He seldom spoke beyond the call of duty and even avoided the bull sessions around the bridge coffee pot. That last was considered unnatural in a white hat.

He never went ashore as a normal man would, for one thing. He didn't even spend money aboard ship. In those days, for instance, men passed out cigars when they were promoted, as new fathers do at the birth of babies. George did not do even that. None of this made him very popular with the rest of us.

It presented a problem, too, when it came time to assign an escort for George's body. The Navy required that escorts "shall be of the equivalent rank or rate of the deceased so nearly as may be practicable, and, when possible, a friend or associate."

The question of equivalent rate was no problem. George was a signalman second class. That was my rate at the time, as well. That was all right. And the fact that we were both members of the signal gang made us associates, I suppose. But I was not his friend. Neither was anyone else on the ship, so far as I knew.

Nevertheless, I got the job. I didn't even know where I was going until I reported to the Navy hospital. George, by that time, was embalmed and placed in a standard Navy coffin. He was dressed in new blues. The Navy thoughtfully provides new uniforms for those whose own uniforms are too worn to be suitable.

The Navy was not so thoughtful, though, as to provide new shoes for its dead. Presumably on the assumption they would not be doing much walking and their feet wouldn't be visible in the casket anyway. But it did stir in me an irreverent mental picture of barefooted sailors padding about the streets of heaven. Or, more likely, skipping gingerly over the hot coals of hell without shoes.

Anyway, it was a small, very small, town in Arkansas where I was to deliver George's body. A Navy ambulance delivered me and him to the Los Angeles Union Station where I watched the checking in of the coffin on the baggage platform. The Navy had words for that, too, specifying that a copy of the bill of lading "be securely pasted on top of the shipping casket with a dextrin paste, similar to that used by the express company, and then covered with shellac or varnish."

After that, there was nothing to do except find my own car and settle down for some forty-eight hours of riding across half the country. At least, the Navy was good enough to provide Pullman fare. Enlisted men, on their own, seldom had money for more than chair car travel.

Since I was riding on the Navy's tab, I could afford a little time in the bar car. This drew some dubious looks from the better dressed civilian types, but sailors were used to dubious looks from civilians. I ignored them and began thinking about what the hell I would do when I got to George's home town.

The Navy gave me instructions on what to do, of course. It didn't amount to a hell of a lot. The civilian undertaker in the little town was alerted to my arrival and would meet the train with his hearse. If he didn't know what to do he could check with one of his buddies in a bigger town. It wasn't my pidgin.

As the bar car drinks followed one another through the afternoon, I came to try for some feeling of mourning for George riding the baggage car up forward. George wasn't getting any drinks at all. George was never going to get any drinks.

After it became dark and I could study my own reflection in the car's windows, I came to feel something like grief for George. He was a shipmate, after all. But, after a good meal in the diner, the feeling went away and I turned in to my berth.

I don't remember the name of the Arkansas town where I took George. It was somewhere in the northern part of the state. I got off the train at a town in Missouri. The civilian undertaker was there to meet me. I helped him load George in his hearse. The undertaker was a pale little guy who tried to be friendly, but I didn't help him much with that.

"You know Martin?" I asked him as he drove us south out of town. It was pretty country, what the locals called the Ozark Mountains. *Mountains?* For Christ's sake! California has sand dunes higher than those mountains.

"Everybody knows George Martin," the undertaker said, jumping at my opening for conversation. "Born here. Grew up here until he joined the Navy. Lived up the holler a ways from town. Used to date the Clark girl. Some say he's the daddy of the baby."

"Baby?"

"Yeah. Lela Mae Clark. She had a baby about six months after George left. Kid don't look much like George, but I guess that can happen sometimes. Couple of my kids don't look much more like me than a coon dog. Ha, ha. Guys down at the feed store kid me about that sometimes."

The undertaker was just being friendly, I guess. Lots of people, especially in small towns, find it hard to be loose around undertakers. It must get lonesome sometimes. But I didn't much take to talking about George like that, him being dead right there behind us and everything. Even though I never cared much for George when he was alive, I still felt like we ought to be a little more respectful of him now that he was dead.

"Sounds like you didn't think much of George."

"Not many around here did. Not after what happened with him and his daddy."

"What was that?"

"Oh, nothing much, I guess." The undertaker looked sideways at me. "Not unless you call killing his daddy something."

"What?"

"Shot his daddy. Said it was a accident. Said they was out hunting and his gun went off." The undertaker paused. "I put the old man away. Bullet hit him square between the eyes. Hell of a hole to cover up for the viewing. One undertaker come all the way down from Joplin to see how I done it."

"You saying it wasn't an accident?"

"Ain't only me. This whole part of the country knows damned well George killed his daddy on purpose."

"Why? Why would he kill his old man?"

"I never figured that out," the undertaker said. "Some said the old man was beatin' up on George's momma and George killed him for it. Some think it was because the old man didn't take to George's fooling around with the Clark girl. Others think they was just drinkin' and got in an argument. I don't know. I just know it wasn't no accident."

"What happened? Was there a trial?"

"Had a inquest. I had to testify at it. Nature of the wound and such like. We didn't have no coroner at the time."

"But there was no trial?"

"No. We didn't have no witnesses that seen what happened. Sheriff couldn't do nothing. But George's daddy was pretty well-liked around here. And George never had gone out of his way to be nice to anybody. People didn't need no trial. They made up their own minds about what happened."

"That's when George left to join the Navy?"

"I reckon," the undertaker said. "I don't know if he left to join the Navy or not. All I know is he got the hell out of here. Folks seen to it he couldn't get a job or nothing. They let him know what they thought about him." Then, abruptly, he asked, "You on the same ship with George?"

"Yeah, same ship." I didn't say anything else and the undertaker didn't say anything else the rest of the way. When we got there, he drove straight to his undertaking parlor and a guy came out and helped the undertaker wheel George inside on a little cartlike thing. There was a blue neon clock sign on the lawn outside of the undertaking parlor and a kind of porch to one side, with extra-wide doors opening into the building. That's where the undertaker parked his hearse.

I looked around, but there was no one else in sight. If everybody in that town knew George, they had a funny way of showing it. There wasn't a soul there to meet him. The Navy's instructions told me what I should say to the family, but they didn't say a thing about what I should say if there wasn't a family to say it to.

It was getting dark by that time. "When are the services?" I asked the undertaker. "They going to be here or in a church?"

"Tomorrow," the undertaker said. "Far as I know, they'll be here. Ain't no church in town would have 'em. Not for George Martin, they wouldn't. Matter of fact, this ain't going to help my reputation much. If he wasn't already embalmed and in a box, I wouldn't touch the case neither."

"There a hotel in this burg?"

"Yeah. The Regal down the street to the right. Or you might try the old lady. She knows you're coming. She might have room for you to stay the night."

"The old lady?"

"George's momma. She lives up the holler south of town. Clark girl lives with her, I understand. Takes care of her. The old lady ain't too spry anymore. I'll give you the loan of a car, you want to drive out there."

"No, thanks," I said. "I'd just as soon take the hotel. How far is it?"

"Block and a half. Can't miss it. It's the only hotel we got."

Well, that was the truth. Nothing in that town was far from anything else. If it was, it was out in the country. Actually, it wasn't a bad little town. One or two business blocks that seemed active enough. Some decent houses under big trees on the high ground off to the right, and a messy straggle of more modest houses on the ground sloping down to a creek to the left. Some churches and a big brick high school with white limestone trim. A couple of corrugated iron shops of some kind just about finished it off.

I saw a dirt road winding off through the trees to the south and figured that must be where George's mother lived. I was tired. A good hot bath and a country supper sounded pretty good to me right about then. I headed for the hotel.

Before I got there, though, I met a gawky woman in a cotton print dress whose color and body had long since been washed out of it. She was wearing what looked like men's work shoes. Her almost colorless hair straggled down from her scalp like the strings of a Navy swab that has been left too long in the sun. Her eyes were pale blue, hardly darker than white, and her voice when she spoke was hard and unpleasant. She was leading a little boy by the hand.

"You the one that's brung George home?" she said.

"Yes. He's at the undertaker's."

"I'm Lela Mae Clark. I'm staying with George's momma. She can't rightly do for herself anymore. This here's John. He's my young-un."

"Pleased to meet you, Mrs. Clark," I said. The boy was eight or nine years old and something around his eyes looked like George. He was barefoot, thin and wore bib overalls that didn't touch him much more than where the straps crossed his shoulders.

"It ain't Mrs. Clark," Lela Mae said defiantly. "I ain't married. I ain't never been married. You want to see the old lady, I'll show you the way."

Well, that didn't leave me a hell of a lot to say. I figured the Navy would want me to see George's mother. We were only steps away from the hotel. "Wait a minute until I register and drop off my bag, and I'll join you."

The desk clerk pointed out where I should sign and let me stash my traveling bag behind the desk. "Them two ain't with you, are they?" the woman said with a jerk of her head at Lela Mae and her boy.

"No," I said.

"Well, this is a respectable house. I just wanted you to know that."

"Okay," I said. "Anything else I ought to know?" I've known people who could get my back hairs up, but I never knew anyone who could do it so fast.

"Room's a dollar. Checkout time's eleven o'clock. Bath when the door ain't closed. Breakfast, starting at six, supper at five."

I nodded without speaking.

There were few people on the street but those that were gawked at me enough to make me uncomfortable.

Lela Mae led me out of town along the dirt road to the south. It was only about a mile or so through wooded hills that pressed in on the road and made the night seem darker than it was. A little creek gurgled alongside the road. It was really pretty nice, but I still wished the hell I was back on the ship.

"Sorry I wasn't at the undertaker's to meet you," Lela Mae said once. "Mrs. Martin was having one of her spells. I had to stay and take care of her."

"That's all right," I said. "Wasn't anything you could do." She didn't say anything after that. The boy didn't say a word the whole time.

The house was an unpainted wooden shack of a place, set back off the road in some trees. The only light was from a coal oil lamp. It shined, dim and yellow, through the windows. A dog barked at us without much interest, and we went in, Lela Mae calling out ahead of us.

"It's me, Missus Martin," she called. "I brung the man from the Navy. George is here now. He's at the undertaker's in town."

George's mother was a seemingly lifeless lump in a tottery rocking chair she didn't bother to rock. I looked for some resemblance of her son, but found none. She was dressed in a washed-out cotton print dress and soiled cloth house slippers. Her hair was thin, gray, and dirty. She looked real old. Her head hung from humped shoulders. She looked up at me with weak and watery eyes. She didn't say anything, but ducked her head in what was a kind of hello, I guess.

The house itself was like nothing I ever saw. My own family was sure as hell not rich, but we never lived in such hard ugliness.

"Missus Martin can't talk much," Lela Mae said. "She's had a lot of strokes. Once a body gets to knowing her, you can tell pretty much what she's thinking. She's right glad you come to see her."

I tried to think of what the Navy instructions said to say to George's family, but none of it seemed right. I just nodded and smiled.

"Well, I reckon it's just about supper time," Lela Mae said then. "We ain't got much, but I wrung the necks of a couple of fryers, and we got some garden peas and new potatoes I can cream up for us. That, and some biscuits and brown gravy and fresh cow's milk ought to make a right nice bait."

"I don't want to put you to any trouble," I said. "I can get something in town."

"Ain't no trouble," Lela Mae said. "We got plenty. Missus Martin would take it nice if you was to eat with us. You being George's friend and everything." She was talkative and friendly after the stiffness between us on the way from town.

From the looks of things, they *didn't* have plenty. And I sure as hell wasn't George's friend, but there was a kind of pleading in Lela Mae's voice which made me want to stay. It was not so much in anything she said, but more her way of saying it. The poor woman was lonesome, and there was not one grain of hope in her eyes. I guess she was looking into all the years staring her in the face after the funeral was over and I was gone and everything.

"All right then," I said. "Long as it's no trouble."

Lela Mae smiled. Smiling made a world of difference in the way she looked. When she smiled she even looked pretty. She would be especially so, I thought, if she were cleaned up and had something decent to wear and did something to her hair.

"John, you run out now and finish your chores while I get things on the table." She turned to me then. "I don't know your name," she said, embarrassed.

"Damon Thomas," I said. "Everybody calls me Thomas."

"I don't," Lela Mae said. "Damon's a nice name. I'll call you Damon. You can go out with John if you want to. He's got to slop the hog and fix things for the night. Watch where you step, though. The old cow's had the runs for two days now, and it wouldn't be nice to mess up them nice shoes. John, you light the lantern for Mister Thomas, hear? Don't let him step in anything."

It was funny how Lela Mae's spirits got better with the thought of having company for supper. There was even a little color in her cheeks as she stirred up the fire in the old black wood stove and rattled her pots and pans.

"You ready, Mister Thomas?" the boy said. It was the first time he said anything. His voice was low, and he still couldn't bring himself to meet my eyes, but he was warming up to me. He took down a coal oil lantern and lighted it to show me the way.

Outside, it was full dark. Bright sparks of stars showed through black trees. There was no wind, and only the smell of smoke from Lela Mae's cook stove. That and the manure and wet-straw smell of barns I had not smelled for years. A lot of memories came back with that smell. I lived on a farm when I was little, but I had not been on one since I joined the Navy.

The boy took up a bucket of slops from beside the door and led the way. He was still barefoot, but walked with a calm confidence, never looking where he put his feet. "Cow's in here," he said as we came to the barn. "I got to give her some shorts. Then we'll take care of the hog."

I stood and watched as he went about his work.

"Did George wear clothes like that?" the boy said, nodding toward my blues.

Yes," I said. "Just like these. He even had one of these on his arm." I touched my rating badge with its white eagle and red chevrons with crossed white flags in the middle.

"Did you know him good?"

"We were on the same ship. We ate at the same table and slept in the same compart — same room." I did not want to lie to the boy, but I sensed that he wanted to hear more about George, who, I was beginning to believe, was his father.

"Did you like him?" the boy asked in that straight forward way kids have sometimes.

"Well enough, I guess," I said.

"Did he ever talk about Momma and me and the place here?"

That slowed me down. "Well, no. Not exactly, John. Guys don't talk much about stuff like that on ships. We're usually pretty busy and everything. Most of us have been away from home a long time. We don't talk much about things like that."

That was a damned lie, of course. Home and what we did before we joined the Navy was about the only thing we did talk about. Although George never did.

The boy thought about this for a little while. He poured a mixture of slop and water into the hog's trough. Then, as though forgetting the subject, he asked me about the Navy and the world beyond the wooded ridges hemming in the place, a world he had never seen.

Relieved at the change of subject, I told him about ships and oceans and the big towns and foreign countries I saw. I tried to keep it all in terms he understood, but I didn't need to worry about that. Except for the ships part, he was way ahead of me.

"Where'd you learn all this stuff, kid?" I said.

"Momma told me most of it. George used to write her letters and tell her about what he saw and everything. And Missus Rhine in town lets me read her books sometimes. She explains things when I don't understand."

Well, that was a surprise. I didn't remember George getting mail on the ship. "Did your Momma write to George?"

"She would have, but she didn't know his address," the boy said. "Sometimes she wrote him letters, but she didn't know where to send them. She's got them all in a box under her bed. She was going to give them to George when he came home."

My feelings for George Martin were changing. I looked at the boy I was sure now was George's son and was surprised to find myself getting mad. Not at the boy, but at the God-damned people who drove George away and left this boy alone and fatherless. And the woman cooking supper inside the house to fend for herself without a man.

I don't remember much of what we talked about after that, but it made us friends, I think. The boy warmed up to me, and I came to think of what it might be like to have a wife someday, and a boy like this one. But I put a quick stop to crap like that. I was in the Navy. I meant to stay in the God-damned Navy. I had seen guys try to have families on Navy pay, and moving all over the world and everything. I didn't want any part of that.

"We better be going in," the boy said then. "Momma'll have supper ready. She don't like it when I'm late." He stepped toward the house and I followed after.

"Well, did you two have a good time?" Lela Mae said, smiling. "You been out there long enough to slop a hundred hogs."

"We been talking, Momma," the boy said. "Mister Thomas was on the same ship with George. He knew him and everything. He's been telling me about the Navy and all the places he's been."

"Well, you just wash your hands now and set down to this table. Damon — she blushed at having said my name — you can wash up there at the pan by the door. Stuff's ready when you are."

I noticed George's mother was still in her rocking chair, but a cloth was knotted under her chin and a small table had been brought alongside her. While Lela Mae and I sat down, the boy took food in a shallow bowl and fed the old woman, patiently waiting out her halting motions.

I tried to connect George in my mind with the boy and Lela Mae and the old woman in the rocking chair, but the stretch was too far. The George I knew did not square with the George I was learning about in that little Arkansas town. Not worth a damn, he didn't.

The table was a little wobbly. It was covered with a cheap oilcloth whose surface had peeled in round rings where hot dishes were put down on it, exposing the woven cloth underneath. The dishes themselves were cracked and stained and none of the knives and forks matched, but you would have thought Lela Mae was a lady somewhere, serving company in a fine house.

She served me the crisp fried chicken and creamed garden peas cooked with new potatoes, and big glasses of fresh milk to go with them. God-damn, it was good!

Lela Mae smiled and talked. You would not have thought her the same woman who met me in town. "Did you really know George in the Navy?" she asked.

"Yeah. We were in the same gang, on the same ship."

"I guess he told you why he run away and joined the Navy?" She said that very tentatively.

"No," I said, "but that undertaker in town did."

"It was a accident, Damon," Lela Mae said pretty strongly. "George loved his daddy. And his daddy loved him. They used to go hunting and fishing together all the time. His daddy used to whittle things for George, from the time he was a little boy. There wasn't nothing George wouldn't do for his daddy."

"That undertaker said people were pretty rough on George."

"They was," Lela Mae said bitterly. "They sure as hell was. And they wasn't much better to me. They ain't a half dozen people around here that will speak to me on the street. I still can't get a decent job around here. They . . ."

"Hell, nothing was your fault, for Christ's sake. What are they holding against you?"

"They knowed how I felt about George," she said softly. "They knowed we was going to get married." she paused before going on defiantly. "And we would have, too, Damon, if all this hadn't come up. George wrote to me all the time. We was still going to get married just as soon as we could."

I wasn't sure how much of that I believed about George Martin, but I didn't say anything. I never saw him write a letter, and sailors live pretty close together.

"George was always so good to me, Damon. George wouldn't have hurt a hair on anybody's head, much less his own daddy's. He was good to his Momma, too. They wasn't a month since he got in the Navy that she didn't get a check."

So, George had an allotment for his mother. Hell, no wonder he never had money to spend chasing around with us. I didn't remember a time he went ashore or bought anything for himself, except maybe, for socks and underwear.

"George knowed I was taking care of his momma for him. We never got much from him, but it was enough to keep us going. We got us a garden patch and the cow and the chickens. We couldn't have made it, though, without George's Navy check," Lela Mae said. "And that's the Lord's truth."

"How about the boy?"

"I never told George about John," she said bleakly. "I never wanted him to feel like he had to come back or nothing like that."

"You know if he had any insurance?"

"No, he never said."

"Well, most of us do," I said. "I'll have the Chaplain look into it when I get back on the ship." If George had an allotment for his mother, I felt pretty sure he would have had insurance, too. It didn't cost much.

We talked on for quite a while after that. Lela Mae did most of the talking. I don't remember much of what we said, but it was a good time. I remember that. I was so full I was uncomfortable. Two cups of pretty weak coffee — by Navy standards — topped me off right up to the loadline.

The boy had long since finished feeding George's mother. He took away the cloth from under her chin and cleaned her face and lap. He moved the little table away, and took the shallow bowl to the dishpan. I don't know when the boy ate. I guess he took bites from time to time as he fed the old woman. I never saw a kid take care of an old person like that. That kid was okay.

It was getting late. The funeral would be the next day. "Guess I better be heading on back to the hotel," I said. "Thanks for that supper. I haven't eaten that much in a long time. The Navy sure as hell doesn't cook like you do, Lela Mae. That was *something*."

"You're welcome, Damon," Lela Mae said. "I'm glad you liked it." She blushed again with my compliment.

"I'm sorry we ain't got no place for you to sleep. It would save you the walk to town."

"Oh, that's all right, Lela Mae," I laughed. "I need some exercise after all I ate.

"I'll come out in the morning in the undertaker's car and take you to the funeral home. Thanks again for the supper. It was good."

I lived in towns most of my life before I joined the Navy, but I liked to walk at night on country roads. That night reminded me of when I was little. It was cool and there were little clouds here and there, but not so many I couldn't see stars through the trees. There were not many lights that far out from town, and what there were were coal oil lamps that were not bright enough to dim the stars. Once I even thought I heard a whippoorwill. I hadn't heard a whippoorwill in a long time.

The evening with Lela Mae and her boy and George's old mother left me in a sour mood. I wasn't sure I wanted to know all I learned about George. We were pretty hard on him in the ship. I guess I was feeling guilty for that.

I went back to my room and stayed there until time to go to the funeral home. I dug in my bag for the carved peach seed I took from George's locker on the ship. Lela Mae said George's father used to whittle things for George when he was a little boy. Maybe his father carved the peach seed for George. Maybe that was why he had kept it in his locker. Maybe Lela Mae would like it for a keepsake.

The undertaker drove me out to the Martin house in a dusty black Buick.

Lela Mae had George's mother up and dressed in what probably was her only decent dress. And it wasn't very decent. Her feet were so swollen she couldn't wear shoes. She still had on the same cloth house slippers I saw the night before. The boy had on clean bib overalls and worn "tennis shoes." But he wore a white shirt buttoned to the neck.

Lela Mae had on what I guess was her best, but it was a poor best. She had on runover shoes and a straw hat with a couple of faded blue silk flowers. She smiled at me. "Morning, Damon," she said as we helped George's mother into the car.

There wasn't a living soul in the dimly-lighted room where George lay that morning, staring with closed eyes through the open top of his casket. Somewhere a record player played scratchy funeral music. I remember "The Old Rugged Cross." There were no flowers. I cussed the God-damned undertaker under my breath. He could have dug up flowers somewhere. The Navy was paying him, for Christ's sake.

I helped George's mother to a seat near his casket. I am not sure she realized what was going on. But she did keep her watery eyes fixed on the casket. I guess she knew more than I thought.

There was a preacher. But not much of one. He didn't say much more than the Lord's Prayer before he came and mumbled something to George's mother. He motioned to me and we helped her to stand beside George's casket for a final look upon her son's face. Lela Mae and the boy came, too. Except for the fact he was dead, George looked fine in the new blues the Navy gave him.

I remembered how he looked lying on the signal bridge deck the day he died. Except for the way his neck was bent, he looked fine then, too.

After all that, we went out and got into the undertaker's car to follow the hearse to the graveyard.

Country graveyards are all pretty much alike, I guess. The stones and graveled drives and the evergreen cedars with their symbolism of eternal life. The hearse stopped beside an open grave with its mound of damp earth alongside it. Two guys in overalls leaned on shovels a short distance off, impatient to get at the business of closing the grave and on to their regular jobs, whatever they were.

I gave George's mother the American flag the Navy gave me to deliver to her. She brushed it with her veined and trembling hands and looked up to me from her chair. "Much obliged," she said. The words were slurred, but understandable.

I got the undertaker to one side then. "Don't you have a Legion Post or something in this God-damned town?" I said as calmly as I could. "You're burying a Navy sailor here, for Christ's sake. He deserves something better than this. You could at least have a bugler to play Taps for him."

"I done what I got paid to do," the undertaker said. "Nobody at the Legion Post wanted anything to do with this."

Well, there wasn't a whole lot more I could do. I rode in the undertaker's car to take Lela Mae and the boy and George's mother home. There, I helped get the old woman back into the house, but I didn't have much time to talk with Lela Mae or the boy. The God-damned undertaker tooted his horn for me to hurry up.

"I'm sorry, Lela Mae," I said. "I got to go now. I wrote my address down on this paper. You let me know if there's ever anything I can do for you. All right?"

She nodded. "I'd like it if you was to say good-bye to John," she said. "John was George's daddy's name. John has taken a shine to you, Damon. He ain't got many friends."

Mention of George's father reminded me of the carved peach seed. I dug it from a pocket and gave it to her. "George had this in his locker on the ship. He didn't have anything else. Maybe it was important to him. You can have it."

Lela Mae's eyes filled at sight of the little carving. "George's daddy whittled that for him," she said. "I'll give it to John when he gets bigger. He ain't got nothing from his daddy."

I did say good-bye to the boy, but he hung his head and would not look at me. I guess he thought I was deserting him after the fine time we had together the night before. Maybe he thought things would be different with me.

Anyway, I did the best I could. I hitched a ride in a pickup back to the town in Missouri where I caught a train back to the ship. My orders did not leave me much time. It was not a very pleasant ride anyway. I was sunk in a black mood of bitter regret that we knew nothing on the ship about George. We would have been different to him, I think, if we knew.

Then I went to the old man and made out an allotment to Lela Mae. I never in the world thought I would do anything like *that*. But I did it for the boy.

THE ASIATIC

In the years just before World War II the Navy's ships were
stripped of experienced men to form crews for the new ships
being built in preparation for the war, and to serve as
trainers for the hundreds of thousands of new men being taken
into the Fleet.

This led inevitably to a lessening of competence in
existing ships. It also led to a less predictable division between
the remaining old-timers and newcomers. Old hands found
themselves often a minority in their own ships, outnumbered by
brash newcomers who did not yet think the Navy way — and
who sometimes held a less than reverent appreciation for the
hard-won skills and knowledge of the old hands.

As do minorities everywhere, the old-timers found
themselves drawn together in sometimes strange unions strong
enough to reach across differences in personality and values.
This, in fact, was what happened between our chief signalman

and a signalman second named Joe Harter, two men who, under normal circumstances, would have been natural enemies.

Joe Harter joined the ship in late 1939. We were lying alongside Ten-Ten dock in Pearl Harbor at the time, and were one of nine heavy cruisers along with a squadron of destroyers — cans, we called them — sent out as a deterrent to Japanese aggression in the Pacific, a move that proved notably futile.

I had the signal watch that morning. We were expecting a new second class signalman to replace a guy named Geiger who was ordered to new construction in the States. Most replacements came from the east, raw new men fresh from schools and training stations, men whose total sea time was five or ten days as passengers between California and Hawaii, but this new guy came from the west.

The minute I saw him I knew he was our new second class. With the starboard forty-five-power glass I saw the crow on his right arm and the two black chevrons. Even from that distance, I also saw trouble in the making. Joe Harter had Asiatic written all over him.

This was all during the time when Japanese pressure was pushing our Navy out of China. The river gunboats were first to pull out — but not before one of them, the *Panay* was sunk by Japanese bombs. Little by little the larger ships followed, and we began to see sailors from them filtering back into the Fleet. Joe Harter was one of those sailors. We called them *Asiatic*.

That was not because they had served in Asia or anything so logical as that. They were called Asiatic because they didn't act or think like normal sailors. They had served too long in the unreal world of the China Station. The rate of exchange out there made even low Navy pay enough for men to live far above their accustomed stations. There was lots of *cumshaw* stuff, too, making life easier for men who, for the most part, had not known much ease before in their lives.

Even more corrosive to character and morals for underlings in any society, they lived in China among a population they saw as inferior to themselves, and over which they enjoyed a good deal of power, unofficial though it was. Gooks and slopeheads, they called the Chinese.

The Navy's river gunboats had coolies living on board to do the cooking and laundry and bilge cleaning and other donkey work. Larger ships did not go quite that far, but duty even in them was more relaxed than it was in the Stateside Navy. Returning to the Fleet with its strict and often petty disciplines, its uniform regulations and working parties, was not something old China hands handled with much grace.

Joe, for instance, stood erect in the boat bringing him to us, hands on hips, his lashed hammock and seabag at his feet, in a challenging stance, as though daring us to do our worst. His white hat was pulled down onto the bridge of his nose and his black neckerchief, folded down and pressed flat as paper, blew in the wind about his face. Even at that distance, the cloth of his whites was one hell of a lot better than regulation Navy whites, and they fit him like a sheath. I have seen snakes back home in Texas with more hips than Joe Harter had. And his hair grew about his ears in a way no Fleet chief petty officer could abide and sleep soundly at night.

Studying him through the glass, I smiled. I couldn't wait until Joe Harter met up with Fred Holmes, our crusty old chief signalman. That promised to be a lot of fun at a time and place where diversion of any kind was welcome. To Holmes, Navy Regulations were little less holy writ than the Bible itself, and uniform regulations were a part of Navy Regs. Right down to how buttons are buttoned and neckerchiefs knotted.

More important in his view was Holmes' perception that his own life would be a lot easier and maybe even a little bit more profitable if his officers saw how zealously he kept his men garbed and groomed in the prescribed Navy way. He might even hope for promotion to warrant officer someday, maybe even to ensign. It didn't happen often, but it did happen. Sometimes. If a guy kept his nose clean, it might.

I watched Joe's boat hook on to the starboard gangway. That side was usually reserved for officers' use, but since we were tied up at the dock, port side to, the lower orders were sometimes allowed to board there. With the unthinking savvy of a veteran sailor Joe heaved his lashed seabag and hammock to his left shoulder, leaving his right hand free for saluting the colors and the quarter deck as he came aboard.

That's when I saw his bucket. Although washing machines were beginning to appear in Navy ships, a lot of white hats still did their own laundry to save money. The Navy thoughtfully issued us galvanized iron buckets for the purpose. At sea, when on water hours, we even took our baths in buckets. When on a move, as Joe was that morning, we simply lashed them to one end of our bundled seabag and hammock, letting them dangle as they would. A sailor's bucket in those days was just another part of what the Limeys called his kit.

Joe Harter's bucket, though, was not like any bucket I ever saw. It started life as a regulation Navy-issue bucket but it sure as hell was not a regulation bucket when he came aboard. Most sailors' buckets were dulled and dented and thickened with dried soap accumulated over the years. Their handles were bare of anything like the knotted and interwoven ropework which encrusted the handle of Joe's bucket, all enameled white as porcelain and knobby with turksheads and other fancy work.

The body of his bucket glistened in the Hawaiian sun, bright and shining as polished chrome could make it. And, coiled about it, a fierce Chinese dragon in red copper was worked and braised onto the chrome with the detailed care of fine jewelry. Some Chinaman spent a hell of a lot of time on Joe Harter's bucket. Later, guys from other parts of the ship came through our compartment just to see the wonderful thing.

In short, Joe's bucket topped off the image of a sailor who was about as Asiatic as a sailor could get. And a sailor who didn't figure to get along very well with Chief Signalman Fred Holmes. To say nothing of the flag lieutenant, who was the staff officer in charge of the signal bridge. The old man, the ship's captain, was not going to be happy either. The admiral, of course, would be above the fray. Or so I thought.

Officers didn't like it when white hats had anything which set them apart from everybody else. Neither did they like it when we found some way to do that in ways the officers couldn't do anything about. There was nothing in Navy Regs which said a man couldn't decorate his wash bucket. That bugged the hell out of the old chiefs. Including Fred Holmes.

Joe didn't make things any better by rubbing Holmes' nose in the fact every chance he got. But, in the end, it was not his bucket which got Joe's mammary gland in a wringer. It was his fancy Ross glass. And the admiral did get involved in that.

Joe was lucky in the first place because Ensign Woods had the Deck when he reported aboard. Woods was one of the pilots we carried for our four seaplanes. Aviators were more lax in matters of uniform and other regulations than black-shoe officers were. (Aviators wore brown shoes. Surface ship officers wore black.) He returned Joe's salute and took his brown orders envelope with little more than a glance at his whites and an open, though silent, appraisal of his splendid bucket.

The quarterdeck in those old cruisers was amidships between the catapult silos. I saw what went on from where I had the watch on the signal bridge. Reporting aboard a new ship for duty was, like everything else in the Navy, routine. I could not hear what was being said, but I knew what it was.

A messenger was sent with Joe's orders to the Exec's office. A master-at-arms was told off to show Joe to his compartment and the bunk and locker which would be his home with us. He would be told where the heads and washrooms were, and the Signalmens' mess. For a sailor like Joe Harter, that would take all of about five or ten minutes.

His Billet Number and place on the Watch, Quarter and Station Bill, along with his assignment to a liberty section would be left up to the chief. That was the power which gave Navy chief petty officers such importance in a white hat's life. It was a power which, in practice, went well beyond the limits specified by regulations.

Joe was in the Navy — his three hashmarks, signified at least twelve years — long enough to know all that, and he did nothing overt upon meeting Chief Holmes to agitate him. He didn't have to. His sharkskin whites, his haircut, his overall Asiatic look and manner were enough set Holmes off.

"Signalman Second Joe Harter," Joe said as he stepped off the ladder onto the bridge and met Holmes for the first time.

Usually guys reporting on board would go through a little dance of swapping dope on the ships they served in and the sailors they knew. The Navy was small then, and men often knew sailors from other ships. This was especially true of signalmen who, while in port, did a good deal of unofficial — and forbidden — signaling between ships by means of short-arm semaphore.

In short-arm semaphore, we used no flags and moved our arms only from the elbows down. It could not be used at such distances as regular semaphore could, but it was faster and less likely to be noticed by officers who would make us knock it off if they saw us doing it. We called it PVTing.

As it happened, Joe Harter served in China under a chief who was a good friend of our Holmes' from some earlier time in battleships. That was a plus for Joe, going in, but it was about the only thing that was. After a couple of minutes of relatively warm discussion of his old friend, Holmes got down to cases.

Tailored whites, custom shoes, creased neckerchief, and relaxed haircut, our Holmes took them all in with a kind of pained expression on his face and he hadn't even seen Joe's beautiful wash bucket yet. "First thing you got to learn, Harter," Holmes said, "is you're not in China anymore. This is a three-star flagship in the United States Pacific Fleet. We are expected to dress and conduct ourselves accordingly. The Flag has to set an example for the other ships. Do you understand?"

Joe grinned pleasantly. "Yeah. Sure, Chief," he said easily. "You got a joe pot on this bridge?" Joe was one of several names we had for coffee.

This encounter took place by the log desk, amidships and aft in our ship's big airy signal bridge. The coffee gear was forward on the starboard side by the pyrotechnics gear locker. It could not be seen from where Joe stood talking with our chief, but he knew damned well there would be coffee somewhere on the bridge. There was *always* coffee somewhere on a signal bridge.

Holmes bristled at Joe's flippant response. "Forget the God-damned coffee," he said. "You got about thirty minutes to get a regulation haircut. And you got about two days to get your ass into some regulation whites. Any questions?"

Still grinning, Joe said, "Yeah, where's the joe pot?"

Sailors on the old China Station, by their very isolation from the Fleet, developed a certain independence of thought and action which made them impatient with regulation and what they called look-see pidgin. They were usually proficient in the duties of their rates, but they were almost defiantly resistant to military discipline — inspections, uniform and haircut regulations and anything else they saw as being unimportant in the actual performance of their jobs.

Still, they were smart enough to know things were different in Fleet ships. They just wanted to find out, as early as possible, how far they could go. Short of a court-martial conviction, they knew they could not be "fired," a knowledge which gave them a maddening insolence in the eyes of men like our chief. Being "busted" to a lower rate, of course, was always a hazard, but most of them had been busted before.

Holmes accepted Joe's challenge. He was a stocky man who came into the Navy during the Great War. He was not long on patience. "Get your ass off this bridge, Harter," he said sternly. "And don't come back until you got a regulation haircut. That's an order."

Joe continued grinning. "Does that mean I ain't on the watch list, Chief?" he said. "I can use a little sleep tonight."

"You're on the watch list," the chief said. "You're on the watch list so God-damned good you got the mid tonight."

The "mid" was the least popular of watches. It was the one from midnight until four in the morning. It knocked the guts right out of a good night's sleep. You got only an hour or so of sleep before being called for the watch, and you got back in your sack for about the same amount of time before reveille sounded the next morning.

Joe left the bridge then, but the challenge was passed between him and Holmes. Passed and accepted. And Holmes had not even seen Joe's Ross glass yet.

Non-reg and glitteringly obvious as it was, Joe's wash bucket did not make much of a problem for him. It hung in the relative obscurity of our living compartment and thus was never seen by officers or chiefs, except during inspections. It never became a serious issue. His Ross glass did, though.

Ross glasses were lightweight telescopes, made in England, which were better for the job and easier to carry on watch than the Navy's standard black long-glasses. Those monstrosities were more than three feet long, bulging out big at the field lens ends and tapering to eye pieces that were three or four inches across, and heavy as iron and thick glass lenses could make them. They were the badge of office for officers of the deck who carried them tucked under their left arms. But they were a pain in the ass for working signalmen.

Ross glasses, on the other hand, were of even diameter throughout their length. They were made of some bright-finished light metal and weighed maybe a quarter as much as the Navy's glasses. Their field was not so wide as that of the Navy glasses, but that made them even better for signal work. All you looked at in signaling was the semaphore guy, or the signal flags snaking out of their bags. Anything else was distraction.

To tell the truth, I never saw a Ross glass before I saw Joe's, but I had heard a lot about them. I don't even know if you could buy them in the States, but you could get them in China. Joe got his in Shanghai.

I didn't know, either, that all Ross glasses did not look like Joe's. In fact, they were made of plain chromed metal for their full length, although that could not have been told from looking at Joe's glass. Joe's glass was covered, from one end to the other with intricately worked silk cord, twisted and twined in coxcombing, turksheads and other fancy knotwork, all of it enameled white and hard as fine china. Ross glasses were nonregulation as hell. Dressed up as Joe's was, they were even more non-reg.

I don't know if Joe carried his Ross glass on the mid that night or not. Glasses were not so important on night watches. Not in harbor, anyway. If we did carry a glass at night, it would be out of little more than habit. Joe and I were not in the same watch. And Chief Holmes seldom came to the bridge at night

— although he could not be counted upon not to do so. If Joe did carry his glass that night, it caused no problem.

But, having the mid watch one night meant a sailor would also have the twelve-to-four watch the next afternoon. And just about everyone was on the bridge for the afternoon watch, either on watch or for drills or simply shooting the bull around the joe pot. This included Chief Signalman Fred Holmes, although he was still below at the noon meal in the chiefs' quarters when Joe relieved the watch that day. Joe did carry his beautiful Ross glass for that watch.

He had not yet had time to get regulation whites. Dressed as he was in rich Chinese silk sharkskin and carrying his fancy Ross glass, the guy made a picture I remember yet as he stood there at the center of all our attention. In fact, everyone on the bridge, watch and all, crowded around him in open admiration. We were beginning to get a lot of young guys in the ships then, as the Navy cranked up for the coming of World War II. These young guys had never seen anything like Joe before.

Joe graciously let us admire him and handle and look through his beautiful glass. He let us study the intricate hand-stitching of his whites and the luster of his custom horsehide shoes. Word of his splendid wash bucket had already passed through the ship. He was the star of our show that day.

But his star dimmed quickly when Chief Holmes stepped off the ladder onto the bridge and yelled: "Who's got the God-damned watch? The Tower's been flying our call for five minutes, for Christ's sake."

Pearl Harbor's water tank was a round cylinder with a conical top, raised on tall steel legs. It was the same kind of water tank seen in a thousand small towns back in the States. But on top of Pearl's tank there was an open structure with a mast and signal yardarms, semaphore platforms, and signal searchlights. This was what we called the Tower. From it, the whole harbor, as well as the entrance channel and several miles to sea were visible. It was the Yard's signal station and was meant to be watched constantly by all ships present. If you had to miss a call, you sure as hell hoped it would not be a call from the Tower.

Worse than that, that day, the Tower had started to make our call by searchlight as well. There was no greater insult for a ship's signal gang — to have someone hoist your call sign flags and then to have to use a signal searchlight to call attention to them. Chief Holmes would hear about that the next time he met chiefs off other ships on the beach. He wouldn't enjoy it, but he would hear about it.

"I said, 'Who's got the God-damned watch?'" Holmes said again. He knew damned well who had the watch, of course. He looked straight at Joe Harter.

"I got the watch, Chief," Joe said easily. "Run up the answering pennant," he said to a striker. "Somebody stand by to write." In semaphore one guy reads the words and another one writes them down. He propped his fancy glass against a stanchion and took the Tower's message calling out the words with no sign of concern for Holmes at all.

The rest of us drew away to other parts of the bridge, but not so far we were unable to hear what was coming. We expected the next few minutes to be interesting.

"What the hell is that?" Holmes said, once Joe took the Tower's message and saw to its logging.

"What is what?" Joe said innocently.

"That," Holmes said, nodding to Joe's glass.

Joe held up his glass as though surprised that it should be the subject of any question. "This?" he said. "This is a long-glass, Chief. You look through it here and . . ."

"Knock off the smart-ass, Harter," Holmes said, red coming to his fleshy face. "Where did you get it? What is it doing on a flagship bridge?"

"I got it in Shanghai. It's on this bridge because I brought it here. I got the watch. I always carry a glass on watch, Chief," Joe said as though explaining something to a particularly slow child.

"We got regulation Navy long-glasses in the locker," Holmes said.

"This one's better. And it don't weigh so much," Joe grinned good-naturedly, although I noticed his eyes narrow. "Want to take a look?"

"I've seen Ross glasses before," Holmes said. "Silly tin sons-of-bitches that they are. Regulation glasses will be used on this bridge as long as I'm chief. Is that clear?"

"Clear as whale shit, Chief," Joe grinned. "Okay if I carry it for the rest of this watch?"

There could be no question as to the outcome of the impasse between Joe and his chief signalman. White hats don't win arguments with chiefs. Joe was in the Navy long enough to know that. But Holmes should not have said what he did about Joe's never using his Ross glass on the bridge. That didn't leave him any way out if anything happened later. And things *always* happen later.

If Holmes had not become sick just about that time, Joe would have got his hair cut, he would have bought regulation whites, and he would have kept his Ross glass off the bridge.

But Holmes did get sick. He got a case of the crud, or something, and was put in the hospital on the beach. We put to sea just after that for two or three weeks of battle practice and tactical maneuvers. Old Tom Harris, our largely ineffectual first class took over for Holmes, and we settled down to enjoy Holmes' absence while we could.

Joe did not go back to his fancy whites or let his hair grow long, but he did bring his Ross glass on watch with him as long as Holmes was not there to bug him. Old Harris didn't much give a damn, one way or the other. He just growled to Joe that he better have the damned thing out of sight when Holmes came back from the hospital.

That was all right with Joe. He knew it couldn't last, but he clearly meant to enjoy it while it did. All the rest of us envied him the efficient little glass, but he wouldn't let any one else use it. We could pick it up and examine it and tell him what a great little glass it was, but no one could have it for a whole watch, or even handle it if Joe were not there. He took it with him when he left the bridge. I sometimes thought his glass was Joe's link to a sweetly remembered life — made even more sweet by the fact that it would never again be anything other than remembered. There would never again be a China Station for Navy sailors.

Things went beautifully on the bridge in Holmes' absence. Within hours — two or three days at the most — Joe became the effective leader on the bridge. He was only signalman second, and we had a first class, old Tom Harris; but it was to Joe we all looked. Even the ship's Signal Officer, a young ensign fresh from Annapolis, and the Flag Lieutenant, a lieutenant commander on the Admiral's staff, came to pass their orders through Joe and looked to him for answers.

Harris didn't care. He was getting close to going out on twenty anyway. The rest of us were glad to be away from the chief's endless nitpicking and harping on regulations. The bridge became a happier place.

I was always glad to get away from harbor every now and then. There was a sense of freedom at sea, even for Navy sailors. That was especially true in those final days before the War when time in port was apt to be fuller than usual with inspections, gas chamber lectures, fire-fighting school, and a lot of other stuff like that. It was good to get away to sea. To get a little rest, if nothing else.

We fired eight-inch day practice and five-inch night battle on that time at sea. We also spent long daylight hours on the bridge, hoisting flags, hauling them down, stowing them — then hoisting them all over again — until our backs ached and our eyes watered and turned red with the strain of binoculars and telescopes — as the ships twisted and turned in seemingly endless high speed tactical maneuvers. The fact that nothing went really right anymore made the work even harder and more frustrating.

A lot of old-timers were taken from the Fleet for new-construction in the States or as instructors in schools and training stations. Their replacements in the ships were raw and fresh from boot camp, still awkward in what, for them, was a strange and demanding world. Performance slipped all to hell and gone. Even our firing became erratic as experienced gunners were transferred away.

On the signal bridge, hoists were lost, flags misread, ceramic heads burned in the big twenty-four-inch signal searchlights, and, in general, things got screwed up. Close quarters maneuvering in fast ships is a chancy thing at best. Officers in tactical command came to allow extra safety margins, but still we had close calls with near collisions. Nerves were noticeably tight on the bridge.

Still, fast ships on a trade wind sea are soothing to mind and eye, in daytime at least. The ships were not yet painted wartime black and were kept to glistening yacht-like standards of paint and polished brass. To see them twisting and turning, bright hoists of snapping signal flags arcing up to yardarms, sugar-white wakes extending to the horizon at times, was to see something which would never be seen again. A way of life was ending.

We did not know that at the time, of course, but I think we sensed it. Too much was changing. Some ships went to cafeteria feeding for white hats, and bunks from three-high to four. More lockers were crammed into our already crowded living compartments. Washrooms were more congested than ever and life, in general, was no longer so pleasant.

The new guys didn't notice it so much, I guess. They didn't know any better, but for the old guys among us, it was rough.

Through it all, though, only Joe remained as unaffected as ever, an equanimity based upon his sure knowledge of what to do in any situation. We of the lesser orders saw that even the officers were coming to rely upon him. This promised to make new problems for Joe once Holmes came back on our return to Pearl, but he gave no sign of either knowing or caring.

As was true in any bureaucracy, the peacetime Navy prized conformity above all else. Passed inspections, proper uniforms and haircuts, shined shoes, and *no* mistakes were the things upon which successful careers were built. Of course, it had all to be reworked once war started, but war had not yet come.

Holmes was never likely to be accused of being the smartest man in the Navy. Nor could he be blamed for having much in the way of imagination. His rise to chief was due to the workings of seniority and the Navy's appreciation for his slavish devotion to Regulations and the minutiae of military discipline. Holmes succeeded, not because he ever did much right, but because he never did absolutely anything chargeably wrong, or which was not justified somewhere in the Navy's voluminous manuals and instruction books.

Once Holmes laid down the law, he couldn't back down. Not in his and the Navy's peacetime world. Face was involved all to hell and gone in the matter.

In the end, it was the admiral, of all people, who tossed the stuff into the fan. Joe carried his Ross glass on the bridge while the Chief was in the hospital ashore. One day the admiral saw it.

We were engaged in tactical maneuvers and Joe was spotting flag hoists on the port side of the bridge, using his Ross glass. He braced it against a stanchion not far from the admiral's padded chair on that side of the bridge. That particular admiral was no more chatty with white hats than any other of his breed, but he was attracted by Joe's glass.

Once we knocked off for the noon meal and were steaming a sedate ten knots in our usual station at the rear of the Sixth Division column, the bridge became quiet. The admiral beckoned Joe to his side. "I have been admiring your Ross glass, son," he said in what was probably as close to friendliness as an admiral could get in speaking to a white hat. "Mind telling me where you got it?"

"Shanghai, Sir," Joe said, all formal as hell. I suppose he thought the admiral was going to climb his frame for having a non-reg glass on the bridge, the way Holmes did.

"Lately?" the admiral said.

"Four years ago, Sir."

"You were Asiatic Fleet?"

"Yes, Sir. *Tulsa*."

"Do tell?" the admiral said. It was an old-fashioned expression of the kind admirals often use. "I was in the old *Asheville* out there. Fresh out of the Academy." He paused. "Before your time, of course."

The *Tulsa* and the *Asheville* were sister gunboats both commissioned in the early twenties, and both usually operated out of Canton. This set them apart from the bulk of Asiatic Fleet ships which usually were to be found farther north.

The admiral clearly was recalling more pleasant times in his career, before age and the responsibilities of command ate into the animal pleasures of a healthy young man enjoying the options of youth and often independent operations on distant stations. He brought his attention back to Joe's handsome glass. "You do the fancy work yourself?" he said.

"Yes, Sir."

"Mind if I take a look through it?"

"No, Sir." Joe handed his glass to the admiral who put it to his eye and swept the horizon before settling onto a close study of the next ship ahead in column.

"I had a glass like this once," he said quietly. "Not as pretty as yours, but a good glass. Lost it a long time ago. Don't let yours get away from you."

"Yes, Sir."

The admiral returned Joe's glass and continued his distant study of the sea abeam. God knows what he thought, but I suspect he remembered the long ago time when he had a Ross glass, too.

Joe stood, uncertain, for a time, but the admiral did not speak again and Joe returned to his station in the bridge wing. Shortly after that, he was relieved and went below.

So far as I know, the admiral spoke again to Joe only one other time, but what he said this time was enough. Some of us were close enough to hear the exchange. Those who weren't were soon told of it by those who were. The word spread with all the incredible speed of scuttlebutt, the Navy's word for rumor. The admiral admired Joe's Ross glass! Hell, he even had one of his own one time.

This soon was improved to the admiral *approved* Joe's glass for the bridge, and that set up a whole new situation for when Holmes returned from the hospital and found Joe carrying it on watch. We all knew Holmes and his unnatural awe of admirals. When he learned that our own three-star admiral *approved* Joe's glass for the bridge, the entire structure of his life would be put at risk. It would be interesting to see how he would wiggle out of the dilemma.

We finished our exercises in another four or five days and set our course for Pearl. Again at our fuel-saving ten knots when on passage. Somewhere well short of Diamond Head, we hoisted an information signal meaning "Disregard Movements of This Ship." Then, shearing out from our normal station at the rear of the column, and ringing the engine room for turns to make twenty-five knots, we passed close alongside the leading ships and left them in our wake. Hauling ass for Pearl, as the white hats put it.

We would be secured alongside in Pearl, with harbor watches set and liberty parties ashore long before the other ships made their stately — and slow — entries. Flagship duty had its advantages sometimes. Not that the men in the more plebeian ships were all that impressed. Some of them made rude gestures as we steamed past.

We were in Pearl that time for almost a week. Holmes returned from the hospital soon after we docked, but the admiral seldom appeared on the Flag bridge while we were in harbor. The looming confrontation between Joe and Holmes was put on hold. Joe left his glass below, during that time. I don't suppose the chief yet heard about the Admiral's interest in it.

But, during that time in port, Joe came to wear a troubled expression and lost some of his usual go-to-hell cockiness. I thought he had the pip or something. But, as I learned later, it was something a good deal more important.

Guys sometimes get into some pretty deep stuff when they talk in slow night watches. Joe did not tell me all at one time, but, little by little, and one way or another, I found out he was worried about the problem of his Ross glass and Holmes.

I was surprised as hell to learn that he did not dislike the chief. He even respected him for some things. "It's guys like Holmes that have kept this God-damned Navy together for the past ten or fifteen years," Joe said one night.

"But what about your Ross glass, Joe?" I said. "You wouldn't hurt anything by carrying it on the bridge. And, after the way the admiral drooled all over it, you can carry the God-damned thing all you want. You know Holmes ain't going to question anything an admiral approves. Carrying that Ross glass on the bridge ain't going to hurt anything, for Christ's sake."

"Maybe not," Joe said. "But I could hurt a hell of a lot if I got away with doing something the chief said I wasn't going to get away with."

"I don't get you."

"I get away with something like that, how in the hell you going to keep everybody else from getting away with stuff. And, if everybody else gets away with whatever he wants, you ain't got a signal gang anymore. You got a bunch of assholes that think they're as good as anybody else."

"What's wrong with that, for Christ's sake?" we young guys went out of our way to be as profane as the old-timers. We thought it was a way to get their respect.

"Nothing, I guess," Joe said quietly. "It's just that, in the Navy, everybody ain't as good as everybody else." He paused. "I did that one time," he went on. "Out in China I once caught a pretty damned good chief with his tit in a wringer. I rubbed his nose in it. It broke the poor son-of-a-bitch before it was over." Joe paused again. "He was a better man than I was."

Well, that was all too much for me. Holmes, for me, stayed a nitpicking bastard who made our lives rougher than necessary. But we were relieved of the watch about that time, and I never talked with Joe about it again.

We all knew that, after what the admiral said, Joe could carry his Ross glass on the bridge all he wanted. But he never brought it to the bridge again.

One time, even, the admiral noted its absence and asked Joe where it was. (That was the other time he spoke to Joe.) Holmes was standing nearby. He probably heard the scuttlebutt about the admiral's interest in Joe's glass by then. He watched closely for Joe's answer.

Joe looked directly at Holmes before he replied. In fact, he let Holmes squirm pretty good before he answered the admiral. "I got a kid brother back in the States, Sir," Joe said. Hawaii was still a Territory then and we referred to the Mainland as the States. "I sent it to him for a birthday present."

"Too bad," the admiral said. "Ross made a good glass."

Signalmen are accomplished eavesdroppers. It wasn't five minutes until everyone on the bridge knew that Joe gave away his Ross glass. Another twenty minutes, and it was known throughout the ship. Such is the efficiency of scuttlebutt. Scuttlebutt might not be accurate or reliable, but it sure as hell was fast.

Everybody was surprised that Joe gave up his glass so easily, but I wasn't. I remembered our night watch conversation. I just hoped to hell Holmes appreciated what Joe did for him.

I needn't have worried. Around by the coffee gear that afternoon, Holmes brought up the subject in an oblique way. "I saw Wright in the hospital. Son-of-a-bitch had the piles," he said.

Wright was Holmes' old friend from battleship days. Joe knew him in China. I remembered they talked about Wright the morning Joe reported on board. "We talked about you some," Holmes said.

"Yeah?" Joe said, spooning sugar into his coffee.

"Yeah. He told me you don't have any family, Joe. No mama, no papa. Not even a kid brother." They grinned at each other then. Joe handed Holmes the sugar can. "Sugar, Chief?" he said.

WHITE HAT CONFESSOR

Although it would come as a jolt to my drinking buddies in the ship to know it, I was once an altar boy. It was in a poor South Boston parish, and so great was my tender young faith in God that Father John encouraged me to become a priest and arranged for my education to that end.

I might well have followed that path in life, I suppose, had not the God I loved so much decreed, or, at least allowed, my widowed mother's slow and agonizing death of cancer before my disbelieving eyes. I could never, after that, bring myself again to believe in Father John's stories of a loving and merciful God.

As I tore myself free of his consoling arms and fled from his old red brick Church, he called after me that I could never travel so fast nor go so far as to escape God's tender love for me.

I don't know if I escaped God's tender love or not in the intervening years, but I went fast and far enough, on a voyage which found me, at last, in the small-ship Navy where chaplains never came, to escape what I saw as the hollow teachings of His priests.

Still, in the darkest depths of my disillusion, I never entirely lost my reverential awe of priests. It was only after many years I learned that priests, too, may sin and find themselves in need of confession. That discovery, when it came, was at a time and place I least expected.

We steamed that day, to the west, under low-hanging clouds which made of the sea a vast and gloomy chamber. Then, at sunset, the sun shot its slanting brilliance through a narrow slit which suddenly opened between clouds and horizon with such a brightness that we winced, turning our eyes away to look back along the way we came.

Had we not done so, we would never have seen what appeared there, and the man we rescued would, in all likelihood, have died in the coming night for he was worn and spent by thirst to the point of exhaustion. Although conscious, he was but barely so.

It was strange that we did not see the foundering boat in which he lay. Its position was such that we passed it by not more than a few hundred yards, and, in that time of approaching war, we kept a good lookout. True, the boat was awash and lying low in the sea, but we should have seen its masts and its remaining tatter of sails.

We were steaming at our best speed — which was not fast at all. By the time we maneuvered into position and lowered a boat, the quick tropical night was upon us, and we used a signal searchlight with its shutters held open to keep the derelict boat in view and guide our own rescuing boat to it. The sea was not at all rough, but there was a sizable swell rolling out of the southeast. Small craft are not easily seen at night in such conditions.

The foundering boat was one of the small island schooners used by missionaries in the servicing of their remote stations. We were used to seeing them among the islands where we steamed. Little more than thirty feet long, and ten wide, they were stoutly built, but seldom well-maintained or expertly manned. Their cotton sails, more often than not, rotted in the tropical sun to a frailty unequal even to moderate winds, much less the violent squalls so often met in those seas. Their size alone made the schooners pathetically vulnerable, even though they sailed under the presumed protection of a God likely to be caring of those on His holy business.

The man, when we came upon him, was so weak he seemed but slightly aware of our presence. As a young signalman I was assigned to our whaleboat whenever "Away, Fire and Rescue Party!" sounded. Since I had no part in the actual handling of the boat, I was free to help the hospital corpsman we brought along. He and I leaped lightly onto the sinking schooner from our own boat which then hauled off to avoid banging alongside.

We did not know then the man was a priest. We learned that only later. Any habit he might once have worn had long since gone to rags. Only a large crucifix of ebony and silver hanging from a golden chain about his neck suggested religion at all. But, somehow, I suspected even then he was indeed a servant of God. This may have been because of the weird way in which we were led to find him.

It is perhaps fanciful to think of it in such terms, but I came to believe, even then, that God, in seeing us pass by His servant without discovering him, parted the clouds and issued a directing beam of sunlight to show us to his salvation. It is possible, I suppose, that the long gloomy day and the quick falling of night over a heaving sea conditioned me to this conclusion, but it was real enough.

Nor do I think I was alone in the fact, for the others in the boat's crew seemed strangely subdued, as though in the presence of something unnatural and beyond our understanding.

We did not carry a doctor. Anything to be done for the man would have to be done by the corpsman, with whatever rudimentary help the rest of us could give. The corpsman moved with an oddly respectful tenderness in examining the exhausted man and those in the boat kept silence as they watched. We all had an eerie aspect in the weird blue-white glow of our ship's searchlight. This added to our sense of the supernatural.

"Is he alive?" Ensign Salter, the boat officer called across in a muted voice.

"Yes, Sir," the corpsman said. "But he's pretty far gone. We need to get him back to the ship."

Ours was a small ship. One of the Navy's old minesweepers from World War I, it had little in the way of guns or speed or much of anything else ordinarily thought of in connection with warships. Nevertheless, the old "Bird boats," as they were more or less affectionately known by Navy sailors — because they were named for birds — seemed to be everywhere in the Far East during the period just before the War. They were used for target-towing, tugboat duties in Philippine harbors, supply missions to outlying bases, and sometimes mysterious assignments to remote islands. Ironically, about the only thing they did not do during that time was minesweeping, the function for which they were designed.

Our mission found us somewhere south of Mindanao on an assignment I no longer remember. War with Japan seemed daily to come nearer, but we had neither knowledge nor power to do anything about it. Most of us thought it would be a short and simple war, in any event.

Such inferior people as the Japanese were not expected to give the great American Navy much in the way of trouble. After a while the sense of dread and impending doom we felt upon first learning of the probability of war became a new norm and little intruded upon our conscious thought, though never sinking far beneath the surface of our minds. Most of us were on the China Station. We saw for ourselves what the Japanese were capable of doing to anyone unlucky enough to find himself in their power.

"Flags," Ensign Salter called across to me. "Tell the ship, 'Boat in sinking condition. One survivor in need of medical help. Request Instructions.'" *Flags* was the Navy's generic term for signalmen. We were seldom called by our real names.

Ensign Salter was a young officer, but he was an Academy man and thus capable. More to the point, he was in the Yangtze gunboats before coming to us and well-schooled in independent action. Still, this was a matter he did not want to handle himself.

Ordinarily, semaphore was not used at night, but it was really the only practical means of signaling from a small boat at that time. We did not then have portable radios. Semaphore was possible that night only because our ship's searchlight made me and my flags visible from the ship. I quickly sent off the question.

After a brief pause, the reply returned by means of the searchlight. "Bring survivor on board. Search vessel for identification and registry."

Since Doc was busy with the man, it fell to me to make the examination for the information the ship wanted. Water by that time was well over the bunks in the schooner's small cabin. Each dip of its bows seemed to settle the boat deeper into the sea. There was little time for searching. Besides, most of the vessel was flooded and little could be reached in any event. After I helped the corpsman hand over the weakened survivor I went below.

With only the indirect blue-white glow of our ship's searchlight coming through cabin hatchway and side ports, I could see little. All was silent except for the gurgle and wash of seawater sloshing about inside the boat. Standing in water to my waist, I found, as much by feel as by sight, a wooden rack just inside the companionway hatch. It was built over a small table, which I took to be the boat's navigation station. The rack held three or four books. Unable to read their titles, I stuffed them inside my dungaree shirt.

It was only when I turned for a final look about that I saw the body of a woman lying in a starboard bunk. Long black hair alternately covered and washed away from her face with the sloshing about of water in the eerie light. I drew back and called up the companionway hatch. "Hey, Doc. You better come down and take a look at this."

As *Flags* was the generic name for signalmen, so was *Doc* the name for Pharmacist's Mates. Anyway, Doc already had crossed over to our motor whaleboat and did not hear my call.

When he did not answer, I turned again to the woman's body. Even in my medical innocence, I saw she was in an advanced stage of pregnancy. She was an island woman and her belly humped up under her thin native dress.

Before I could do anything further, something carried away somewhere below the waterline. With a sudden lurch, the boat went downward. Seawater rushed through the companionway hatch with such force I was knocked from my feet and well forward in the instantly flooded cabin. It was a near thing I got out at all. Our boat fished me out of the suddenly empty sea where the schooner once was.

Back on board the ship I went below and changed into dry dungarees. Even tropical nights are chilly in wet clothes. I tossed the books I recovered from the sinking boat onto my bunk while dressing. Once dry, I took them to the Captain. It never occurred to me to tell anyone of the dead woman.

I found the Captain, with two or three other officers and a half dozen white hats, in the wardroom where Doc had stretched the rescued man out on a transom bench and covered him with a white Navy blanket. Officers and men stood about in watching silence, or talked together in muted voices. The sanctity of the wardroom was not so observed in the Bird boats as it was in larger ships. Besides, anything out of the ordinary was welcomed by sailors as a relief from boredom. I suppose the officers realized that and let us watch for a while as an affordably modest treat.

"How is he, Doc?" the captain asked as I came up.

"Vital signs are good," Doc said. "We'll have to get some fluids in him and keep him warm. I'll . . ."

As often happens when men are saved from one kind of ordeal or another, the rescued man remained conscious until Doc and I jumped on board his boat, only to faint dead away at being relieved of the necessity for holding on. But, at the feel of Doc's warm soup in his mouth and the sound of the captain's voice, he came feebly awake.

"I am all right," he croaked through his parched throat. "Where — where am I?" He rolled his head to look about the small wardroom as though searching for something.

"Was there anyone else in your boat?" the captain said. He was only a lieutenant, but it is a Naval courtesy that commanding officers, regardless of rank, are addressed in their ships as captain. "Should we make a search of the area?"

The man did not answer at once. Again, he looked about the compartment. I don't know if he remembered me and Doc as the ones who rescued him or not, but he seemed to hold his eyes on us for a time before replying. "No," he said. "I was alone." He explained that the two Mission boys who were his crew were swept over the side in the same shrieking squall which blew out his sails and left him adrift. His auxiliary engine, as they often do, failed.

I thought I saw tears in his eyes, and his voice certainly was more strained even than before. He made no mention at all of the dead woman I saw in his boat's cabin. I thought then he probably meant he was the only *living* person on board, to save us the trouble of a useless search. I assumed the woman was the wife of one of the lost crewmen. In any event, she was dead.

Doc continued holding warm soup to the man's lips until, after a time, he fell asleep even as he ate. Whatever lay behind his lying about the dead woman, he was aboard the ship now and it was the Captain's pidgin not mine.

No one spoke for what seemed a long time. The sleeping man stirred now and then, as though trying to come awake. Once he actually did waken and tried to sit up, his face working in panic.

Gently, Doc pushed him back. "No. Rest," he said. "You've had a rough go. Just relax. Get back your strength. You are all right now."

The man protested for a moment, but only weakly, and lay back. "Sorry to be a bother," he said.

"No bother," Doc said. He stood and motioned for us to clear the wardroom. Medical people are quick to assume authority at such times. The last I saw was the man lying there, his eyes again closed. There was an expression of great sadness in his face. But that may have been no more than fatigue.

During the next day or two I came to know the rescued man. Signalmen on ships steaming alone have little to do other than keep a lookout. The captain told him that I was the one who, along with Doc, rescued him. Oddly, the man never referred to that fact at all, and never, in any way, thanked either me or Doc for saving his life.

In the meantime, the captain learned from the books I took from the sinking boat that the man we saved was a priest. He was pastor of an island Mission some two or three days to the south. The captain told me all this before the man wakened from his exhausted sleep. He also told me Cavite had diverted us to deliver the man to his home Mission. That meant he would be with us for some days to come.

This fact — that the man was a priest — and my own past as an altar boy and a prospective priest myself, may explain how quickly we became friends. Ordinarily, civilians in a naval vessel live and associate with the officers. White hats are lucky to get a perfunctory "Good Morning" from them. But our rescued priest went out of his way to be considerate of enlisted men.

He resisted our Captain's efforts at an explanation as to how he came to be alone in the little Mission schooner so far from his home island. All the Captain wanted was to get information for proper log entries, but our rescued priest would not cooperate. He became especially upset when I told him we were diverted to take him home and gave every evidence of not wanting to go.

Once back on his feet, the priest and I spent long hours in a bridge wing or sitting on a forecastle mooring bitt where we were alone and the wind of the ship's speed tempered the tropic heat. I no longer remember all we talked about, but much of it grew out of his fascination with men who chose for themselves careers of war and the preparation for war.

He discovered quickly my own religious past, but never reproved me for my loss of faith or tried to bring me back to the

Church. Nor did he so much as comment upon my choice of a Navy life, a life of which he clearly disapproved.

He was from somewhere in Ohio and was ordained out of Notre Dame. He even played football there. He went into Mission work, he said, to escape what he saw as the boredom of routine parish work. His Bishop approved of his assignment in an effort to "save" him for the Church.

A dozen times I had it on the tip of my tongue to bring up the question of the dead woman, but I failed in the end. I have often thought it was some lingering after effect of my early religious training which kept me from questioning him. Priests still held some of the awed respect I had for them when I was young and undoubting. The woman was dead in any event, probably from the exhaustion, hunger, and thirst which so nearly killed the priest himself. It never occurred to me that he had something to do with her death. If he failed to mention the woman's presence in his boat I assumed he had good reason. Still, I was uneasy about it.

I was made uneasy even earlier by the priest's demeanor after he became strong enough to talk more extensively with the captain. I was in the wardroom at that time only because the captain called me there to introduce me to the priest as one of the men who saved him.

"Good evening, Father," the captain said. I didn't know then — I still don't know — if the captain was Catholic or not, but his demeanor towards the priest, both then and later, certainly suggested he was. "I am the captain," he said.

The priest seemed wary at being addressed as "Father."

"We recovered your ship's papers," the captain explained. "Some books and things. Sorry we couldn't save more, but your boat was going down. We got what we could for you."

"Books?" the priest asked closely.

"Yes. Log. Azimuth and sight reduction tables. Things like that."

The priest spoke pointedly. "You didn't find a diary?"

"No. Only what I just said." The captain turned to me. "Did you see a diary, Flags?"

"No, sir," I said. "Just what I gave you."

The priest relaxed visibly, lying back against his pillows. "It is not important," he said. "Thank you for saving what you did. Thank you very much. God bless you." Then, and more prosaically, "I suppose there will be an inquiry."

"Not as far as the Navy is concerned," the Captain said. "As for your church, that is between you and your Bishop. Again, the captain seemed comfortably conversant with church affairs. His manner towards the priest was completely deferential, "You may be happy to know we were diverted to deliver you to your island."

The priest protested. "That is not where you were bound, is it?" he said.

"No, but it will be a welcome diversion for us," the captain said. "We have never been to your island. I have heard it is beautiful."

"But I can't put you to that trouble. You have done quite enough as it is. Please, I beg you, Captain. Continue on as you were. I understand you are based at Cavite. Cavite will be quite all right for dropping me off." The priest all but pleaded.

"There is no point in arguing, Father," the Captain smiled. "I have already reported your rescue, and the Navy, in its infinite wisdom, has decreed your safe return. I'm afraid there is no appeal from Naval wisdom, even from the Almighty."

The priest seemed about to speak, but thought better of it. "You embarrass me, Captain," he said with a weak attempt at a smile. "But, it seems I am in your hands."

"That you are, Father. I suggest you relax and enjoy it, as we often say in the Navy — in another context entirely." The captain laughed. I never saw him so expansive. Then, more seriously, he said. "I have directed you be moved to my cabin. You will be more comfortable there. We will have you home in a day or two."

"Captain, I must insist . . ."

"When you are up and about, you can repay us by conducting Mass for us, if you will be so good, Father. In the meantime, should you need anything, you need only ask."

The priest conceded, but was clearly not happy with the way things were going. I had the clear impression that he did not want to return to his island at all.

"Is there anything more, Captain?" I said. I was strangely uncomfortable in the priest's presence and glad to be clear of him. Doc and I both left. I still remembered the dead woman.

I did not see the priest the rest of that day nor well into the night. He was, of course, the great topic of conversation among us, but I saw no more of him until very late that night.

I had the mid watch — the one from midnight to four in the morning — and it began to rain. We were permitted in the Bird boats to go to the bridge through officers' country during bad weather to avoid becoming wet before starting our watch. That is why I was in the passageway outside the captain's cabin. And that is why I saw the captain kneeling with his head against the bulkhead beside his door.

His door was slightly ajar. I was behind the captain and could not actually see his lips moving, but I heard the indistinguishable murmur of his words. And, sometimes, I thought I heard an answering, though less distinct, murmur from beyond the door.

This was all very strange, and I could think of no explanation. I thought at first that the captain might be sick, until I heard a familiar phrasing. I remembered then Father John, my parish priest when I was a boy growing up in an orphanage in Boston. Father John used that same phrasing all those years ago. God knows I gave that poor priest practice enough in hearing confessions, but I remembered that particular phrasing when I heard it again outside the captain's cabin.

Then I realized the priest was hearing the captain's confession. In the absence of the conventional "box," he was to one side of the captain's door and the captain to the other.

Embarrassed, I made the sign of the cross and backed quietly away and out onto the weather deck, getting soaking wet as I did so. I have never mentioned the episode to a living soul from that day until this.

It is always uncomfortable in a Navy ship when a stranger, especially a civilian stranger, is on board. A priest is even worse. We had to watch our language for one thing. White hats are not altar boys. We used bad words sometimes, and priests have an inhibiting effect upon an otherwise natural flow of conversation. About the only thing worse would be having a woman on board.

The next day, steaming alone as we were, meant little work for the signal gang. With no other ships in company, there was no one to signal *to*. It's easy that way, but it gets boring. That is when the priest and I came to have our long conversations. I wasn't all that upset when the captain passed the word, sometime that afternoon, to "Rig Ship for Divine Services." It was a break in routine, though I had no intention of attending.

Rigging ship for divine services is partly a signalman's job in the Navy. The deck force sets out chairs and benches and digs up something to use as an altar, but it is the signalmen who hoist the Church Pennant and who drape signal flags around the area set aside for the purpose.

The Navy Church Pennant is a long white pennant with a blue cross. It is the only thing ever hoisted above the American flag in a Navy ship. During Divine Services the flag is lowered a few feet at the gaff and the Church Pennant is run all the way up on an adjoining halyard. Not even the Church Pennant is hoisted above the flag on the same halyard.

We didn't have chaplains in the Bird boats, of course, so we almost never had Divine Services. Commanding officers might or might not do so. Ours never did. Although most of our signal flags were well worn and somewhat faded, our Church Pennant was bright and clean.

I didn't attend the services that afternoon, but a lot of the guys did. Hell, it was something to do on a dull day, and it got them out of a little work. I was always dubious about church services in ships built for killing, but I didn't mind other guys going. I saw them from the bridge and knew when it was time to go down and get back our flags.

After the priest finished with his services, he came again to talk with me. I still remember those conversations. Civilians seemed never to know how to talk with white hats, especially on board ship. It was seldom a profitable exercise for us since we were either patronized all to hell or looked through as though we were not even there. But this priest talked with me as he might have with any other human being. He reminded me very much of Father John in that respect.

We continued talking, the priest and I, at every opportunity until we arrived at his island around noon the next day. By that time, he didn't look too much the worse for wear, except for a drawn look which was perfectly understandable under the circumstances. That, and a haunted expression in his eyes. Otherwise, in the starched khakis the Captain gave him, he looked like an officer, except he didn't have a cap and wore that big black and silver crucifix outside his shirt.

The island, as we came up on it, was little different from all the thousands of other islands out there. Green mountains shadowed dark by a swathing of clouds about their shoulders. Tall coconut palms leaning out over white beaches. Neat brown houses of dry palm fronds and other native materials. Canoes pulled up on the sand.

But the little bay on which the priest's Mission faced was prettier than most. Cleaner, anyway. There was a small stone jetty where Mission schooners might tie up, although there were none present as we came in. There was not water enough for us to come alongside. We had to anchor out.

Fishing canoes dotted the pastel lagoon waters to either side of the pass we entered, with the priest serving as pilot to show the way. The people in the canoes shouted glad cries when they recognized their priest standing on our bridge and dropped their nets to hurry alongside and escort us in. Their enthusiasm spread quickly ashore as well, and all activity stopped as the people rushed to the foreshore and sang welcoming hymns in deep resounding voices. Soon the church bell added its ponderous glee to the din. The priest obviously was well-loved by his flock who must have thought him lost.

Immediately our anchor was down, we became the center of a swarming mass of canoes. Younger islanders swam out from the beach, clinging to our sides, shouting and waving to their priest who, for his part, stood erect on a mooring bitt and blessed them with a solemnity which slowly stilled their joy.

Ashore, the dominant building was the church, a wide low building with a high-pitched roof of thatch. Its walls of plaited fronds were little more than three or four feet high, with the remaining space between them and the overhanging eaves left open for any breeze chancing by. A wooden cross rose from an open belfry set astride the roof's ridgepole near the front.

To the left of the church, a second imposing building sat back against a dark green treeline. It was low as well, but with a hipped rather than a gabled roof. A veranda stretched the length of its front, furnished with white rattan tables and chairs and long cushioned settees, all ranged behind a white-painted wooden railing in a diamond pattern of a style common in the colonial islands.

To the church's right there was the school. Of similar design to the church, it was not so big, but had the same low walls and doorless ends. A small hospital finished the Mission establishment itself.

Ranged all about, the plaited and thatched houses of the people formed tidy ranks. All were planted on broad tended lawns sloping to the water's edge, studded with beds of lush flowering plants. White crushed-shell walkways, with edges of on-edge shells, laced the smooth green of the lawn. It was a most handsome place, hemmed in by a dark walling of jungle trees.

Once we were secured and riding quietly to our anchor, the priest came to the bridge and spoke to the captain. "Thank you, sir," he said with an odd lack of emotion. "Thank you for your kindness, and for that of your crew. In the name of my people — and in the holy name of God — I invite you all ashore that we may thank you in a more substantial way. We would like to have you to a feast tonight. Please, do not deny us that pleasure, Sir." Despite the warmth of his words, their delivery remained flat and lacking in any real warmth, though I could think of no reason for the fact, since he was home safe again among people who obviously loved him.

At first, I thought that denying those simple people was exactly what the captain was going to do. But, as he listened, his face softened. "We are under orders, Father," he said. "We are not free to do as we might like."

"Surely, your ship can be spared for one evening of thanksgiving and worship," the priest said. "Surely, your Navy will be able to spare your ship for that long."

The captain laughed and turned to our engineering officer who came to the bridge just then to report his engines secured on standby — and catch a breath of relief from the stifling heat of his station. "How long has it been, Mister Craig, since we've had anything wrong with the engines'?"

"Months, Captain," Ensign Craig smiled knowingly. "I don't remember the last time."

"Then it would not be surprising if we were to suffer some engineering casualty this afternoon? Something which might take, say, twenty-four hours or so to remedy?"

"Not at all, Sir. All this tropic steaming, something can go down just about any time," Mister Craig said with mock seriousness.

Thus it was we stayed the night at the priest's island Mission. Duty in the Asiatic Fleet was never so straitlaced as it was in the Stateside Navy anyway. Especially not in the Bird boats and other small ships. Our guys whooped when the word was passed that we were staying the night. Holiday Routine was declared. Swimming call followed soon after, and we were, for the most part, like so many school boys for the rest of the day.

The Captain went ashore with the priest in an island canoe and took up station on the Mission house verandah over what looked through my telescope to be very tall and very cold drinks. The priest changed into an ankle-length white robe which buttoned with many buttons down the front. His big crucifix stood out against the white cloth of his robe. He was a handsome figure of a man, though still thin and not yet recovered to full vigor.

Women passed to and fro from the Mission gardens, arms and head-baskets heaped with fruits and vegetables of all kinds. Children dashed about in happy chase of scrawny jungle chickens. Laughing men dragged and carried wood to fire pits and killed and gutted pigs to go in them. Others set up torches for light and brought flowers and foliage to make the place pretty for us. It was fun just to watch it all. I suppose it was as welcome a break in monotony for them as it was for us.

Soon, the air ashore turned blue with wood smoke and fat with the smells of cooking meat. Sometimes, wisps of breeze brought the smells out to us in the ship as well. Our mouths watered at the promise of what was to come. There probably would not be any booze, but everything else was *ding hao*.

We didn't bother shifting the watch from the bridge to the quarterdeck. No one on the bridge pretended to be on watch anyway. I suppose there was someone in the engine room to keep an eye on boiler water, but that was not my pidgin. Most of us corked off or showered and got ready to go ashore, jostling each other in the crowded washroom and laughing at the thought of liberty in a new port.

A steady parade of guys came to the bridge to use our telescopes and binoculars for what white hats called "long-glass liberties," a close study of things ashore without leaving the ship. Since we were anchored so close in, that was almost as good as being shore, except, as some of the more horny of us pointed out, "You can't touch nothing."

Most times Navy sailors were not allowed on ships' bridges unless on watch or part of the bridge force, but we stretched things a little in the Bird boats. It wasn't long before the bridge was crowded with sailors carrying on a spirited and physiologically detailed evaluation of the quality and likely availability of the women on the beach. Individual talents were pointed out and claims staked. Since it was a Mission station, dress was modest. But, since it was the tropics, dress was flimsy, too, and followed contours in teasing outline if not in great detail.

Ensign Salter had the watch. He smiled at the goings on and excused himself on some pretext so as not to be an inhibition. Ensign Salter would be a good officer someday.

Sometime around two in the afternoon, liberty call was sounded and the ship was virtually abandoned. We lowered a boat, but no one bothered manning it. The islanders fought amongst themselves for the privilege of hauling us ashore in their canoes. That was an adventure in itself.

I volunteered to take the bridge watch, content to view things through a long-glass for a while. And confident, too, that it would not be me who was stuck with the watch on board when the fun started after dark.

The priest still entertained on his veranda. All of our officers were with him by that time, with the exception of one engineering officer left on board to keep an eye on things below. Girls in loose white dresses trotted out in giggling procession with trays of fruit and more and more drinks.

As I watched through my glass, only the Captain and the priest seemed at all constrained. They sat to one side, quietly talking, smiling only from time to time at some offering from the other officers. I was reminded of old photographs showing colonial white men enjoying their privileged lives before everything changed with the War.

But, though the Captain and the priest might be constrained, our guys ashore were not. In big ships Navy sailors tend to know only their messmates and associate only within small groups. In the Bird boats, though, everybody knew everybody. I knew all the guys I watched making fools of themselves that day. Mister Salter had sternly warned all of them before going ashore that this was a Mission and that we were to keep our hands to ourselves. No condoms were handed out at the gangway that day.

The odd thing was the guys didn't seem to mind. Much. They played simple things like tug-o-war and kids' games. I could not help smiling as I watched from the ship. The Mission's men tried to get up a cricket match once and show our guys how to play that British game but that did not work at all. The game quickly deteriorated into a kind of bastard baseball, which itself suffered from the distraction of laughing young women hanging about the fringes and poking fun.

That is the way things went until shadows stretched out from the clouded inland mountains. The little bay assumed a quiet waiting for the night. Harney, our chief quartermaster, relieved me. Navy chiefs then were apt to be old guys. It was easier for them to stay aboard than it was for us younger guys. At least that's what the younger guys thought.

We were not long at sea that time, but it is always good to take a run ashore. Especially so on shaded lawns, clipped short and scented with flowers. By that time the scent of flowers was not the only smell. The pigs and chickens would soon be ready. Everybody drifted toward the fire pits. The play became less raucous. Even the Mission children became quieter.

I felt a great peace there amid the laughter and glad shouting of children. The sheer beauty of the place. And, capping it all, the sight of our ship lying to her anchor with no sign of life save for a wisp of white steam playing about her silent whistle. There is nothing in the world so serene as the sight of an anchored ship in still waters.

Still, there was a disquieting sense of foreboding I was unable to shake from our first sighting of the priest's sinking boat, spotlighted as it was by that remarkable ray of God's sun. Thinking of the priest, I looked to the veranda. He was no longer there. I assumed he was away on Mission business. The ship's officers were there, still presenting their picture of white men's colonial privilege, but the priest was nowhere to be seen.

Darkness came fast as it does in the tropics. I was not far from the front of the church. Certainly, I had no intention of going in. I was away from the Church so long I no longer was drawn to it, except for transient twinges when I was troubled by something and a Church was near at hand.

Well, this one was near at hand. I knew my mother would be pleased if she looked down from heaven. I went in. Mary Lou probably would be pleased, too, damn her. Mary Lou cried when she told me she was going to marry someone who doubted God less than I did. But, with the war coming on and everything, it couldn't hurt to pray a little.

Inside the building I dabbed at the Holy Water and stepped onto a crunching floor of crushed shells. Already, dark shadows were gathering in corners and under benches, moving out in viscous black advance to meet the night. Others sagged down from the shadowy heights of the roof where lizards rustled in the thatch in search of bugs. Gloom settled over all.

The only resistance offered the night was that of votive candles at the altar. Some were in glowing red glasses. More were in coconut half shells. Together, they formed a dim light at the forward end of the Church to remind of God's unending love and man's equally unending longing for that love.

The candles' glow was not enough to show much in the way of detail. But it did show the priest kneeling before the altar. I made to move back, not wanting to intrude upon his devotions, but as I turned to go, either he sensed my presence, or he heard the sound of my feet on the crushed shell floor. He looked over his shoulder to where I stood.

Quickly, he got to his feet and greeted me warmly, though still with the same reserve which marked him from the time we took him from his sinking boat. "Flags?" he asked. I suppose I showed as a black bulking against the lighter black of the church door.

"Yes, Father," I said. "Excuse me. I did not mean to intrude." I had not before used the word "Father" with him, but I thought it appropriate in his own church.

"No intrusion," he said. "Would you like to join me? Please, Flags. I would like it very much if you would."

I had not foreseen this. I thought simply to kneel a bit and to say a prayer or two among the backless wooden benches of the church. I was doing that, I told myself, only because it would please my dead mother.

"Please, Flags," the priest said again.

In the end, I joined him in prayer, but we prayed only briefly when he asked if I would like him to hear my confession. Certainly, I had not counted on that.

I laughed, embarrassed. "We are sailing in a few hours, Father," I said. "There is not nearly time enough to hear my confession after all these years."

He did not reply at once, nor did I speak. We heard the sounds of the people down by the cook fires. We saw through the church's open walls the flaring glare of coconut fiber torches and the glowing piles of the fires themselves. Their flames had long since died down. We smelled the cooking odors and the sweetish scents of the jungle beyond the rows of huts.

Without responding to my attempted joke at all, and without further comment, he said. "Then, will you hear mine?"

"What?" I blurted.

"I know it is irregular," the priest said. "But the situation is irregular, as well. It has been a long time since I made confession." He paused. "The need is great, Flags," he said. "I would not have asked you otherwise."

"But I am not a priest, Father," I said. "It would mean nothing for me to hear you, Father. Isn't there a priest somewhere near? Someone we could get to . . ."

"There is not time, Flags," the priest said. Later, I recognized the ominous sense of what he said, but I did not recognize it then.

"But I am not a priest," I said again.

"I know that," he said. "God knows it as well, but God will understand. No one else need ever know . . ."

In the end, I did as the priest wanted. I even sat in the "box" and listened, aghast, at what I heard. Never had I heard such anguish in a human voice, but, as he talked on, he seemed to find a measure of peace. Maybe what I did was of some help to him. I have often since hoped that it was.

Although I defiled the sanctity of the confessional with my non-ordained presence, I could not bring myself to give the priest a penance. I remained seated in the close space of the confessional until certain he was gone. As it happened, I never saw him again, though I remember him still, sometimes with an aching poignancy.

Troubled as I was by what I heard, I could not join the merry throngs about the cooking fires. The night turned even blacker for me than it was, and I returned to the ship without eating. After taking a shower and turning in, I found sleep was as difficult as eating. After a time, I slept, but it was fitful and uneasy and ended with someone tugging at my shoulder. "Come on. Old man wants to see you."

I sensed, even then, that it had something to do with the priest. "You sent for me, Sir," I said upon reporting.

"Yes. Come in, Flags." But the captain did not close his door, nor did he ask me to sit down. Nor did he speak in any other way for a time.

In that waiting silence, I steeled myself. "Captain, there's something I got to tell you." And, lest I lose my nerve, I hurried on. "The priest was not alone in his boat, sir."

The captain was not surprised at all. "You mean the dead woman?"

"Yes, Sir. She was below in the cabin."

"She was the wife of one of the native sailors who was lost," the captain said.

"Is that what the priest told you, sir?"

"Yes." The captain paused. "Why? Is there something else?"

Certainly there was something else, but it was something I heard in the confessional box. I knew real priests are required to keep secret anything they hear in the confessional. I was not sure what my status was since I was not an ordained priest. In the end, I said, "No, sir. I don't know anything else."

We would be sailing early the next morning. With any luck at all, none of us would ever hear of the priest or his island or anything else of what happened.

"Is that all, Captain?" I said.

"Not quite," the captain said. He turned in his chair then and took down his pistol holster from where it hung on its belt beside his desk. The holster was empty.

"You were up here this morning, I believe, Flags."

"Yes, Sir." The priest was living in the captain's cabin. I came in to see him about something.

"Was the priest here?"

"Yes, Sir. You both were here when I left."

"Did you see my holster?"

"Yes, Sir."

"Was it empty?"

I hesitated, trying to recall. "I don't know, Sir. I didn't notice."

The captain studied me for a time. "You carried the priest's bag down for him, didn't you?"

"Yes, Sir." We all contributed things for the priest and his Mission. Shirts, underwear, shaving gear, combs, towels. We stuffed it all into a regulation Navy laundry bag for him to carry ashore.

"Did you feel anything unusual in the bag, Flags?"

"No, Sir. But, come to think of it, when I put it down on deck at the gangway, something did make a funny noise."

The captain was again silent for a time. A conviction was growing in his face. "Who has the Deck?"

"Ensign Woods."

"Have him call away a boat's crew. *Chop chop.* We're going ashore. On the double."

"Yes, Sir."

The time must have been near to midnight. The coconut torches had burned down to glowing nubs. Only one of the cook fires kept going. Around it islanders sat or lay on the grass, singing their own words to old church music. They sang quietly so as not to disturb those who went to their houses, but the sound came easily across the water to where we lay at anchor. The beauty of the night was almost hurting in its intensity. The singing was part of the beauty.

The captain was at the side before our boat was. He stood impatiently studying the dark island off which we lay. A single oil lamp burned in a back room of the Mission house. The gentle glow of votive candles showed through the Church's open sides. Otherwise, all was dark beyond the one cook fire and the embers of coconut torches. All was quiet, save for the singing.

Then, as our boat came alongside, we heard a muffled shot from ashore.

The singing ended abruptly. Somewhere in the treeline beyond the Mission, wakened birds cried out in alarm. We on the ship stopped short and looked to the captain as though he would know what had happened. Captains are supposed to know everything.

The captain did not speak for a time. His shoulders sagged and he became somehow smaller. "Secure the boat," he said sadly. "Make all preparations for getting underway."

We could not sail then, of course. The pass was not lighted. It would have been foolhardy threading reefs and coral heads in the dark. But we would be ready to sail, once daylight came.

Except for the captain, who seemed somehow to know, none of us had any idea of what happened, and he volunteered nothing. Those of us on deck moved to go below. Only the watch remained. All again was quiet.

I do not remember how long the silence lasted, but it seemed a long time. It ended with the starting of a slow tolling of the Mission Church bell. That, and the resumption of singing by the group by the one remaining fire.

The singing, though, was no longer happy. The deep island tones sounded in those rich mourning notes cellos sometimes make. For the rest of the night the singing and the slow tolling of the bell continued.

It was still going on when we were wakened by the boatswain's mate's call: "Now, go to your stations all the special sea detail." It soon would be full day.

The signalmen's job upon getting underway is to lower the jack forward and the colors at the staff aft and run them up to the gaff, but since morning colors had not yet been made, all I had to do was to hoist the flag to the gaff.

As I was aft by the mainmast, and the anchor chain was almost up-and-down, a man in a canoe came out from the beach and lifted up a sack to a sailor at the gunwale. Bird boats had very low freeboard aft. It looked like the same sack the priest took ashore filled with our gifts, but I paid little attention. It was not my pidgin.

At dead slow ahead, we felt our way out the pass at day's first light and made for the open sea. The sounds of singing and the tolling of the Mission bell, like the slow beating of mourning hearts, followed us out. I watched as the Mission buildings drew together in the form towns show the sea. I was glad to be underway. Too much had happened I did not understand.

It was not over, though. I was at breakfast in the crew's mess when a messenger stuck his head in the door and called, "Captain wants to see you in his cabin, Flags."

The captain's face was expressionless as I reported. He sat at his desk with the rough log before him. The sack I saw the islander hand aboard lay empty and pushed to one side. I glanced to the captain's holster. It was no longer empty.

The captain saw me look at the gun, but he didn't say anything. Instead, he handed me a folded piece of paper. "This is addressed to you," he said.

The paper was addressed simply to "Flags." There was neither salutation nor signature. When I opened it out, it read, "As you have done, I might perhaps have lived with the bitter knowledge that my God had failed me, but I could not live with the even more bitter knowledge that I had failed my God. Good-bye."

I handed the note back to the captain, but he refused it.

"No, that is yours," he said. "So is this." He handed me the priest's ebony and silver crucifix on its golden chain, a crucifix I carry still in my seabag wherever I go.

From that day until this, I have spoken of this to no one, certain that it is unlikely to occur to anyone now — anymore than it had occurred to me then — that the priest had anything to do with the dead woman's being pregnant.

WING NUT

Even in the States, old Navy white hats had remarkably little contact with civilians ashore. Except for bartenders, B-girls, cab drivers and the like, we seldom met or became friends with anyone on the beach. We knew, too, that our friendships with those characters seldom lasted much longer than our money. We lived amongst ourselves behind the steel walls of our ships and the chainlink fences of our yards and stations, content to be apart from a world many of us found to be both hostile and contemptuous.

The situation was even worse on the China Station. Language and cultural differences kept us apart there, as well, but our willingness to remain separate in China was based more upon a feeling of our own superiority than of any shunning on the part of the Chinese. Most of us felt we were a damned sight better than the often starving slopeheads and gooks we saw swarming in the port cities at which we called.

Even in the old gunboats, steaming the narrow upper reaches of China's rivers, the separation held true. There, the Chinese were never far from us. Some of them actually lived in our ships to do the donkey work for us: the laundry, cooking, scrubbing and bilge cleaning which we would have had to do for ourselves in Fleet ships.

In all the time I was in China, for instance, I remember only once when any kind of personal friendship developed between me and a Chinese. And that was with a Hankow ricksha coolie.

He was similar in appearance and manner to other ricksha coolies. Thin, small, partially clothed in tatters of rags and straw sandals, with strands of white mucous draining from his nose in cold weather, he was like all the others. Towards American white hats his manner was one of cringing servility.

His only difference was that he had a name. His name was Wing Nut. No other Chinese I saw out there had a name. At least, for me, they didn't. I came to know, too, that he had a wife and three small children in a dirt-floored hut in a squalid Hankow *hutong* or back street.

Wing Nut wasn't his real Chinese name, but it sounded like Wing Nut and that is what I called him.

How I came to know him in the first place was a fluke. All Navy ships have more men in their crews than are necessary to keep and sail them. The service of their guns and the possibility of battle casualties make it necessary but the practical result in peacetime, even in Fleet ships, is that finding work for so many hands becomes a problem.

The only grandmother I ever knew said, "Idle hands are the Devil's work tools." This, I learned, was even more true for Navy sailors than it was for children.

The situation was worse in the river gunboats where we had coolies to do a lot of our work for us. Especially when we wintered in Hankow or Changsha or some other cold, dank river port and did not have even the duties of steaming watches to keep us busy. Boredom often hung heavy over the ship.

There were bars on the beach, of course. And whore-houses well-stocked with ready and inventive women of several races and assorted ages and sizes. Sometimes women even came out in sampans to secure alongside and do away with the need for going ashore.

The rate of exchange in China made it possible for us to pay for diversion — if we could but find it. There were times when the exchange rate was as high as ten Mex for one American dollar, and we were paid in American dollars. But respectable white society was effectively closed off to us and the Chinese we met had little to offer save whiskey and women.

Still, there was a limit to how much a white hat could drink, and a variable but definite physiological cap to how many times he could wrestle to much advantage with a woman on soiled blankets and filthy mats. Especially so when the women could not speak even our form of English. Oddly, sexual passion, to be good, we learned, must have a verbal content as well as a physical one.

Anyway, we found ourselves at loose ends sometimes. That is how I came to meet Wing Nut. Lloyd Nations, a machinist's mate second, and I were drinking most of the day in a retired chief petty officer's bar. It was called The Eagle and Chevrons, for white hats' rating badges. We called it The Crow because that is what we called our rating badges.

Nations was a pretty good guy — for a machinist's mate. He came from a town in Arizona, not far from the Mexican border. We drank together pretty often.

This particular time we drank so long we were late for our watches and had to take rickshas back to the ship. Another reason we took rickshas was that we were too drunk to walk.

By chance, Wing Nut's ricksha, along with three or four others, was parked outside the bar. I kicked him awake and jumped in, yelling at him to "Makee shipside! Chop-chop. All-same moto-car!"

Nations got into a ricksha of his own and we chop-chopped our two coolies as much as we could — to chop-chop meant to hurry. We both knew old Chief Harry Baxter had the Deck watch and he could be a bastard on guys late getting back from liberty. Both Nations and I had crossed swords with him before. Drunk as we were, we did not want to do it again.

The streets were crowded, of course. *All* Chinese streets were crowded. Wing Nut and Nations' coolie fell into single file in order to make their way through traffic, but that was not good enough for Nations and me. No. In a brilliant flash of drunken inspiration, we decided to make a race of it.

"Last man back to the ship is a rotten egg," Nations called out to me in the classic challenge of children. At the same time he leaned forward and beat at his coolie with his white hat. Laughing and shouting out in drunken excitement, I did the same, and we forced our way through the streets, scattering Chinese right and left as we went, overturning push carts and upsetting market stalls.

Wing Nut and Nations' coolie ran for their lives. Although used to the antics of sailors, they had not before known this particular form of harassment. But they did their best, and we came, gasping and panting, to the river pontoon where our motor pan, by chance, lay with popping engine to take us out to the ship.

Wing Nut won. We beat Nations' coolie by almost fifty feet. Wing Nut's wizened face grinned up at me. "Maskee, sailor man?" he said. "All-same catchee race."

"Maskee," I grinned back. "All-same race." It was the first time I ever exchanged a personal word of any kind with a coolie. On impulse, I said: "What name you, coolie?"

That was when he told me his Chinese name which sounded like Wing Nut. "Maskee," I grinned. "All-same numba one coolie." I gave him two dollars, Mex, for the ride. That was several times more than the usual fare. I would have caught hell from the guys in the ship if they knew I did that. It was not smart to overpay coolies. It could break a lot of rice bowls and spoil things for all of us.

Wing Nut's grin grew even wider.

That would have ended it, probably, if Nations and I had not come aboard, still drunk and falling down laughing over our ricksha race through Hankow. The way we told it, it sounded like fun. It wasn't long until we started bragging about how fast "our" coolies were.

And that, in a day or two, led to more races to settle the question of which of us had the fastest coolie. It wasn't long after that that other guys in the ship got into the act with coolies of their own and a regular tournament developed. Before it was over other ships got into it as well. Even the Limeys did. And some of the Standard Oil guys.

Naturally, money was bet on the races. Even the Chinese came to watch and — with their love of gambling — bet, as well. All this made the Hankow streets, crowded as they were, impracticable for racing. We moved operations to the big horse track at the edge of town. Someone — I think it was a Chinese — got permission for us to use the track if there were no horse races being held. It worked out fine for us. Sometimes we even had sizable crowds in the stands.

With all this new interest, morale — we had never heard the word before — hit new highs in the ships. We soon had ricksha races almost every day the track was available.

Inevitably, this led to refinements. The first thing we did was to improve the rickshas. Chinese rickshas were neither things of beauty nor much in the way of mechanical efficiency. Wheels were lopsided and misaligned for the most part. Hubs and axles were rough and starved for grease. The shafts were placed with little thought of efficient balance. Some of the older ones had iron or even wooden tires.

Nations, being a machinist's mate, was the first to get into the mechanics of rickshas. He sneaked his coolie's wheels and axles into the ship's machine shop and completely reworked them; reducing friction and making them roll truer. He even fitted smaller and harder rubber tires, realigned the shafts and made the rain hood removable for race days. Hankow, in all its long history, never saw such a ricksha before.

Naturally, Nations won everything for a while, but he was decent enough to help me recondition Wing Nut's ricksha, too. Still, rickshas were simple structures. There was a limit to how much they could be improved mechanically. That left the power plants. The power plants were the coolies.

Half-starved as they were, exposed by their near nakedness to cold and wet, shoeless or wearing rotting straw sandals, they offered little in the way of real physical strength. It was hard to believe, from looking at them, that they ran as well as they did. I suppose it was the threat of starvation which kept them going.

Wing Nut was in no better shape than the other coolies then, but I made sure he got a good share of whatever winnings he made for me. I hoped he would use the money to buy better food and build his strength, but I soon found he saved most of his money toward getting his family into better quarters. That is when I took to bringing stuff from the ship for him, things like butter and meat and eggs, stuff that would put a little muscle on him. Even then, I suspected much of the food would go to his family if I did not make him eat it on the spot.

I didn't want him giving the food to his family. Not then, I didn't. I wanted to fatten him up, build up his strength and stamina, so he could run faster. I had not yet come to see Wing Nut's family as any concern of mine. Hell, China was full of starving women and kids.

God knows Wing Nut needed better housing. One day when he failed to appear at the pontoon, I sought out Nations' coolie and asked where Wing Nut was. It was a measure of how we felt about coolies that I had a hard time picking out Nations' coolie from the others. Except for Wing Nut, they all looked alike. "Where at Wing Nut?" I said.

"Wing Nut in housee," Nations' coolie said. "Wing Nut sickee."

"You takee me Wing Nut housee," I said. Friendship already had taken hold between me and Wing Nut. I know I was worried about his being sick. And it was not just because he won a lot of money for me, either. I liked the little guy.

Nations' coolie took me in his ricksha to Wing Nut's house. To call the place a house was an exaggeration. Its street was narrow and slanted to a central open drain where whatever offal escaped the nightsoil gatherers made a playground for small naked children who drew back from me in a conditioned reflex of fear.

The front of Wing Nut's house was largely open, with only a loose arrangement of unpainted wood and rough burlap hangings to keep out wind and wet. The walls were of coarse mud bricks, receding into unlighted darkness, even in bright day, under a rude roof of the drab gray-black mud tiles seen so often in China. Wing Nut's ricksha, gleaming from the special treatment we gave it in the ship, took up much of the crowded space. For a time, I saw nothing else in the gloom.

A woman I took to be Wing Nut's wife was at a straw fire on a built-up mud hearth. She drew back at my approach and looked to Wing Nut as though for some explanation for a white hat's being in her house. The kids ran to her, hiding behind her soiled cotton pants and peeking out with big black eyes.

Wing Nut himself lay half unseen on a raised earthen platform — the Chinese call them *kangs* — along one wall. He was covered by a thin pile of blankets and burlap bags. Our forced feeding put meat on him, and he had lost much of his former look of starvation, but he was sick. He tried to sit up as I entered, but fell back with a grimace of frustration.

His wife and children continued cowering against the far wall which — given the size of the place — was not far at all. "Whasamatta Wing Nut?" I asked her. Her only reaction was to draw even farther back. The kids ducked completely out of sight behind her. The warm richness of my blues made me feel out of place in the squalor of the place.

"Whasamatta you, Wing Nut?" I said.

Again, he tried to rise, but with no more success than before. Worse, the effort brought on a spasm of coughing which left him pale and gasping in his blankets. The guy was sick. Even I could see that. And, if he was sick, he wasn't going to make much money for me in any ricksha races for a while.

I knew the Chinese had their own doctors who stuck them with pins and needles and had them drink teas made of bits and pieces of dried plants and animals. But, as did most white hats then, I thought that was all superstition and witch-doctoring. I wanted something better for Wing Nut. I wanted to get him back on his feet so he could start winning races again.

There were European doctors in the Foreign Concessions. And Americans in the Missions, but they were not likely to follow some white hat down into Hankow's slums to treat a ricksha coolie. Besides, they would charge an arm and a leg.

That left Doc Weldon in the ship. Doc was our pharmacist's mate, the closest thing we had to a doctor. And he had access to the ship's medicine chest. Besides, he owed me some favors. Doc did not have a racing coolie of his own, but he made some money by betting on Wing Nut.

"You what?" Doc blurted when I told him I wanted him to go see Wing Nut. "For Christ's sake, Flags," he said. "They got crud down there that ain't even made it into the medical books yet. You ain't been down there yourself, have you?"

"Yes, God damn it, I have," I said. "And Wing Nut's sick, and you're damned well going back down there with me and see what's wrong with him."

There's little point into going into detail about how I did it, but Doc saw the light after a while. From my description of his symptoms, he guessed Wing Nut had the Navy's universal disease of catarrhal fever — cat fever — normally treated with a white pill called an APC. Doc grabbed a handful of APC's and came with me to see Wing Nut. He wasn't happy about it, but he came.

That was the only time I got him to go, but it was enough. He left the APC's with Wing Nut's wife and, with a mixture of sign language and pidgin English, we told her how and when to give them.

Later, I came to think that was the beginning of my trouble with the guys in the ship. White hats didn't have much to do with coolies in China. They didn't like to see anybody else have much to do with them either. I knew Doc sure as hell did not take kindly to my dragging him down into Wing Nut's hovel. Sometimes when I came into the mess and he was talking with the guys they fell silent and looked away from me.

Even Nations was pretty cool toward me, and he was a good friend and drinking buddy before.

Anyway, Wing Nut got well, and we began winning races again. He used the winnings I shared with him to find better quarters for his family, and to feed them one hell of a lot better. I found out later he bought two more rickshas and hired other coolies to pull them for him. He became a *businessman* for Christ's sake, but he continued pulling his racing ricksha for me, even though it cost him "face" to do it. A proper Chinese businessman could not be seen pulling rickshas.

Wing Nut's new house was not far from the river. It was nothing compared with the fancy houses in the Foreign Concessions or the mansions of Chinese merchants, but it was a hell of a lot better than what he had before. There was more than twice as much room, for one thing, and it was warm and dry — by Chinese standards. There was even some furniture.

His wife, getting fat and fluffed out in the quilted blue cotton garb of the time, became shyly welcoming as Wing Nut more and more often invited me into their home for meals. And she cooked on a real charcoal fire. I didn't know Chinese food could be so good, nor the Chinese themselves so laughingly warm and friendly.

That period became the best time I ever had in China. Things got to be pretty chilly between me and the other white hats in the ship, but I came as close as I ever did in the Navy to having a family.

I found out the Chinese are not so much different from anybody else except that they could be one hell of a lot friendlier to white hats than a lot of people I saw, in China or anywhere else. Especially so, their kids.

In the streets, Chinese kids were wary of foreign devils — that's what they called us. God knows they had reason enough. But it did not take much to win them over. A bit of candy or a cheap toy or, sometimes, nothing more than a smile would do it. Easy.

Except for the kids in the orphanage where I grew up, I never knew any children. I didn't know how to act around them, I guess. But, like a lot of white hats, I was a pushover for kids. I liked watching kids in school playgrounds in the States, but you had to be careful about that. Somebody might get the wrong idea.

I never had any trouble with Wing Nut's kids. Not after he invited me into his house and the kids got used to me. I always brought them little presents of one kind or another.

They swarmed over me in a laughing tangle of arms and legs trying to find what I brought each time.

Wing Nut laughed as hard as any of them. Even his wife laughed softly at us, while making a look-see effort to get the kids to behave.

Those were good times. They were for me, anyway.

I knew it would not last, of course. With the coming of Spring and the rise of the rivers, we would be off up the river and not see Hankow for another year. Maybe not even then. Sometimes we wintered farther upstream. It was all a function of water levels. In the meantime, I fell back upon the white hat's one sure defense: I didn't ask any dumb questions. I enjoyed what I had while I had it.

I spent most of my time ashore in Wing Nut's place. All that did was make things worse than ever with the guys in the ship. Few guys shot the breeze with me anymore, and I almost never went ashore with anybody. Not even with Nations. Coolie-lover was the nicest thing they called me.

About the only thing which kept any kind of connection between me and the guys in the ship, in fact, was the ricksha racing. That kept up all Winter, and Wing Nut won almost every race. The guys might not like my friendship with Wing Nut, but they didn't mind cashing in the bets we won for them. But that is all it was, the money. They couldn't bring themselves to anything more.

One reason Wing Nut won so much was that I made sure he ate. None of the other guys in the ship fed their coolies the way I did. To them, a coolie was a coolie. Sometimes, they took whichever coolie was first in line. They might spend a little time and money fixing up a ricksha to be faster, but they didn't much give a damn about who pulled it. Their coolies wouldn't pull as hard for them, either.

Still, when the stuff did hit the fan it happened in a way I did not expect. We were already getting the ship ready to move up river. Every day the water rose higher. Finally, it was decided to have one last ricksha race before we shoved off.

It was the biggest race of them all . . . and as far as I know, the last one ever held in Hankow. Several hundred people yelled from the stands. There were fifteen or twenty rickshas at the starting line. Some of them were pretty impressive, but their coolies were no match for Wing Nut's smooth-muscled condition. I put down every dollar I could on him to win. So did just about everyone else in our ship. Even the chiefs and officers.

The race went about as I expected. Wing Nut won going away, and I whooped and hollered from my seat in his ricksha like a crazy man. I don't remember how much money I won that day, but it was a pot full, and I meant to leave every penny of it with Wing Nut. I would not need it up in the rivers anyway, and it made me feel good to know how much good it would do him and his family.

Wing Nut and I went directly from the track to The Crow to settle all our bets and have a few belts, but I didn't stay long. Wing Nut pulled me home in his shiny ricksha for a dinner of pork and rice and vegetables. I had no chance to pick up anything for the kids, but they were soon over their disappointment and climbing all over me in laughing play, satisfied with the few *cash* I had in my pockets.

That is the way I best remember Wing Nut and his family. It was also the last time I saw them. Fortunately, I did not know that at the time and had at least that final day to remember.

I knew I was in trouble the minute I got back to the ship and the quartermaster of the watch told me the chief wanted to see me in the quarters. Navy chief petty officers on the China Station in the nineteen-twenties and -thirties had a significant lot of power over white hats.

This particular chief, Carl Hoffman was his name, was usually pretty easy to get along with. About the only thing which got him worked up was if one of us did something which brought the old man — the captain — down on him.

Captains, on the China Station, liked to leave things up to the chiefs, but they did not expect the chiefs to goof off so that The Flag — Commander of the Yangtze Patrol, ComYang in the Navy's graphic shorthand — was made aware of their ships' existence.

That was pretty much the Navy way — white hats did not like to be brought to the attention of their chiefs, chiefs did not like to be brought to the attention of their captains, and captains sure as hell did not want to be brought to the attention of The Flag. Low profile was the word. As in any bureaucracy, that's how people stayed out of trouble and got ahead.

The trouble was I did not have the dimmest notion of what I did wrong. I knew I had no trouble with the Shore Patrol. I didn't have a shack job on the beach and stayed pretty much in the usual bars and whorehouses. Still, if it were not important, the chief would not have sent for me. I figured he would tell me soon enough. He did.

"I've seen guys out here get their tits in a wringer with the God-damned missionaries, Flags," the chief began. "I've seen guys out here get their ass in a crack with the God-damned Limeys. But I've never seen anyone do both those things at the same time. You must have a talent for getting yourself screwed up."

"Limey" was our word for the British. It came from their longtime practice of serving lime juice as a preventative against scurvy. The British had a presence of longer standing even than our own in China. Ordinarily, American Navy sailors got along pretty well with our opposite numbers in British ships. Certainly we got along a hell of a lot better with them than we did with the French or the Germans. And one hell of a lot better than we did with the God-damned Japanese who were beginning to throw their weight around.

"I don't know what the hell you're talking about, Chief," I said.

"I'm talking about a God-damned ricksha coolie on the beach, that's what I'm talking about."

"Wing Nut?" I said. Wing Nut was the only Chinese I knew on the beach — other than for a couple of pretty good whores. "What the hell has he got to do with anything?"

"The God-damned missionaries are complaining to the old man that you're *degrading* the poor son-of-a-bitch, that's what he's got to do with anything," the chief said with some emphasis. "In case you don't know it, we are not supposed to *degrade* anyone, much less the noble Chinee."

"I didn't degrade anyone, for Christ's sake, Chief," I said. "What the hell am I supposed to have done?"

"The missionary guy said you and the other guys, especially you, are treating ricksha coolies like animals. He said you are organizing ricksha races out at the race track. You are laying bets and playing hell with ricksha fares." The chief paused. I felt the other chiefs in the quarters staring at me. I suppose they were judging Hoffman on his technique for chewing out a white hat. "Well, how about it?" Hoffman growled. "You do all that?"

"Yeah. Yeah, sure, but what the hell's wrong with that? We split our winnings with them. This is probably the first time in their lives the poor bastards have had enough to eat and feed their families. Wing Nut's even bought a couple more rickshas. He's going into business, for Christ's sake, Chief. Hell, he's never had it so good."

All that wasn't news to the God-damned chief. He made bets on Wing Nut. He knew damned well what was going on. So did our old man, for that matter. It only became news when some God-damned missionary blew the whistle.

"The missionary guy says you are treating coolies like horses or dogs. It's undignified. Human beings are not supposed to be treated like animals. Besides, what you're doing is encouraging gambling. Gambling is a sin."

I laughed outright at that. "God damn it, Chief," I said. "You chiefs bet as much as any of us on the God-damned races. So do the officers."

"I ain't talking about what the chiefs and officers do, Flags," Hoffman said. "I'm telling you what the missionary guy said. And the missionary guy said it's a sin. But the only thing you got to remember is that the old man don't like missionaries writing letters to Congressmen about guys in his ship. The only other thing you got to remember is that the old man says you are to stop it. Right now. You think you can get that through your thick skull?"

"Human beings race all the time back home, for Christ's sake, Chief. We call it track. Runners are big heroes in the Olympics."

"You been out here long enough I shouldn't have to point out, *we ain't home.*"

I didn't know what the hell to say. Maybe, if I talked with the old man myself. Maybe, if I explained how much good it was doing for Wing Nut and his family. "How about if I talk with the old man, Chief?" I said. "How about you put me down for Request Mast in the morning? Okay?"

"You got an order, Flags," the Chief said. "You ain't going to question an order, are you?"

"Yes, God damn it, I am, if that's what it takes."

Hoffman paused for a minute, as though finding what I said too silly for comment. "You want to hear the rest of it?" the Chief said. "The part about the Limeys?"

I had forgotten about that. "Yeah. Yeah, I guess so. What's their beef?"

"Their beef is what you're doing figures to break one hell of a lot of rice bowls."

Breaking rice bowls is what we called it when you did something that upset somebody's apple cart. Something that made waves or dinged somebody's way of making a living. I didn't see how our ricksha races could break anybody's rice bowl. Especially not for the God-damned Limeys. They kicked the coolies around more than we did, and they sure as hell had a lot more going in the trading line than we did.

But, as the Chief didn't waste any time in telling me, there was still a lot I didn't understand about China. I still didn't know, for instance, what I did to bring the Limeys down on me.

"You got any idea how many Chinamen there are in this God-damned country?" Hoffman demanded.

"No," I said. "And I don't really much give a damn. We figured out a way so at least some of them can eat better and have a dry place to sleep. What's so God-damned bad about that?"

"The Limeys ain't complaining about that. They're complaining about the fact you was pulling and the coolie was riding. That's what the God-damned Limeys is complaining about. Jesus Christ, ain't you got a lick of sense in that thick head?"

"I was pulling a ricksha?" I said. I was puzzled.

"That's what the Limey officer said. He said he saw you. Someplace on the beach. You and a couple hundred white hats. And God knows how many Chinamen. You even had a band, for Christ's sake, to call attention to the fact, I guess."

It came clear to me then what the Chief was talking about. It was one hell of a race. There were a thousand or so people in the stands, and God knows how much money was bet that day. A lot of it by the Chinese themselves. And Wing Nut won the God-damned thing going away. I pulled down more than a thousand dollars, Mex, on that one race alone. That was damned well worth a celebration.

And that is all it was, a celebration. We put Wing Nut in his ricksha and I pulled him all the way back to The Crow for some serious celebrating. Wing Nut wasn't allowed in the bar, of course, but we gave him enough of the winnings that he didn't have to worry about eating for a while. But, come to think of it, he did look scared when I picked him up and plunked him down in the ricksha. I guess Wing Nut was smarter than I was.

As for the band. Sure we had a band. A drum and three or four screechy Chinese horns. Toward the end, we always had a band play at the races. Not that you could call the noise they made music. Not by American standards anyway. And we didn't pay the musicians. They passed the hat. But that day was the only time the band had ever paraded back to The Crow with us.

And once the Chief mentioned it, I remembered seeing the God-damned Limey officer. He stood with two or three others on the sidewalk, looking down his nose at us as though something smelled bad. There's nobody who can look down his nose like a God-damned Limey. But I didn't pay any attention at the time. Hell, I had just won a thousand dollars, Mex.

I tried to explain all that to the chief, but he ignored me, "Nobody knows how many Chinamen there are in China," he said, answering his own earlier question. "But there ain't enough bullets in the whole God-damned world to shoot them all, and we're sitting here — fat, dumb, and happy — with a couple of thousand guys in a half dozen obsolete ships."

"What the hell's that got to do with me and Wing Nut, Chief?" I said.

"What it's got to do with you is that, if the Chinese ever get it into their heads to kick us to hell out of China, that's damned well what they'll do. The only thing we got going for us is face."

"Face?"

"Face. We got the Chinese thinking they ain't got a chance against us. Anytime they get to thinking they're as good as we are, we're going to be in deep trouble," the chief said. "And when the Chinese see a white man pulling a Chinaman in a God-damned ricksha, they can get to thinking stuff we're better off they don't think."

"You're kidding, Chief," I said.

"Maybe so," the chief said, "but *you* are packing your God-damned seabag and reporting to the Flagship in just about thirty minutes."

Hankow was more than five hundred miles up-river from the South China Sea, but there was enough water for ships as big as cruisers to visit sometimes. In fact the heavy cruiser *Augusta*, flagship of the American Asiatic Fleet, was there at the time. I logged her present just the day before.

Anyway, that's what happened. The Navy, the Limeys, and the God-damned missionaries all landed on my back. They did not even give me time to go ashore and tell Wing Nut good-bye. And all I was trying to do was to help the poor little bastard.

THE RUSSIAN EGG

"Treat a whore like a lady and a lady like a whore and you won't never have no trouble with women." I heard this bit of Naval wisdom a thousand times, but saw it specifically demonstrated only once in all the time I was a white hat. The guy who demonstrated it was Chief Gunner's Mate Honk Taylor. It was in Hankow.

I don't know if Honk ever treated a whore like a whore or not, but he did treat a lady like a lady one time, and it cost him one hell of a lot before it was over. It started with the Russian Revolution.

Sometimes, great storms send out violent gusts of dry winds ahead of the rain, filling the waiting air with dust, feathers, blown leaves and other debris. The great storm which was the Russian Revolution, though not a storm in the meteorological sense, blew out ahead of it a pathetic human chaff which swirled about the world until settling back to earth wherever fate and a seemingly unfeeling God deemed best.

White Russians they were called, in distinction from the Bolshevik Red Russians from whose vengeful brutality they fled for their lives. Many were aristocrats and others of means little fitted by prior lives for the rigors of making torturous ways across Siberia and Northern China, nor for the struggles of life without money when they arrived.

Many of them lodged in the coastal cities of China and there sometimes met with sailors of the American Navy's Asiatic Fleet, often with strange and unpredictable results.

Zena Tretchnikoff, an actress long celebrated not only in Russia but through all of Europe and much of the world for her talents and classical beauty, was one of them.

Chief Gunner's Mate Oliver Taylor — known throughout the Asiatic Fleet as "Honk" for his deep and sonorous voice — was the American sailor she met.

Zena was no longer young at the time, but the remnants of her once great beauty and aristocratic bearing hid from obvious view the scars of hardships she suffered since being driven from her great house in Moscow. She remained outwardly proud and disdainful of a world turned hard against her, but by not so great a margin as once she had. Though she would little admit it and struggled hard to hide the fact, Zena was near the end of both her wits and her strength.

Honk, for his part, was not proud at all, and disdainful of virtually nothing. More than twenty-four years in the Navy, sixteen on the China Station, left him with few illusions and even fewer hopes for human betterment. Women, individually and as a species, reigned at the very peak of his hard and practiced cynicism. Except for the frankly purchased sexual release they offered, he avoided them wherever possible.

A solitary and debasing childhood in various orphanages across America, all of which he escaped at first opportunity, was long lost to conscious recall. His life, prior to joining the Navy during The Great War, no longer existed. Even his Navy years before coming to China were but dimly remembered and seldom recalled. Taylor was a China Sailor.

There was little of degradation and human venality he had not seen in his time, much of it practiced upon himself —

or had himself practiced on others. His only fear, apart from that of women, was of the looming time when he would have to leave the Navy. He had no idea what he would do then. His only sureness in life was the recurring four year segments of certainty represented by his reenlistments. With those coming to an enforced end, nothing offered but loneliness and return to the alien and hostile world of an America he remembered only with pain and bitter resentment.

A gunner's mate by rate, Honk exercised an influence in his ship well beyond its guns and ammunition — not that the old river gunboats in which he served had much in the way of guns in the first place. By sheer force of natural leadership qualities, he was accepted by white hats as the Law on board, and by officers as a convenient channel through which they could get done easily what otherwise took work.

Clarence Howard was the closest thing Honk had to a rival. Howard was chief boatswain's mate in the ship. Ordinarily, boatswain's mates took military precedence over gunner's mates, but not in Honk's ship. This is not to say there were not some sparks from time to time, but once the dust settled, Howard accepted the fact of Honk's rule with but a slight grating now and then between the two old sailors.

When Howard retired on twenty however, and opened a sailor bar not far from Hankow's French Concession, the two of them became the best of drinking buddies, with never a cross word between them.

The old river gunboats did not often get so far down-river as Hankow. Most of their time was spent as far inland as the height of water allowed, moving upstream with the rising waters of Spring and retreating before the lows of dry seasons. But they did sometimes winter in Hankow.

That's when Honk and Clarence Howard would get together in Howard's bar and drink. Honk practically lived in Howard's bar, for that matter. He had what was called an open gangway in his ship, which meant he came and went pretty much as he pleased.

Howard's bar, in fact, bleakly functional as it was, became a shoreside home and social club for all of us, save only those shacked up with Chinese or White Russian women in houses or apartments. Even they often were present.

Old Howard took care of all sailors off his old ship, but he took special care of Honk. The two of them sat at a corner table and drank with a dogged, though relaxed, intensity through the night. And, sometimes, the days, as well.

Despite his impressive capacity for whisky — especially the kind of expensive Scotch whisky Howard kept for him — there were times when even Honk took on too much and had trouble finding his way back to the ship.

When that happened, Howard would clear a whore out of an upstairs room and let Honk sleep it off, though the old Gunner's Mate brayed indignantly about sleeping in a whorehouse when he woke up.

Sometimes, Honk refused to go upstairs. He could be stubborn when in drink. Especially so when accused of being drunk. "You ain't seen the day Honk Taylor can't get back to his own God-damned ship," he would yell, staggering to his feet and reeling out the door, hitting both sides and bowling over Chinamen right and left on the street outside.

Most times, he commandeered a ricksha and belabored the poor coolie all the way back to the riverfront, screaming and waving his arms with good humored, but thoughtless, cruelty.

Other times, he sank in the morose depths so often known to aging sailors when they come to realize the emptiness of their lives — and the fact that there is never going to be any less emptiness. At these times, which grew closer together for Honk as his retirement drew ever nearer, he shoved his hands deep in his pockets, shoulders hunched and cap awry, and barged his way blindly through the near-solid press of people which were Hankow streets. He seemed to find his way back to the ship without conscious thought, much in the way homing salmon find the gravel beds of their hatching streams after four wandering years in the ocean. It was like an instinct, or, at the least, a conditioned reflex.

Inevitably, as he grew older, Honk lost some of his acquired senses. He feared he could not handle his drink anymore. And, sometimes, worst of all, he got lost finding his way back to the ship.

One time, for example, he came out of Howard's bar after a particularly serious night of drinking — night and half of a morning to be exact. The sun was half as high as it would rise that winter's day. The night's freeze was melting, making footing treacherous in the streets. Honk became lost and found himself wandering through Frenchtown.

Hankow's French Concession was its most handsome quarter. Substantial two and three story stone and brick houses lined the streets of winter-bare trees. Some had walled gardens for front yards, with ornate gates and entry ways. In many ways Hankow's French Concession looked much like the better sections of Lyon or other prosperous towns in France.

That is where Honk found himself the morning he met Zena Tretchnikoff.

The first thing that penetrated his befuddled senses was that the street was not crowded. China streets were *always* crowded. Except in the foreign concessions. The French Concession was always quieter than the others in that regard. Except for the Chinese in blue robes who were obviously house servants out for their morning shopping and other errands, the street in which Honk found himself was virtually empty.

Especially so of Europeans. Europeans kept late hours, both for going to bed and for rising. They were not likely to be found walking, in any event. To do so was to lose face. If out at all, they were in rickshas or other vehicles. That knowledge was what first drew Honk's attention to a tall Caucasian woman walking toward him.

Thin to the point of emaciation, the woman wore a severely tailored black suit dress of an outdated cut reaching to the tops of buttoned shoes. A black broad-brimmed hat shaded graying hair drawn into a prim bun at the nape of her neck. In one black-gloved hand, she carried with studied dignity an embroidered bag of some soft material.

A bearded old man in what China sailors had come to know as the garb of Russian servants, long white coat with off-center buttons and soft leather boots, followed the woman at a respectful distance. White Russians were common in China, and Honk paid the pair but little attention.

Nor was Honk concerned at being lost. Hankow was not so big he could not find the river, and if he could find the river he could find his ship. His interest in the European woman was only slight in any event. She looked more like officer gear to him than anything else and, thus, beyond any reasonable hope of his getting her into a bed. Besides, she carried herself with an almost contemptuous aloofness which became even more contemptuous as she drew back from Honk's approach with clear evidence of distaste.

This was nothing new for Honk, of course, nor any other China sailor, for that matter. Caucasian women in China were good at drawing back from Navy sailors, even when those sailors did not look as Honk did that morning: white shirt soiled, cap alop, blues wrinkled, his face bleared with whisky. Disillusion, and the weight of twenty-four hard Navy years, combined to make him a good deal less than an appealing figure.

This particular woman's hauteur, however, was made somewhat less impressive by the fact that she suddenly swayed and collapsed almost at Honk's feet.

In old China, it was said, a drowning man should be left to die because it was felt a rescuer would be responsible for the saved man for the rest of his life. This may not have been true, but American sailors on the China Station *thought* it was true, and that made it true enough.

Streets in Hankow's foreign concessions were swept clean every morning. They never really became dirty in the first place. Not in the way streets in the native quarters did. Still, it was unnerving for Honk to see the women fall. Especially since she was a white woman, and one so expensively, although out-modedly, dressed.

Those Chinese in the street appeared not to see. This was in keeping with their custom of shunning the fallen. Few Chinese could afford to assume responsibility for anyone else, even had they wanted to save them. The Chinese are practical people. It made more sense to let drowning men drown.

Honk hesitated. He sure as hell did not want to become responsible for anyone, much less a woman like the one lying in the street before him. He would be out of the Navy in two or three years and gone from China.

The old servant leaped forward — as much as he, in the feebleness of age, could leap at all — and fell to his knees beside his fallen mistress. His face worked in an expression of great fear and pain. Taking the woman's head in his hands he lifted it clear of the paving stones, looking up as he did so to beg in silence for Honk's help.

Still, Honk hesitated. Navy sailors learned not to touch lightly the bodies of white women, unconscious or not. Of course, White Russian women were not considered to be *really* white. Even enlisted men shacked up with them. Some married them. They were not the same as British or French or American women.

The White Russian women didn't have any money, for one thing. They went with Navy sailors to have a place to stay and something to eat. It was Honk's opinion, often voiced in the chief's quarters, that the other white women in China would go with Navy sailors, too, if they were cold and hungry.

It was accepted lore that all White Russian women were Tsarist princesses. Some of them may actually have been, but China sailors called them pigs, more or less affectionately. Still, whatever else she might be, the thin woman lying at Honk's feet that morning was nobody's pig. Even senseless as she was, and even hungover as he was, Honk recognized the woman as something well out of the ordinary. Her face wore unmistakable marks of refinement, and her clothes, though out of current style, were once expensive.

He also saw that the old servant kneeling with the woman's head in his arms was not going to be much help. That left things up to Honk.

"You speakee English?" Honk said to the old man.

The old man shook his head, his panic seeming to grow. He said something. Honk had had a few White Russian princesses himself and knew a few words of Russian. He recognized the language.

Honk looked up and down the tree-lined street, flanked to either side by the bland fronts of what, by China standards, were rich homes. All the doors and windows remained tightly closed and those Chinese in the street continued studiously ignoring the whole thing.

"Where at missee live?" Honk asked the old man. He clarified the question by pointing to the fallen women and pantomiming the opening of a door and resting his head on his hands to signal sleep.

Still distraught, the old man pointed with his head to a house three or four doors away in the direction from which he and the woman came.

Honk bent then and gently brushed the old man aside, lifting the woman in his arms. Thin as she was, she weighed startlingly little. Honk shifted her in his arms and motioned for the old man to lead the way. "Chop chop. You savvy?" Honk said in the expediting phrase known throughout the East.

The old man bent to pick up the woman's fallen hat and bag and trotted out ahead. He looked over his shoulder from time to time as though making sure Honk were still coming.

"Missee live," the old man said as he stopped at a closed gate before a house more pretentious than most others in the street. It was equally mute, though, with tall windows and doors closed and muffled by heavy draperies. Its walled garden was unkempt and overgrown with that particular look of places long abandoned and left untended.

"Chop chop," Honk said again, motioning with his head for the old man to open the gate and the door beyond. He followed the old man into what was an elegant, though gloomy, house made dark by heavy maroon velvet draperies at windows and doors.

To one side Honk saw a sitting room fitted with heavy chairs and ornate sofas and love seats and paintings in massive frames on papered walls. He put down the fainted woman on one of the sofas and stepped back, looking about. Honk had never been in such a house. He had seen its like only in movies.

Only then did he see the meager figure of a second old man sitting, half-obscured, in a maroon wing chair. This old man was a Caucasian, lean also to the point of lankness. His face, though still handsome in a theatrical way, was rigid. The thumb of his right hand moved obsessively in the telltale pill-rolling gesture of advanced Parkinson's disease. He wore a dark red velvet smoking jacket of the kind Honk had seen only in movies. A lap robe buried his legs and lower body.

"What name this fella?" Honk asked the serving man.

"Him name all-same Missee," the old man said.

This did not tell Honk much. He could be brother, father, uncle, or husband to the woman. Convenient and ingenious though it might be, pidgin is not a precise language. But the old guy could wait. The woman was the immediate problem. And, from all Honk saw, he was as alone in the house as he was in the street so far as effective help was concerned.

"You catchee coffee?" Honk asked of the old serving man, falling back on the Navy's universal cure for all conditions. "Hot coffee," he said. "You catchee hot coffee?"

"No catchee coffee, Mastah."

"Tea? You catchee hot tea?"

The old serving man shrugged without bothering to speak.

"I want neither coffee nor tea." The woman's voice was surprisingly strong for someone who so recently fainted dead away. But she remained weak. After a tentative attempt to sit up, she fell back on the sofa. "You have my leave to go," she said to Honk. "Yuri, show the gentleman to the door."

Honk bristled at the curtness of the woman's dismissal. "Look, Lady," he said. "You just fell flat on your ass out there in the street. I don't give a damn what you think of me, but you need something warm in you. That's all I . . ."

"I said, you have my leave to go," the woman said again, even more coldly. She managed to sit up on the sofa, but swayed even so. "I will be quite all right now."

That was enough for Honk. He had been stiffed by hoity-toity white women before. "Okay, Lady. Have it your way." He turned to leave, but was stopped short by a little cry from the old man the woman called Yuri.

The woman had fallen again. This time right off the sofa and full length onto the carpeted floor. Yuri tried to lift her again onto the sofa.

Honk pushed him aside and returned the woman to where she had been. She was completely spent insofar as physical strength was concerned. She struggled against Honk's touch. "I am perfectly all right," she said.

"Yeah? In a pig's ass," Honk said. "Lady, you are just about as all right as a fart in a whirlwind." He stood back and studied the defiant woman. Okay, so she was a bitch kitty, she was human. And she was just about as helpless a human as Honk had seen in a long time. He softened.

And, in so doing, Honk placed himself in the woman's power. The same power the Chinese so feared when they allowed drowning men to drown. The same power we all yield to those we help. But Honk did not yet know that, nor would he ever much realize, to tell the truth.

"You catchee chow-chow? Hot chow-chow?" he said to the old man named Yuri. "Missee all same makee chow-chow. Maskee?"

"No catchee chow-chow," Yuri said.

"You mean there ain't nothing to eat or drink in this joint?" Honk said, reverting to English and speaking to the woman.

"That is no concern of yours," the woman said. "Please go now." She looked away and her voice failed. She was embarrassed at having been found out. "We will be all right."

Honk looked then to the slumped old man in his wing chair and back to the woman. "Lady, I ain't no doctor, but I been in China long enough to know it when I see somebody starving to death. You look to me like you are pretty God-damned hungry."

The woman made a weak, but bravely dismissive gesture to the room and its furnishings. "If we were starving, as you so rudely put it, would we be living in such a house?"

"People can't eat houses and furniture," Honk said. Then, turning to Yuri, he pulled money from his pocket and handed it over. "You catchee chow-chow. Savvy? Catchee chow-chow. Chop-chop."

The old man took the money timorously, but looked to the woman. Already, his face had brightened. He licked his lips hungrily.

The woman looked to the old man in the wing chair, as though for permission to accept Honk's money. There was pain in her face. Then, with an obvious effort, bringing forth only the slightest of nods, she bade Yuri go, telling him, in Russian, what to bring back — meat and milk and eggs and sturdy vegetables. She did not look at Honk at all.

The great house became still then. The woman lay back on the sofa. The old man remained slumped in his chair. Honk studied the house and its furnishings. His hangover, though repressed by what happened, had not gone away. His head hurt like hell, and nausea which bothered him in recent years when he drank too much, churned his stomach. He stared hungrily at a side table with bottles and glasses and a seltzer bottle. All of the bottles were empty.

"You got a name?" Honk asked the woman.

"I am Zena Tretchnikoff."

"Him?"

"Alexander Tretchnikoff. He is my husband. We were actors. Have you not heard of Zena and Alexander?" She lifted her chin dramatically. "We played all over the world. Even in your country at one time. Chicago, it was. And New York and San Francisco. We did Shakespeare and all the great play-wrights."

"I ain't all that big on Shakespeare, Zena," Honk said.

The woman reacted to the familiarity. "You would have known us on sight had you been cultured at all," she said coldly. "Everyone who was anyone knew Zena and Alexander."

Honk took the slap good naturedly. "Nobody ain't never said I was cultured, Zena. I'm just a dirty-assed American sailor who put up the money for what I'd say is going to be your first meal in a long time. Come to think of it, how in the hell do you eat when I ain't around?"

Zena hesitated. "We — we sell things. We managed to get some things out with us from home."

"What kind of things?"

"Paintings. Icons. Jewelry. Eggs."

"Eggs?"

"Yes. Easter eggs." She reached to where Yuri had placed the small bag she was carrying when she fainted in the street. From it she took an artificial egg of some four or five inches in diameter. It appeared to be made of porcelain, but was so encrusted with gold and pearls and other jewels the fact was hard to see. The Russian Orthodox Church made much of Easter. Such decorated eggs played some part in its rites, Honk had heard. Fabergé eggs, they were called.

"It's pretty," Honk admitted.

"It is exquisite," Zena corrected him. "We had several when we reached Hankow. We have been living off their sale. But people know we must have money. They do not pay much now."

Honk knew that for the truth. Hankow was full of portable Russian art and other valuables. Prices were so low even sailors could buy it, if they wanted. Honk had not wanted. The egg to him was no more than an interesting bauble.

"How many you got?" he asked.

Zena was reluctant to reply.

"This is your last one?" Honk guessed. "You was taking it to sell for chow?"

"Yes. We didn't want to," Zena said softly. "It is all we have left of home. But we must eat. Alexander is not well."

Honk motioned to the room and its furnishings. "How about all this stuff? Can't you peddle some of it for chow?"

"It is not ours," Zena said. "The house belongs to a wealthy Frenchman who admired our work a long time ago. He is in France now. He gave us the use of the house while he is gone. We cannot sell what is not ours."

"What are you going to do after you sell this?" Honk said, looking again at the ornate egg.

For the first time, Zena let down her guard. Despair came into her voice. "I don't know," she said so softly Honk hardly heard her. "The good Lord will provide."

"Yeah?" Honk said skeptically. "Don't look like the good Lord's been doing too good a job lately."

"He got us across Siberia. He got us this far," Zena said defiantly.

"Well, I don't see a hell of a lot of difference between starving to death in China and starving to death in Russia."

"We will not starve."

"You got a pretty damned good start on it right now, Lady," Honk said. "The stuff Yuri is bringing ain't going to last long."

"There will be something else," Zena said. "There is always something else."

"Yeah? Well, maybe you are right, but I got to get back to the ship. You got enough dough for right now?"

"If you mean money," Zena said stiffly, "Yes, we have enough for the time being."

"There may not be an American sailor handy next time you take a nose dive. You think of that?"

"We do not want your money, Mister — Mister —?"

"Taylor, Zena. Chief gunner's mate, United States Navy. You can call me Honk."

"Honk?"

"It's a nickname. Don't let it bug you."

"A nickname?"

"Yeah. It's just what guys call me on the ship. It don't mean nothing."

Zena pondered this strangeness for a time. Then she straightened and regained her former coldness. "We do not want your charity Mister — Mister Taylor," she said, ignoring Honk's offer of his nickname. "If you will return tomorrow, after I've had a chance to sell the egg, Yuri will see that you get back what you have lent to us."

"You don't have to pay that back, Zena," Honk said. "Hell, that wasn't nothing."

"We do not accept charity, Mister Taylor," Zena repeated, stiffly. "I will see that you are repaid."

"Okay, if that's the way you want it," Honk said. "But what if you can't sell the egg? This Russkie stuff is a drug on the market here. Hankow is full of it. You ain't going to get much for it, you know that?"

"Yes, Mister Taylor, I know that," Zena said. "But, if you will but return tomorrow, you will get back your money. You need not worry on that score."

Yuri returned, his arms burdened with food. Within minutes he had charcoal burning under a wok. The smells of cooking food worked their way through the house. In the interim, Yuri brought large glasses of milk to the woman and the old man in the wing chair. Both of them were beginning to look stronger at the mere prospect of food.

"I ain't worried," Honk said. He was silent for a time while Yuri brought out plates of food and more milk on little serving carts.

Honk smiled at seeing Zena, unable to control her hunger any longer, eat with more than ladylike haste. Even the old man in the wing chair recovered enough to permit Yuri to feed him. His trembling hands did not permit his feeding himself.

Honk watched the three of them eat. Yuri interspersed his patient and loving feeding of Alexander with spoonfuls to his own mouth. For a time, there was no talking at all. Honk grinned to see Zena struggle to resist her hunger-driven urgency lest she appear undignified. That is what a matron in one of Honk's childhood orphanages said of people who ate too fast — they were undignified.

Alexander did not bother with such pretense. He gulped at his food, spilling it down his chin so that Yuri had to wipe it away.

Honk looked again about the house. He did not remember the last time he was in a private home. Certainly, not in China, and he had been in China sixteen years. He figured it was in San Diego. He picked up a woman in a bar there one time. She took him to her small stucco bungalow somewhere in El Cajon. Her husband was away to sea. It was a neat little house, with bottles and jars of cosmetics on the dresser in the woman's bedroom.

It was nice, being in a real house again. Maybe, after he left the Navy, he would get a little house of his own somewhere back in the States. It would be nothing like this house, of course. Navy pensions would not buy anything like this in the States. But it would be big enough for him. Maybe a woman somewhere would — Loneliness can give a man strange thoughts.

Honk looked at Zena appraisingly. Old Alexander did not look as though he would last much longer. But, no, Zena was a mule-headed old broad. She had already shown that. More than likely she would starve to death before having anything to do with anyone like Honk. Besides, she was too skinny. Of course, that could be fixed with regular chow. She would not be bad looking if she had a little meat on her. Already, she had the fatal, though still unrecognized charm, for Honk, of the fact he had helped her.

Buried within Honk's sentimental musings of Zena was an accepted responsibility for her. The thought of her fainting away of hunger and falling again in the streets was unbearable. But she made it clear she would not accept gifts. Not from him anyway.

Then, as though saying something which just then occurred to him, Honk said. "I always wanted one of them eggs, Zena. What do you say I buy it?"

Zena stopped chewing. "What did you say?"

"What do you say I buy your egg," Honk said. "How much you figure it's worth?"

"Are you serious?"

"Why not? I got money I ain't spent yet. How much you want for it?" The exchange rate, in fact, gave white hats more money than they could have dreamed of anywhere else. Sometimes it got as high as ten Mex for one American dollar, and the Navy paid in American dollars.

Zena sat as though not understanding what Honk said.

191

"You was going to sell it anyway," Honk said. "How much you figure to get for it?"

"There are dealers," Zena said. "I — don't know what they will offer for this one. It is better than most. I . . ."

"What did you get for the last one you sold? Was it as good as this one?"

Zena was hesitant. It was repugnant for her even to talk of such things. "I don't remember. I . . ."

"Look, Lady," Honk said. "Let's knock off the crap. Okay? You sold the God-damned thing to get something to eat. How much was it?"

"Two hundred and fifty dollars, I believe."

"Mex?" The Chinese used Mexican silver dollars for their money. Local money was still called Mex, when compared with American or other currencies.

"Mex," Zena grudgingly admitted.

"Mex! Hell, that ain't nothing. Not for something like this," Honk said. He took up the ornate egg and turned it over in his hand. "Hell, Lady. I'll give you a thousand Mex for it. I'll give you that much for it right now."

Despite herself, Zena's face brightened. "The dealers will not give . . ."

"The God-damn dealers have been screwing you, Lady," Honk said. "They know you got to sell it. They'll turn around and sell the God-damned thing for fifteen hundred or two thousand."

"Very well then, Mister — Mister Taylor," Zena said as though granting a favor. "If that is your wish, we will sell it to you." She drew herself up and spoke with severe dignity. "You may take the bag, as well. It will be easier to carry. The bag will offer some protection." She looked with yearning poignancy at the jewelled egg, the last remnant of a life long gone.

Honk, calloused and rough though he was, saw the pain in Zena's face. "I ain't got that much money on me right now," he said. "But, if you can send Yuri with me to Howard's, I'll send it back with him."

"Howard's?"

"A bar. I can get the money there. It's not far from here. Yuri can be back in thirty minutes."

Zena measured Honk with cold calculation. Then, as though finding him trustworthy, she said. "Very well. Yuri, you will go with Mister Taylor."

Honk was not used to being called Mister. Enlisted men in the Navy did not rate that courtesy, even from other enlisted men. He took up his cap and turned to go.

"You are forgetting your egg, Mister Taylor," Zena said formally. "You have bought it; it is yours."

Honk stopped short and snapped his fingers. "That's something else, Zena," he said. "I ain't got no place in the ship to keep nothing like this. How about if I leave it here? That way, you would have it here to look at. You think that would be all right?"

Zena studied him as though puzzled by this new development. She seemed to suspect Honk of some trick or ruse. Then, with no unbending whatsoever in her manner, she said: "Very well, Mister Taylor. You may leave it here if that is your wish. You may collect it any time you please. Good day, Mister Taylor."

Thus began as strange a relationship as can be reasonably imagined, a relationship in which Honk came again and again to the house in the French Concession. Through a discreet arrangement with Yuri, he came always at those times when the Tretchnikoffs were at the end of the money they received for their last elegant Easter egg.

And, each time, Zena received him with the same formal coldness. Never did she address Honk as anything other than Mister Taylor. Nor did she ever so much as ask him to be seated in her presence. And, each time, she sold Honk the egg with the same seeming reluctance, before replacing it again on its shelf and bidding him "Good day, Mister Taylor."

Old Alexander had the decency to die a month or so after Honk became involved with the little household, but Zena hung on for as long as I was in China. Honk even paid for the old guy's funeral.

Zena fleshed out on the groceries bought with Honk's money, the money she got for the God-damned egg she "sold" him — over and over again. She bought new clothes on his money. And went to the beauty parlors to get her hair fixed and her hands manicured. She came to look as she did a long time ago in Russia.

She came to look so good, in fact — on Honk's money — that when the French owner of the big house came again to China on a business trip, he took Zena with him back to France.

I tried to tell Honk a lot of times that he was being played for one large-size sucker, but he wouldn't listen. So far as I know, he never got one God-damned thing out of the deal. Even the fancy egg he "bought" so many times became lost in the confusion of Zena's departure. He never saw it again. And, I know for a fact, he never got the old broad into a bed.

TOOFAY

One of the many hazards faced by white hats in the river gunboats of the old Yangtze Patrol was missionaries. Missionaries were forever trying to save what they called our immortal souls. They proposed doing that by making us nicer people, for Christ's sake.

Invariably they got around to the Biblical warning that those who *lived* by the sword surely *died* by the sword. And, we of course lived by the sword.

Usually it was the younger missionaries who gave us the most trouble. You could just see their little faces shine when they got into the short strokes. Sometimes we played along by pretending to listen to what they said, then laughed and went along to our usual bars and whorehouses.

After they were in China for a while, though, they recognized the futility of the effort, or concluded we were not worth saving in the first place. The longtime guys didn't pay much attention to us.

Some of them, though, made sense, sometimes. I remember a fresh-faced young Methodist I met in a river steamer. He talked about the dangers of hating people. The risks incurred by the one doing the hating, that is. It was a pretty standard sermon but I heard him out because other entertainment was scarce that night.

I forgot (I thought) every word almost at once, but the young missionary's words returned to me again and again over the years, sometimes at the oddest times.

One time, in particular, when a boatswain's mate named Adams demonstrated the point dramatically. I had just transferred into the gunboats from the fleet cruiser *Augusta*.

Meeting new shipmates for the first time was always interesting. In the first place, you replaced someone else and were immediately compared with the man who left.

Then, the whole business of fitting yourself into the crew's pecking order started immediately. Some of the old guys saw you as a threat to their own positions, others picked you out as someone to dominate. That was just the nature of the beast. As happens when a dog meets up with a strange pack, a good deal of bristling back hair and sniffing under tails went on until things got themselves sorted out.

This was especially true of small ships on remote stations where sailors were thrown upon their own company for long periods of time without the distractions and social releases of shoreside contacts. The river gunboats of the old Yangtze Patrol met that criterion admirably. The crew was at mess when I reported aboard the *Leyte* at Hankow. It was my first river gunboat, and I remember my wonder at seeing how gunboat sailors lived. I let my seabag and hammock to the deck and stared about me in the way a farm kid sees his first carnival.

The mess compartment was a big room, all light and airy with big square glass windows. The tables, too, were bigger than the standard Navy mess tables and the men sat on *chairs*. In the Fleet ships, we sat on narrow wooden benches with folding wrought iron legs which sometimes collapsed in rough seas. I had not sat in a chair, for Christ's sake, since I joined the Navy. Except for maybe in shoreside restaurants and bars.

The guys at the tables stopped chewing and looked up, waiting, with expressions held carefully in neutral. Even the two mess coolies stopped and turned to me. Everything stopped. I felt like a piece of meat at a butcher counter, being appraised by a shopping housewife.

"Roberts," I said by way of introducing myself. "Signalman second. Off the *Augusta*."

"Adams," a big, red-faced boatswain's mate first class blurted around a mouthful of something. With his fork in his left hand as a pointer he indicated each man in turn along both sides of the table, naming names which came too fast for me to remember.

Gunboat sailors were known in the rest of the Fleet as "river rats" and were supposed to be a rough bunch of sons-of-bitches, but this lot didn't look much different from any other bunch of white hats. A little older, on average, maybe, and, from the looks of them, a touch or two tougher than regular Fleet sailors. But not much more than that.

Adams did not bother to introduce the guys at the second table. "You had chow?" he said without much warmth.

When I shook my head, Adams growled at one of the mess coolies. "Ching. Place for . . .?"

"Roberts," I said. I tugged my seabag and hammock to a place out of the way and sat down to where the coolie put plate, cup and cutlery in a vacant space at the table. Hot food and a cup of steaming coffee appeared before me as though by magic. This was beginning to look good, and I hadn't even seen the sleeping compartment yet.

All gunboat living spaces were on the main deck, I learned, and equally roomy, light, and airy. In the Fleet ships we lived buried deep in a maze of hard metal decks and bulkheads where the only air we got, usually hot and oil-smelling, came out of eternally humming electric blowers.

The only hitch I saw, so far, in what promised to be what white hats called a home and a feeder, was Adams. I spotted that big son-of-a-bitch for trouble. The way the other guys deferred to him told me that. That, and his overbearing manner and loud mouth. And he *was* big — easily over two hundred pounds — with impressive scars all over his whiskey-red face indicating a history of both ring and bar room brawls. Probably a Fleet boxer at one time, I guessed. He had the prominent vertical muscles in the back of his neck for that.

Altogether, none of it looked good. I always had trouble getting along with loudmouths. I had enough fights of my own to know that getting hit in the nose can hurt like hell. I didn't look forward to tangling with Adams.

In the Fleet ships it was easier to keep away from the bad ones. We ate in our own Division messes and, typically, knew only the guys in our own gangs. But it was already clear that in the gunboats everyone, except for chiefs and officers, ate together. Whether I liked it or not, I was going to see a lot of Adams, and everyone else in the crew, for that matter.

"How long you in the *Augusta?*" Adams growled then. It was interesting — and ominous — how everyone let Adams do the talking.

"Came out from Pearl on her," I said. "Six months maybe."

"You Flag?"

"Yeah," I nodded. What Adams meant was, was I in Admiral Hart's flag allowance? Admirals were given extra communications people — signalmen, radiomen, yeomen — called their flag allowance. They went with the admiral wherever he went. Ship's company sailors did not usually like Flag people because Flag people were sometimes given special privileges.

But that was not what Adams was driving at. As a boatswain's mate, he never had much to do with Flag people anyway. No, what Adams was getting at was establishing, quickly, where I would find myself in this ship's pecking order.

"God-damned Flag skivvy-waver," he growled. "Just what we need on this bucket." Skivvy-waver was white hat talk for signalmen. Although the term was mildly derogatory, it was usually used with good humor and we didn't get in a sweat over it. Adams didn't use it with good humor, though.

I let it go. I was resigned to having to fight the big son-of-a-bitch, sooner or later. But, given any say in the matter, I preferred it to be later. One of us might die before we came to blows. I always liked looking on the bright side of things.

I was pretty busy for the next few days getting squared away with a bunk and locker and learning my way about the ship. Not that there was that much to learn about the little vessel. A hundred and ninety-one feet long, and twenty-eight feet in the beam, she drew only six-and-a-half feet, fully loaded. There was not a hell of a lot to learn.

The signal bridge was the top of the wheelhouse, with a spread canvas awning to keep off sun and rain. A couple of signal searchlights, yardarm blinkers, semaphore platforms, and two bags of code flags was, as the British say, the lot. But it was enough for the river.

The other signalmen were decent enough types. Nor was there much problem with any of the other rates. I quickly shook down into the pampered status we all enjoyed in the gunboats. Onboard coolies did most of the dirty and menial chores leaving us to an easy and very comfortable acceptance of the little luxuries and privileges due, by rights, to white men, no matter how lowly they might be in their own world.

I even went ashore regularly with the other guys and learned the loose but definite protocol of gunboat liberty. We tended, even as do white hats off Fleet ships, to frequent the same bars and whorehouses on the beach so that we might become known at least to some one. That was about the only family most of us ever had.

In time, I became friends with some of the guys in other rates. Even with some of the left-arm rates. That would have been a rare thing in the Fleet ships but it was the norm for gunboat sailors. Probably because there were so few of any one rate, we came to live more as members of the whole crew than of any individual division. In a way, it was nice.

The only flaw lay with Adams. We still had not had the confrontation I expected. I caught him staring at me sometimes with a kind of measuring look, but he didn't push it. Our duty time was spent largely apart — as apart as anything could be in so small a ship. He worked the deck gangs, and I spent most of my time on the bridge where the common herd was not even allowed if not on watch. The clash, when it came, would most likely occur off the ship. And that, in fact, is how it happened.

The nineteen-twenties and -thirties were tumultuous years in China. Competing War Lords plagued the land, preying on hapless peasants and wealthy merchants alike with a merciless greed and cruelty which left the country bleeding and its economy in ruins.

I saw War Lord troops prowling the streets of the towns sometimes, each unit with its own executioner, big-bladed sword slung across his back as a badge of office. Executions in China then were peremptory, public, and frequent.

About the only stability in all of China during that time was in the foreign concessions in which Europeans, Americans, and Japanese lived their illusory, but very pleasant, lives insulated by their military forces from the dangerous turmoil in which the native Chinese lived.

One of those military forces was the United States Navy, with its associated Marine units. And one of the things the Navy did in protecting American rights in China was to provide armed guards on the Yangtze river passenger steamers regardless of nationality. These steamers, often old and decrepit, provided most of the transport for China, both freight and passenger. The steamers were considered far safer from the bandits infesting the country than were the few and rudimentary railroads then available.

Usually, these guard units consisted of four or five white hats with Springield rifles, riot guns, and Lewis machine guns from World War I. Normally, they were volunteers. Most of them volunteered as an escape from the boredom of duty in their own ships where they were subject to the nuisance of officers and the burden of Navy regulations.

On armed guard duty, we wore civilian clothes, ate with the first class passengers and lived in staterooms. The steamers provided free whiskey. An oral literature grew up about horny white women forcing their way into Navy sailors' staterooms for incredibly ornate sexual exercises. Sometimes the wives of missionaries, traveling alone to upriver missions, were cast in this improbable role. These enticements were enough, usually, to provide an ample pool of volunteers for the duty.

Especially in its middle and upper reaches, the Yangtze is narrow in places. Even in the river's broad areas, the ships' necessity for following deep water meant they sometimes came well within range of shoreside rifles. We wore civilian clothes to make ourselves less conspicuous to the bandits and Communists who fired ancient rifles from the river banks.

An even closer hazard came from the bandit practice of boarding as passengers, only to break out their guns and attempt taking over the ship at some later time. If the bandits succeeded, what followed was not pleasant for passengers, crew and armed guard alike. The Chinese, we were warned, were ingenious in the development of tortures.

Isolation of native passengers behind iron bars and strong steel mesh barricades controlled much of this danger. The armed guard units on board were at small actual risk.

The greatest hazards were from the river itself which might find a ship grounded, impaled on a rock or otherwise disabled along the shore where bandits concentrated and laid siege to the unfortunate vessel until its defenses wore down. Looting, rape, and murder were then certain.

Still, the duty of armed guards in the steamers was sought after. At least for a trip or two. It was not until some time later I discovered that, for some, the lure of the duty was other than a break in routine. Some guys worked out ways of making money, mostly through petty smuggling. Some devised more complicated schemes which paid off handsomely.

But a more troubling reason some of the guys liked to go in the river steamers was that they enjoyed shooting at people. That was why Adams volunteered so often.

Most times, the bandits fired from hiding places in the vast reed swamps of the lower river or from behind rocks farther upstream. Their purpose was not so much to kill passengers or crewmen as it was to harass and threaten. Rifle bullets do little harm to sizable vessels, but the sounds of them hitting steel plates is unsettling. Being killed by random bullets is just as lasting as any other way.

Sometimes, though, the bandits fired from exposed positions in a kind of macho bravado which dared the armed guard units to return fire. The Yangtze has extreme variations in its height of water, depending upon the time of year. Sometimes broad expanses of exposed sand and mud lay between water and inland cover.

The gunboats used these exposed expanses for their race tracks and baseball diamonds. On the upper river they represented about the only level land available. The bandits and/or Communists sometimes lined up in ranks to parade on these open areas and fire whole volleys at us, or stood without firing in what was meant to be a display of bravery.

When they exposed themselves, the armed guards responded vigorously, whether the bandits fired or not. The Chinese term for bandits was *tu fei*. We pronounced it, with a disregard for the tonal qualities of Asiatic languages, as "toofay."

The working definition of a *toofay* was anyone on the beach, man or woman, armed or not. We were not supposed to fire unless fired upon, but it was a restriction to which little attention was paid.

The white hats' reasoning was: "If the sons-of-bitches ain't firing at us now, that don't mean they didn't fire at us yesterday — or that they ain't going to fire at us tomorrow. Blow their God-damned heads off."

I never heard of armed guard duty in the Fleet ships in which I served. I didn't know what Adams was talking about when, one day at mess, he asked if I wanted to go in a Chinese-flag steamer to Chungking. "You got a choice," he said. "You can volunteer, or I can tell you to go. What's it going to be?" It turned out that Adams, as senior boatswain's mate, was in charge of assigning guys to armed guard.

"What the hell you talking about?" I said.

Once it was explained, I didn't have much interest in the matter, but what did appeal to me was the idea of getting off the ship for a while and seeing China close up.

"Who else is going?" I said.

"You and me and Johnson and Armstrong and Patterson," Adams said. "Draw your guns from the armory and fall in on the quarterdeck at eight in the morning. Uniform, civvies."

"What ship is it?" Patterson, a young seaman first, asked.

"The Loopy," Adams said, glaring.

The name meant nothing to me, but Patterson put down his fork and pushed back his plate. "I ain't going armed guard in no God-damned Loopy," he said.

I learned later that Loopy was the sailors' name for a Chinese steamer named *Lu Pi*. She had an evil reputation on the river, but I did not know that then.

"Me neither," Johnson and Armstrong blurted with equal force. "Last time I went in that tub, I damned near starved to death. God-damned officers didn't know their ass from a hole in the ground. Grounded three times, for Christ's sake." Johnson said.

"That goes for me, too, Boats," Armstrong said. "If I aim to get killed, I aim to do it as comfortable as I can."

Adams grinned his ugly gap-toothed grin. "Like I told Roberts, here," he said. "You bastards can volunteer, or I can tell you to go. It's up to you.

"Either way, you're going. Have your ass on the quarterdeck eight o'clock in the morning."

Naturally, by that time, I was aware something was going on that didn't sound good. "I don't have any civilian clothes, Adams," I said. We were not allowed to keep civilian clothes on board Fleet ships.

"You got about twelve hours to damned well get some," Adams said. "Send a coolie over. Shirt and pants'll be enough. It ain't going to be cold this time of the year."

That didn't leave me a hell of a lot to say. Adams left to take his evening shower. "What's that all about, Armstrong?" I asked. "What's wrong with the Loopy?"

Armstrong finished his coffee and slammed down his cup. "Son-of-a-bitch's old as hell, for one thing," he said. "More rust than paint, and engines shot. She'll be lucky to get up the God-damned rapids at this stage of the river. Feeds pig slop, too. And if there's a white woman passenger, she'll be a pig nobody in his right mind would screw."

"If she's that bad," I said, "Why's Adams is going along?"

"Adams would go on a God-damned honey barge if it give him a chance to shoot somebody," Armstrong said bitterly. (Honey barges were the boats the Chinese used to haul night soil to their fields. Night soil was human waste. Honey barges did not smell good.)

I realized there was something more behind Armstrong's bitter words, but I didn't push it. "How come he picked you and Johnson and Patterson to go if you don't volunteer?" I said.

"He's pissed off at all three of us," Armstrong said. "He's been saving something like this. It's his way of getting even."

"He's not pissed off at me," I said. "Not that I know of. I haven't done anything to him."

"You don't have to do nothing to that son-of-a-bitch," Armstrong said. "He don't like you. He don't like any signalman or quartermaster or radioman or anybody he can't order around. Armed guard is one thing he can order you to do. And, if you don't, he'll find a way to make you wish you had."

Since I didn't really know what the hell I was getting into, I didn't fight it too much. The next morning I drew a Springfield from the armory and fell in on the quarterdeck with Adams and the other three guys. I felt ill at ease in flimsy civilian cotton shirt and pants. It was the first time I wore civvies since joining the Navy.

Armstrong had a riot gun. Patterson and Johnson had Springfields like mine. Adams carried a Lewis machine gun. Coolies dumped some boxes of rifle ammunition on deck at our feet and some pans for the Lewis.

Adams made a cursory inspection of the lot and called away the motor pan to carry us off to the Loopy. I didn't see an officer during the whole thing, but that wasn't all that unusual in the gunboats. Chiefs took care of the details most of the time. Or first classes like Adams.

My first sight of the Loopy made me question Armstrong's description of her. She was worse. I had already seen a good number of River steamers. None of them, except for maybe one or two of the Dollar Line ships were impressive, but the Loopy abused the privilege of being ugly.

She rode at anchor in midstream with the current making a little bow wave under her stem. Two tall and staggering stacks rose over her amidships house. Low of freeboard along her full length, she had three decks — with the roof of the third serving as a fourth deck — all of which were jam-packed with Chinese passengers.

Our coxswain swung us in alongside the poor old ship and we clambered aboard. At close quarters she was no better — and the stench, of course, was much worse. The stink was strong enough, in fact, to be damned near *visible*. But, what the hell, we were there. In a few days we could get off and go home.

The jabber of voices stilled as we came aboard. The people drew back and made a way for us as a skinny ship's officer in limp cotton khakis far too big for him led us up and forward. He was wearing a .45 caliber automatic in a U.S. Army holster hanging half way down to his knee. All the officers wore guns.

The crowd drew back as we came up the ladder. Most were men, in peasant clothes, some with farm implements or other things which could be used as weapons. Some were women and children. The women and children looked at us with flat, expressionless faces. The men, though, looked at us with anything but expressionless faces. It was clear they did not like us worth a damn. The Chinese called us Foreign Devils on the river. Their animosity was damned near tangible.

Fear crawled up my spine as I sensed the mob's hatred but there was little to be done about it. I swore that I would be damned if I ever went on armed guard detail again. Not in a China-flag ship anyway. I fell in behind Adams and the others and followed the ship's officer forward to the barricade which would seal us off from the native passengers.

As the crowd was pushed back for us, a peasant woman with a lumpy bundle of possessions and a baby in her arms, lost her balance and fell. In the turmoil then going on she stood a damned good chance of being trampled, baby and all. Without thinking, I jumped forward to help her.

As though on a signal, the crowd surged against me, an ugly and menacing growl deep in its collective throat. I was shoved bodily back to the wire mesh barricade where Adams and the others turned to help. We all had our weapons but they were not loaded. The crowd surged against us.

Desperately, we clubbed our guns and beat at the snarling faces closing all about us. Adams leveled his Lewis gun as though ready to fire, even though it had no pan rigged.

Slowly, the crowd fell back from us. An ominous silence settled over the deck. I think it was the Lewis which did it. Lewis guns were only thirty caliber but they had an air-cooling jacket which made them look like small cannons. When Adams leveled his gun, the crowd drew back in fear.

"Get your ass behind that God-damned barricade, Roberts," Adams growled. "All of you! Behind the barricade. And close the gate behind you. Move!"

The ship's officer had drawn his own gun and the barricade sentry, tall bayonetted rifle and all, swung open the barricade gate. The Chinese passengers fell back in sullen silence, their eyes following us with deadly intent.

I never felt so *safe* in my life as when that damned gate closed behind me. I never knew what happened to the woman with the baby. I looked for her but I couldn't see her in the crowd. They all looked alike to me, anyway. I followed Adams up the ladder. I needed a drink.

"Look, you stupid son-of-a-bitch," Adams said, once we were clear. He grabbed my shirt and pulled me close to his big chest. "Don't never do that again."

"Do what again?"

"Go after a Chinese woman like that," Adams said.

"I was only trying to help her, for Christ's sake."

"Well, don't," Adams said. "You saw what happened. Lousy bastards probably thought you was trying to steal her stuff. They're Chinese. That's what they would have tried to do. Just don't do nothing like that around gooks. You'll get your God-damned head handed to you, you keep that up."

"The baby could have got killed, Boats," I protested. "You mean I just ought to let them kill the God-damned kid?"

"You think maybe it'd be better if we was all to get killed?" Adams growled. "We could all have been killed down there a minute ago. They got axes and shovels and stuff. We wasn't loaded. Hell, even if we was loaded, we ain't got bullets enough to kill all of them. They make up their minds to kill us, we're dead. You better get that through your frigging head, Roberts, or you ain't going to last long on the river."

I didn't answer. It was all too new for me. I followed Adams and the others to our assigned staterooms. They were not as bad as the rest of the ship, but they sure as hell fell short of even the worst flophouse I ever stayed in back home. After that, we went into the bar. For armed guards, the drinks were on the house in the Loopy. I couldn't help wondering what I had let myself in for.

The ship, by that time, was underway, wheezing its labored way upstream. "Ain't nothing likely to happen until we get away from town," Adams said. He talked to all three of us but he fixed on me. Since this was my first trip as armed guard, that may have been reasonable. "Better get squared away and get something to eat while we can," he said. "Don't let your guns out of your sight for any reason. You hear that?"

The dining saloon was not much better than any other part of the ship, but it was some cleaner. Table linens were white, for one thing, and the European style china and cutlery was clean. Decks and bulkheads, though, were soiled and the red shades of dim lamps were tattered.

The other passengers were almost all whites, with a scattering of "tame" Chinese men. Most of the whites I took to be Standard and other oil company guys, with a handful of missionaries, some of them with their wives, but I saw nothing likely to stir thoughts of romantic adventure in the lot.

Patterson came to much the same conclusion, I suppose. He muttered, "Ain't nothing here I'd screw with Adams' dick."

The chow was not as bad as it might have been, and there was enough of it. The free booze, brought to us in water glasses, helped. The food was actually not too bad. But Adams rose and went outside long before the rest of us. He took a rifle rather than the Lewis gun he carried before.

"Where's he going?" I said.

"Son-of-a-bitch can't wait to shoot something," Patterson said. "He'll set watches pretty soon so one of us will be outside all the time, but five'll get you ten Adams will be outside nine hours out of every ten. He's scared something will show up on the beach and he won't be there to shoot it."

"How come he took a rifle?" I said. We stacked our arms in a corner behind our table.

"Adams likes to kill Chinese one bullet at a time," Patterson explained. "Machine guns throw lead all over the place. Adams likes to see the one he's killing."

"What's eating him?" I said. "How come he hates the Chinese so bad?"

"Nobody knows," Patterson said. "He's been out here a long time. I've heard a dozen different stories but none of them makes much sense. I asked him once and he said he didn't hate the lousy sons of bitches — he just likes to shoot them."

I read in a book somewhere that we can truly hate only those we have harmed or injured in some way. Maybe that was Adams' problem. He abused the hell out of whores and ricksha coolies every chance he got. I had known other guys like that in China. They knew they could get away with anything against the Chinese. I guess knowing that made a mean son-of-a-bitch meaner than ever.

But Adams was the only white hat I ever knew who *actively* hated Chinese. Most of us, I think, viewed them with a careless pity for their poverty and the cruelty visited upon them by their own people. Adams was the only one I ever saw who went out of his way to hurt them.

Before we could explore that fascinating subject further, though, the sound of a rifle shot cracked sharp from outside. "Hot damn!" Johnson yelled. "Old Adams has got him one. Let's go."

We grabbed our guns and ran outside. The missionary types glared at us through the whole meal so we wouldn't forget they didn't like us. The other whites showed little interest. The Chinese ignored us completely from the start.

We steamed past a long, featureless expanse of reed swamps. Adams stood erect, bracing his Springfield against a stanchion while he studied the shore with savage concentration.

His sights were up and adjusted for windage. His eyes glittered, black and hungry under heavy brows.

"What is it, Boats?" Patterson cried, jacking a round into his own rifle's chamber and stepping alongside Adams.

"I don't know," Adams said. "I can't see nothing, but somebody shot at us. I seen the splash in the water."

We were still too close to town to expect anything in the way of serious danger, but if Adams saw a bullet hit the water, somebody fired at us.

Before I could worry that any longer, I saw a faint puff of blue smoke among the shoreside reeds and a rifle bullet hit one of our stacks with an oddly dull plopping sound. I suppose the stack metal was so rusted it didn't make much noise.

Instantly, Adams squeezed off four quick rounds in the direction of the smoke and reached for another clip. The rest of us took stations along the rail. The riot gun was not much use at that range. It was meant for close-in work. But the rifles and machine guns reached the shore. Easy.

We opened a rapid fire, raking the reeds where we saw the smoke. We never knew if we hit anything or not. We could have killed a hundred men and never know the fact.

We saw no more smoke. Adams had a strangely satisfied look on his face. I've seen guys come out of whorehouse rooms with the same kind of a look. But it did not last long and he returned to his hungry watching of the shore.

Shipping traffic on Chinese rivers — especially the middle and upper rivers — did not move at night. The hazards were too great and reliable aids to navigation too few. Since it was coming on to night by that time, the Loopy looked for a wide spot and anchored as far from shore as she could.

That was fine as far as fire from the beach was concerned, but it left her perilously at risk from boarding parties drifting down in sampans. Fifteen or twenty sampans, silent and invisible in the night, might place a hundred or more men alongside in a matter of minutes. Enough men to swamp any resistance five white hats might put up.

That is when the riot gun would come into its own. A single blast from that blunt and ugly weapon would wipe out an entire sampan. And it could be fired fast. I was nervous as hell as Adams explained the danger and set his watches to meet it. I got the mid — midnight to four in the morning. I didn't look forward to it. I was trained to fight from big, fast ships, with big guns, against other big, fast ships with big guns of their own.

The others, though, made their preparations with no sign of undue care. Clear fields of fire were the great concern. Any attack, Adams said, would come from ahead. The ship rode to her anchor heading upstream, her bow interfering with our firing in that direction, from which the enemy would most likely drift down upon us.

The most logical place for us was in the very eyes of the ship, but we couldn't go there because of the passengers. They were as much at risk from the bandits as we, and we were the only protection they had, but I, for one, was not going to go down there and get my head knocked off from behind.

Adams did the best he could, placing us where we could cover the widest possible fields of fire. The son-of-a-bitch was having a ball. I think he wanted the bandits to make a try for us. He was still on deck when I left early in the evening for my stateroom and a little sleep before my long night watch. And he was still on deck when I arrived, at twenty minutes to twelve, for my watch, even though it was Patterson who had the eight-to-twelve.

"Anything doing?" I asked as I came near. Adams had set up along the athwartship railing at the forward end of the superstructure. That gave the best field of fire against anything approaching from ahead. This time he had the riot gun.

"Not yet," Patterson said softly. It is strange how men in the presence of danger speak softly. I have seen it many times. "Boats is right over there. If anything is coming, it will probably come on the mid. Keep your eyes open. The Lewis is right here. Boats has the riot gun."

Adams came to check my taking over the watch but didn't say much. "I'm going to get my head down for a minute," he said. "Call me first thing you even think you see or hear anything." He sat down then on deck, the riot gun in his lap, and leaned back against the superstructure house. It was nice to know he trusted me enough to sleep all of six feet away.

Nevertheless, the river world was black and silent. The dim lights of a shoreside village blinked out. Our passengers lay in a tangled mass on the decks below. Occasionally, a child whimpered or someone coughed, but, on the whole, they were as silent as though already dead. The ship, her engines on standby, made no sound. There was no wind. The river current made only the lightest swishing sound along the ship's sides.

Despite the silent menace of the river, however, the danger, when it came, came from the shore. I saw muzzle flashes. Even guns so small as rifles make surprisingly bright flashes when fired in dark night. And I heard the clanging spatter of bullets hit the ship. Although anchored far from shore, we were hit by a dozen or more bullets.

I sprang at once to the Lewis where it was mounted on the superstructure railing and pulled off half a pan of return fire in the general direction of the flashes on shore, but there was no more firing.

By that time Patterson and Johnson and Armstrong were with me, thumbing clips into their rifles and conspicuous in the night dark in their white navy shorts and skivvy shirts. White hats didn't sleep in pajamas. "What is it?" Patterson said. "Where are they?"

"On the beach," I said. "I saw their muzzle flashes. Must of been twenty-five or thirty of them."

"You hit anything?"

"I don't know. All I saw was the muzzle flashes. They haven't fired any more."

Strangely, through it all, there was no sound from the deck passengers. They lay still and unmoving, but they must certainly have been awake and frightened. People in ships taken by bandits did not stand much chance of living.

Neither was there any sign of the ship's officers. The wheel house forward remained dark and still as ever. They were probably holed up there with their forty-fives, waiting to make a last ditch defense against anything that came.

"You all right?" Patterson asked then.

"Yeah."

"Where's Boats?"

I had not thought of Adams. It was not like him, though, to stay away from any kind of action. "Right over there," I said. "He decided to sleep on deck. He thought it likely something was going to happen."

I stayed at the Lewis gun. It would be our most effective weapon against any further firing from the beach, but Patterson went over and nudged Adams where he sat propped against the superstructure bulkhead, the riot gun still across his lap.

"Hey, Boats?" Patterson said. "You all right, Boats?"

Patterson leaned and shook his shoulder. Adams rolled limply onto his side.

"Son-of-a-bitch," Patterson said. "He's dead."

A rifle bullet, so spent it did not pass completely through his head, took him squarely between his eyes.

Strangely furious, I wheeled back and emptied the Lewis gun in the direction of the rifle muzzle blasts. Patterson, Johnson, and Armstrong did the same with their guns. None of us liked Adams. He was a lousy son-of-a-bitch in most ways. But he was a shipmate.

And — I thought of this many times since — Adams would not have been dead — not that night anyway — had not his hatred for the Chinese led him to sleep on deck. That is when I remembered what the young Methodist missionary told me so long ago about the danger hating has for the guy doing the hating.

Had Adams not hated the God-damned Chinese so much, he would have been in his stateroom. He would not have been hit at all. Maybe there is a lesson in there somewhere.

LOOK-SEE PIDGIN

In the years just before World War II the Navy began taking things a little more seriously. Ships were painted a business-like black over their peacetime horizon-gray; we showed no lights at night, no longer anchored in exposed roadsteads, and never steamed at less than ten knots. Still, as we prepared for the bloody times to come, there seemed always to be time for the silly stuff — for what white hats called *look-see pidgin*.

As had *chop-chop, ding hao, maskee, gung ho* and a lot of the Navy's more colorful expressions, the phrase *look-see pidgin* came out of the old Asiatic Fleet ships in China. *Look-see* is pidgin English for something that is similar to, but not identical with, something real. *Pidgin* is a corruption of a Chinese word for business. Put together, they came to mean something done for the sake of appearances. God knows, there was enough of that in the Navy.

The whole business of saluting with swords, wearing funny hats and making elaborate rituals of simple acts was look-see *pidgin*, for which there was little justification, as was proved during the war when almost all of it was abandoned.

But things were done like that in the pre-war Navy. The officers seemed to enjoy it. Some of the old chief petty officers were worse. Form was rigidly enforced over substance, sometimes with unintended but tragic results.

To see the charade played out in full, all one had to do was be there for an admiral's change of command ceremony. That's when the whole cast was brought out: band, guard, sideboys, officers wearing swords — sometimes even the saluting battery.

Once, in Pearl, I was a Flag signalman in a heavy cruiser that was flagship for a two-star admiral then being relieved at the end of his tour. We were tied up to Ten-Ten Dock. And, although the admirals and their staffs, and what seemed to be every officer in the Pacific enjoyed themselves thoroughly, chatting comfortably before the show started and stiff and proper once it got underway, it was what white hats coarsely called a royal pain in the ass.

It was impressive as hell with all the bugles and pipes and drums and shouted orders, but it didn't just happen of its own accord. Signalmen were especially involved. The whole crew had to make the ship spotless, of course, before the great event, but the signalmen had all the business of flags and reporting approaching boats. The fact we were alongside the dock made it even harder. We had to watch for cars as well as boats.

This was all-important because the officer of the deck had to be notified of the identity and rank of arriving officers so that the right honors could be laid on — the number of side boys, how many ruffles and flourishes by the band, and the like. The OD wanted as much advance notice as possible for all that. God knows what would happen if he gave some guy the wrong number of sideboys. God-damned ship would probably have sunk right then and there.

All this was not so hard in the case of arriving boats. Admirals' barges, for instance, were black and wore the embarked admiral's flag. Captains' gigs had the first three letters of their ships' names in polished brass on their bows. They wore the national ensign aft with special emblems on the flagstaffs to show their ranks: eagles, halberds, globes.

But officers arriving in cars were harder to identify until they stepped onto the dock, trying to keep from stumbling over their swords (swords were not designed for wearing in cars). Admirals flew their flags from the front fenders of their cars but lower ranking officers didn't. By the time they got out of their cars, it could be too late for the OD to get ready for them, and somebody would be unhappy.

In short, the signal bridge was a busy place that morning. Everyone was tense and strained from the pressure. The Flag lieutenant did not help a hell of a lot. Neither did the Flag chief signalman, an old fusspot intent upon avoiding anything that would make him look bad. Both of them got in the way any way they could.

The chief was a special trial for us. He was a nervous man in the best of times, and a change of command ceremony in a flagship was sure as hell not the best of times. He had been in the Navy a long time and loved all the fuss and bother of look-see pidgin. He was also scared spitless something would go wrong for which he could be blamed. He had only a few years to go before retirement, and was determined to go out clean. He was entitled to gold hashmarks on his blues and he meant to keep them. (Men with clean records for twelve years, wore gold hashmarks and chevrons. Things like that were big deals for men like our chief.)

When an admiral moves into a new flagship he is said to "break his flag" in that ship. What happens is the admiral's dark blue personal flag with its proper number of white stars is folded and rolled into a compact bundle. The length of halyard at its bottom is then taken, in round turns, in and about a lashing of sail twine, making a small cylindrical shape which is then attached to a halyard and run up to the main truck. (That means the top of the main mast.)

At the proper moment in the ceremony on the quarterdeck, and on a signal from the bridge — the old cruisers' quarterdecks were amidships and could not be seen from aft —

a sharp tug on the downhaul would "break" the flag and cause it to fly free. What actually broke was the sail twine around the rolled flag.

I was a signalman first class at the time. One of the things the chief assigned me was the job of making up the new admiral's flag for breaking. It is not all that hard. A monkey could be trained to do it in a week or two, but the chief wanted it done right. So he had a first class petty officer do it. Not only that, he stood over me to watch my every move in order that nothing might go wrong. He even took the damned thing in his hand and tugged and pulled at it to make sure it was done right and would not break prematurely. That would have been a fate worse than death for the old son-of-a-bitch. He would be embarrassed in front of the whole damned Navy, you see, including a pot full of admirals, men of whom our chief lived in awe and mortal dread.

Once satisfied, the chief told off Jimmy Broder, a new striker on the bridge, to go with me to BatTwo and hoist the made-up flag to the main truck. BatTwo was a small secondary signal bridge and steering station at the base of the mainmast aft. It had a couple of signal searchlights and two small bags of signal flags. It was meant for use as an emergency ship control station if the main bridge was ever put out of action by battle damage.

Jimmy Broder should never have been in the Navy. Especially, he should not have been on a signal bridge. He was afraid of heights. The fancy word for it, a doctor told me once, is acrophobia. Broder hated to stand on the semaphore platforms, for instance, and they were only seven or eight feet above bridge level. One night when a blinker light burned out on the port yardarm, he flatly refused to go aloft and replace it. I thought he was going to faint at the very thought of going onto the yardarm.

I should have busted his ass off the bridge. His refusal meant someone else had to go up in his place. We were alone on the bridge so I went up and fixed the God-damned light myself.

Maybe what followed was partly my fault for letting Broder get away with that disobedience, but he was a likable kid and, except for his fear of heights, a promising signalman. I hoped he would grow out of his fear, but, tragically, he never did.

I was glad to be sent aft. It was a hell of a lot more peaceful back there, for one thing. BatTwo was a long way from all the hassle forward. There were no officers there. That alone made it peaceful, and all I had to do was to watch for the chief's signal and jerk on the halyard downhaul when I got it. As I said, a monkey could be trained to do the damned thing.

Broder, the striker, wasn't much in the way of help, not that I needed any, but it would have been nice to have somebody to shoot the breeze with while we waited. Broder was in the Navy for less than a year, and most of that time he spent in a deck division. But he was a decent enough kid and I liked him.

The word "striker" meant he was in training to be a signalman. It did not mean he was already a signalman. He was nervous as a God-damned cat at the thought of our enormous responsibility that morning.

"You sure it's made up right?" he asked.

"Yeah."

"What happens if anything goes wrong? I mean if it doesn't break or the halyard gets stuck or something?"

"Oh, nothing," I said. Broder was so nervous I tried to kid him out of his funk. "Worst thing would be they'd hang us from a yardarm, I suppose, but the Navy hasn't done anything like that in a month or two now. Probably we wouldn't get more than five or ten years in Portsmouth and a dishonorable discharge." Portsmouth, New Hampshire, was where the Navy had its brig. It was like Leavensworth, Kansas, was for the Army.

"You're kidding." Broder said. But his face said he was not sure whether I was kidding or not.

I laughed. "Don't sweat it," I said. "If something goes wrong, you can just climb up and straighten it out."

"Climb up there?" Broder said. "Did you say I would have to climb up there?" Broder's voice was tight. When I looked at him, his face was white.

"Yeah. What's wrong with that?"

"I can't climb up there," he said. "I get sick when I get up high someplace."

"Well, you picked yourself a damned poor rate if that is so," I said. I remembered then the night he refused to go up and fix the blinker light. "Signalmen have to go aloft all the time. Didn't you know that, for Christ's sake? Who do you think reeves all those God-damned halyards and maintains the God-damned blocks?" I could not think of anything that could go wrong, but Broder was not convinced. If anything, his fear grew stronger. I realize now the mere possibility of having to go aloft set him off.

On the theory the best thing to do when you got a guy in a funk is keep him occupied, I handed Broder the made-up flag and told him to bend it onto the halyard and run it up.

He did it all right, but he would not even look up to where the small blue bundle twisted at the masthead. I didn't pay as much attention to what he was doing as I should have. I was watching for the chief's signal to break the flag.

The mainmast, incidentally, is the aftermost of the two masts in a cruiser. In our ship it was a relatively slender tripod rising from BatTwo and seems taller than it is. The much more substantial mast rising from the bridge structure forward is the foremast. Although taller than the main, it rises through bridges and fire control stations so that it seems to be less tall than it is.

"Look up there," I said. "It ain't that far, for Christ's sake. You got handholds and steps all the way up."

"I can't," he said. He turned away and looked out over the harbor. I saw his hands shaking. The guy was scared to death at the thought of climbing that God-damned mast. He was not going to make much of a signalman, that was clear. Signalmen not only had to climb masts and go out on yardarms, most of the time they had to do it at sea when the God-damned ship was rolling its guts out and you're left hanging on for dear life fifty or sixty feet over a very deep ocean.

I felt sorry for him. "Don't worry about it," I said. "There's nothing to go wrong. Forget it."

Actually, though, something *was* going wrong even then. I was so wrapped up in talking with Broder that I forgot what was going on on the quarterdeck.

I suddenly became aware of a signal searchlight flashing at me from the bridge forward and saw the chief jumping up and down and waving his arms. He wasn't happy.

Guiltily, I gave the flag downhaul a smart jerk and the Admiral's flag flew free, its white stars shining. I didn't look forward to facing the chief when I got back to the bridge, but, at least, the flag broke all right. Late, but all right. I secured the halyard about its belaying pin and started forward. "Come on, kid," I said to Broder. "We might as well go up and face the music."

I was not more than a few seconds late in breaking the God-damned flag. But it was an *admiral's* flag, you see, and that makes all the difference in the world when you are talking about *look-see pidgin*. In the great scheme of things, it didn't mean diddly. But, in the Navy, it meant a lot.

There's no point in going into detail about what the chief said when we got back to the bridge. He had been in the Navy a long time and developed a large nautical vocabulary. And, since we were in port, there were no officers on the bridge to slow him down.

I was on my third cruise at the time. That meant I had been in the Navy a little over ten years. I had been reamed out before and could comfort myself with the thought that it would probably blow over in ten or fifteen years. But it was still new to Broder.

Of course, I was the main target, but Broder had to stand there and take it with me.

I realized it wouldn't do any good to argue with the chief. Every ranking officer in Pearl saw that flag break late. Every other chief in the fleet would remind him of it for the next year or two. It didn't figure that he would let me forget it any time soon.

Even so, getting chewed on like that gets old pretty fast. Especially so with all the other guys standing around the bridge grinning at me. They didn't grin so the chief saw them. That would mean they didn't take the whole thing seriously enough, but they sure as hell grinned where I saw them.

"Okay. Okay," I said at last. "So I was a couple of minutes slow. What's the big deal, for Christ's sake? The God-damned flag is up, isn't it? The sky's not falling, is it?"

It was like dropping a match into a bucket of gasoline. The chief roared in a voice which might have been heard on the quarterdeck. "Yes," he screamed, "It *is* up!" Then, as though realizing he could be heard even on the dock alongside, he gritted more quietly. "It is also up *upside down!*"

"What?" I said, gaping.

"You heard me," the chief said bitterly. "The God-damned flag is upside down. All in the world you had to do was run up one God-damned flag, and you run it up upside down." There is no way in the world to tell the outrage in the chief's voice that morning. His eyes burned into me. He was a suffering man.

Now, a rear admiral's flag is a plain blue piece of cloth with two white stars on it, arranged in a vertical line. How you could tell whether it was upside down or not, I didn't know. I stood there like a damned fool. "Upside down," I said. "How in the hell can you tell?"

"The stars," the chief blurted. "Look at the God-damned stars."

That ship was six hundred and ten feet long. The signal bridge was a hundred feet or so from the bow and the mainmast was maybe sixty or seventy feet from the stern. That meant the admiral's flag snapped in the wind three or four hundred feet away from us. The stars on it were maybe five or six inches high. As a signalmen I had pretty damned good eyes, but all I saw was a couple of white dots on a blue field.

"I *am* looking at the God-damned stars," I said.

"They're upside down," the chief said. "Look at the points."

"Points, hell," I blurted. "I'm lucky to see the God-damned stars, let alone their points."

"You can see the points if you use a long-glass," the chief said. He handed me his own personal Ross glass, the one that ordinarily you touched at your own risk.

By God, through the glass, you could see the stars with *one* point down and *two* up. But the thing which frosted my balls was the fact the God-damned chief actually used a long-glass to check something which otherwise no one on God's green earth would notice.

Admirals are touchy as hell about things like that, and we had a half-dozen admirals on board that morning. Flag lieutenants are even touchier. None of *them* noticed the flag. Not even our own ambitious flag lieutenant. If they noticed it, you could bet your ass we would hear about it. I learned later that was not exactly true, but I thought it was then.

The only one in the whole God-damned world who noticed it was our crazy chief. I turned away. "Come on, Broder," I said.

Poor Broder stood all this time in silent dismay at what was going on. He moved at once to come with me, glad for any chance to get away from the chief.

"Where the hell you think you're going?" the chief said.

"Back to turn the God-damned thing right side up," I said.

"How?"

"Haul it down, turn it over, and run it back up again," I said. It didn't really seem necessary to explain something that simple.

"No, you are not," the chief said. "You touch that God-damned flag now and everyone in Pearl Harbor will know something's wrong. We will be the laughing stock of the Fleet."

I didn't know what the hell to say to that. If having the God-damned flag upside down was such a threat to God and country, it made sense to me to turn it right side up as soon as we could. But, if no one else even knew it was upside down, what difference did it make if it was ever turned right side up or not, for Christ's sake?

"You got a better way?" I said. I had just about a belly full of the chief by that time.

"Yes," he said, smiling tightly and with no humor at all. "You and Broder are going to fix things. But you're going to do it on the mid-watch tonight when everybody's asleep."

"Broder had nothing to do with it," I said. "I was the guy in charge."

"Broder was with you," the chief said. "This will be a good lesson to him in learning that having three stripes under his crow doesn't mean a man can be relied on to do a job." The "crow" the chief talked about was my rating badge, the black eagle with crossed flags and the three stripes of a signalman first on my right sleeve.

Getting up in the middle of the night was no big deal. Watchstanders did it all the time. I didn't have the mid that night, but it would take only a minute or two to haul down the God-damned flag and run it up again. I could be back in my sack in ten or fifteen minutes.

"Broder will go up and straighten the flag," the chief went on deliberately.

"Broder had nothing to do with it," I said again. "Besides, you don't have to go up the God-damned mast to turn a flag over."

"Broder does," the chief said.

"But, God-damn it, Chief, the kid had nothing to do with it. It was my job to see it was done right. Besides, we can just haul the damned thing down and run it up right."

"An admiral's flag, once broken in a ship, is never hauled down until he is relieved," the chief said.

That was a damned lie and we both knew it. Flags don't last long in fast ships. The wind shreds them. We were always hauling them down to replace them. What the chief was after was our hides nailed to the mast so we'd never screw up again. But, what the hell, if he didn't want the God-damned thing hauled down, I'd go up and fix it.

"I'll go up the God-damned mast," I said.

222

"Maybe you didn't hear me," the chief said. I suspect now he sensed some hidden reason for my not wanting Broder to go aloft. "I said, 'Broder's going aloft.'"

"And I said I would do it." I was getting on thin ice there. As the old chiefs liked to say, they might not be able to make us do something, but they could damned sure make us wish we had done it.

"Oh, you're going to go up the God-damned mast," the chief said to me. "But Broder's going to do it first. He's going to go up and turn that flag around. Then he's going to come down, and you are going up to see that he has done it right."

That didn't leave me a hell of a lot to say. I shut up, confident that when the time came I would be able to go aloft and come back down with no one else being the wiser.

But the chief was ahead of me on that, too. "I know that is what you are going to do because you are going to come to the chief's quarters and call me. And I am going to be there to see that you do it."

Broder stood pale-faced and shaken by what he heard. He looked at me in despair. His lips even moved a little bit but no words came out.

Even then, I began to have a sick feeling in my stomach. There was no telling what a guy as scared as Broder might do. I knew a guy one time who was afraid of the water. Even the chaplain tried to talk sense into him. Finally, they just kicked him out of the Navy. A doctor told me once that being scared like that is what he called a "phobia," and there's nothing to be done for the poor bastard that has it. It's like a disease or something.

I sure as hell didn't know anything *I* could do about it. The chief left the bridge for his lunch and I took over the watch. There wasn't much doing in the harbor. With all the commotion that went on earlier, it seemed the ships were content to lie quietly and rest a while. I knew I was sure as hell ready for some rest.

But there was no rest for me. I could not put from my mind the terror in Broder's eyes on hearing the chief's orders. I think the other guys on the bridge began sensing something wrong, too. They no longer grinned and I saw them look nervously from one to another, as though embarrassed by the fact they grinned before.

As for Broder, I did not see him again until that night in BatTwo. I would not have been surprised had he not showed up, but he was there when I got there with the chief. But he was in whites. I told him to wear dungarees. Dungarees were the clothes we wore for dirty work. The mainmast in those old cruisers was aft of the stacks. That meant its upper reaches are always fouled with a greasy black coating of soot and unburned oil. You get that on your whites, and you never get them completely clean again. The stuff is slick as hell, too, and hard to grab hold of.

"Go change into dungarees," I told Broder. "We got time for that."

"The uniform of the day is whites," the chief said coldly.

"But, Chief, for Christ's sake," I blurted. "He'll ruin his whites up there."

"He should have thought of that before he screwed up," the chief said. Then, to me, he said, "And you can change into whites yourself. I'll wait here. For ten minutes. All right?"

During this whole time, Broder stood silent. I doubt now the chief noticed anything out of the ordinary with him, but I sure as hell did. The kid trembled almost visibly. Even in the dim light you could see the panic in his face.

I was so God-damned mad at the chief, over ruining a suit of whites, if nothing else, that I didn't trust myself to speak to the son-of-a-bitch. He simply stood in one wing of the little bridge and smoked a cigarette. I thought at the time he was enjoying himself.

There was not much room in BatTwo, but I got Broder as far away from the chief as I could. "Just take it easy, kid," I said under my breath. "Don't turn loose of one thing up there until you got a good hold on something else. And don't look down. You hear me? Don't look down. Okay? And, when you get up there, don't worry about the God-damned flag. I'll take care of it when I get up there.

Broder nodded without speaking. I don't know if he understood what I was saying or not.

I was so God-damned fired up that I didn't think to ask the chief if he notified the officer of the deck (O.D.) that he was sending a man aloft. The officer of the deck had to be notified so that he could order the radio transmitters shut down. The chief was the guy sending someone aloft; it was his pidgin to notify the O.D. I assumed he had.

Broder looked at me for one final imploring moment then turned to the ladder on the mast. He didn't look at the chief at all.

"Chief, for Christ's sake . . ." I said then, but he would not answer, and Broder moved slowly upward.

The chief knew by that time something was wrong, but he did not soften. He snuffed out his cigarette and watched intently as Broder slowly climbed higher and higher in the night. We saw him in the glow of dockyard lights.

I remember thinking bitterly to myself that it was all just look-see pidgin. That poor kid was going through the tortures of hell, all because a couple of stars had their points going the wrong way.

"You are one no good son-of-a-bitch, Chief," I said with as little expression in my voice as I could manage. There was no one else there to hear me and I could always deny saying it.

Oddly, the chief did not react as I thought he would. He looked at me. "The kid's a sailor in the United States Navy," he said, as though that made all the difference in the world. "Sailors have to go aloft."

"But it's only a God-damned flag, Chief," I said.

"No, it isn't," he said, his voice still calm and reasonable as hell. "It's about being ordered to do something and doing it. We may be in a war soon. It will be important then that sailors do what they are ordered to do." He paused. "This is the time for sailors to learn to do what they are told to do. We don't know how much time we have for learning that. We can't waste any chance to learn it."

I found nothing to say, and the chief went on. "I am trying to help him. Don't you see that? I'm trying to help you all."

Well, I sure as hell did not see it. But, before I could speak, Broder fell.

I still don't know what happened above our heads as we talked. There came a sickening series of thudding sounds as Broder fell and broke his body on the cross girders of the tripod mast. He didn't cry out. There were only the heavy thumping sounds, followed by the final crushing impact of his body on the BatTwo deck.

There was a Board of Inquiry, of course. There were questions about why a signal striker was aloft, in whites, on the mainmast, in the middle of the night. There were questions, too, about what a veteran chief and a first class petty officer were doing in BatTwo at the time. There were also questions about why the officer of the deck was not informed that a man was going aloft so the radio transmitters could be turned off. That was a Navy requirement.

But not one thing was said about the fact that every officer and watchkeeper on the quarterdeck that morning knew the God-damned flag was upside down. They could not see the stars, but they saw that the length of empty halyard which was supposed to be at the bottom of the flag was at the top instead. That made the flag fly a foot or so below the top of the mast.

A guy named Eddie Williams, quartermaster of the watch that morning, told me that. They all knew the God-damned flag was upside down — and they pretended not to see. Now that was really look-see pidgin for you.

Not long after the Board of Inquiry, the chief was transferred out of the ship. So was I. I don't know if the admiral's flag was ever turned right side up or not. It was just look-see pidgin anyway. But Broder was still dead.

DRINKS ON
THE LEGION

M ost people have read and heard a lot of nonsense about how sailors come to love their ships, but I remember only once meeting a man of whom that might truthfully be said. And he was a special case whose sentimentality sprang more from the idea of ships than from any particular ship.

Ships, after all, are nothing more than steel and wood, shaped to float upon and move through water with as little resistance as possible. Anything like personality or lovability is problematical. I've heard far more sailors cuss their ships for cranky, hard-to-manage rust-buckets than ever expressed words of endearment for them.

It was a saying among old white hats that there are only two good ships in the whole God-damned Navy — the one you just left, and your next one. The one you are in at the moment has all the warts and wrinkles of an old whore.

Nevertheless, I met this one guy who professed love for his old ship. He was forty-five or fifty years old at the time, and the ship he remembered so fondly was one of the old four-pipe destroyers which operated out of Queenstown, Ireland, during the Great War. He had not seen the damned thing since, but had it in his head that the old can was the most beautiful thing in the world. To anyone who ever saw the old four-pipers, that statement alone is enough to cast doubt on the old guy's sense of beauty.

Few events on the beach had noticeable effect upon white hats, isolated as they were behind the steel walls of their ships and the chain link fences of their stations and dockyards. But there was one shoreside event in 1937 which interested the hell out of Navy sailors in Long Beach.

The American Legion held its convention in Long Beach. The Legion was a significant social and political force in America. Politicians reckoned with it in running for office. Police departments *had* to reckon with it when its conventions came to their towns.

The Legion's 1937 convention figured to be especially lively, marking as it did the twentieth anniversary of America's entry into World War I. For the most part Legion members were still young enough to raise hell but old enough to recognize the first signs of the inevitable slowing down. Opportunities for making damned fools of themselves had best be seized.

The tradition was to hurl bottles, glasses, water-filled balloons, ice buckets and, sometimes pieces of room furniture out hotel room windows — not always with the windows open — to shatter among cringing pedestrians in the streets below. Managers of bars and banquet rooms resigned themselves to the burdens of life and hoped that what the conventioneers spent would match the bills for damages.

The significance of all this for Navy sailors was that the war was twenty years gone, long enough for the veterans who fought in it to become sentimental about the brotherhood of arms. If they became sentimental enough, they forced free drinks upon men still in the services. At least, that was the reading I got from my new shipmates when I first reported aboard as a signalman on a heavy cruiser.

Long Beach was then home port for the Navy's battleships and heavy cruisers. The big carriers *Lexington* and *Saratoga* were often there, as well, sometimes rolling their boat booms under in the long Pacific swells outside the breakwaters. As in all things Naval, ships moored in strict order of rank, with the higher ranks closest to shore. Since my ship was Flag for a three-star admiral, we moored close ashore indeed. Inside the inner breakwater, in fact, a scant three-minute motor launch ride from the Big Pico Street Landing. Sailors from ships of lesser status had a sometimes wet and miserable open boat voyage of twenty or thirty minutes between their ship and the shore. In heavy fogs or roaring Santa Ana winds, it took even longer. Rank indeed hath its privileges, even for white hats who sometimes bask in the warmth of blessings meant for their betters.

Painted in the Navy's almost-white peacetime horizon-gray, the ships were a mysterious presence whose deadly power was not obvious at all. From time to time, they slipped silently away, leaving the harbor strangely empty until, one day, they equally silently returned to lie again at rest from the sea. In port, they were an impressive floating city of several thousand men upon whom the good people of Long Beach and San Pedro preyed, to their considerable profit

I didn't even know there was a Legion convention in Long Beach when I reported aboard. When I learned there was, I could not see how the fact made any difference in my life. But, as things turned out, it changed my way of looking at the Navy.

I had reported aboard only that morning. By the time I checked in with the master-at-arms and had my bunk and locker assignment, it was time for dinner. It was at this noon meal that I learned about the Legion convention. This was before the War and sailors, even white hats, still ate like human beings.

We sat at tables and our food was brought to us in Division messes. We ate at the same tables and with the same guys every day. The senior petty officer of each mess kept things on track. It varied by mess, of course, but most of those old petty officers kept a pretty tight lid on dirty talk and rough behavior. The feeling in Division messes was much like that of a family eating together.

The signalmen's mess in my new ship was at the forward end of Number Two mess hall, on the port side. It was in a nook alongside the after furnace uptakes and, thus, set apart from the common herd. We had two tables, each seating eight to ten guys, on benches whose foldable wrought iron legs wobbled precariously in any kind of seaway. We had portholes, too, which were left open in good weather to let in both fresh air and light.

A mess cook from a deck division served us. Mess cooks were not cooks at all, but more like waiters who collected our food from the galley and brought it in nested tureens from which we helped ourselves, a system as old as Navies themselves.

Division Messes were managed by the senior petty officer of the mess. In our case it was a first class named Rogers, a guy with almost twenty years in the Navy — and a well-defined idea of what was and was not proper in the way of language and behavior. Being eager to prove our saltiness, we younger guys were sometimes a trial to Rogers.

We had about sixteen guys in the Signal gang, eight to a table. Flagships were assigned extra signalmen and radiomen to handle the additional communications traffic they generated, but all our ships were undermanned in those days. Most of us were young first-cruise — less than four years — guys, still trying to impress those with longer service.

In any group of men, there is always at least one loud mouth who wields an authority justified by little more than the noise he makes. Our loud mouth was Sam Manes — he pronounced it *Man-ness* — a second class in the first section of the port watch.

Manes already was running a bit to fat, but he remained a strong and willing brawler, another source of his influence in the mess, I suspect. It was Manes who brought up the Legion Convention. "There's no reason in the world why any white hat in Long Beach is going to have a pay for a drink while the Legion's in town," he said past a mouthful of something. Rogers didn't like for us to talk with our mouths full, but he seldom made much fuss about it.

Navy sailors were not paid much in those days. Any mention of free drinks attracted attention.

Even Rogers unbent enough to stop chewing and look questions at him.

"I happened to be home on leave one time," Manes went on, "when the Legion had its convention there. They damned near tore up the town. The cops wouldn't touch them, and they cut one fat hog in the ass for four or five days, I'm telling you."

"What's that got to do with our not paying for drinks?" Rogers growled. Rogers did not talk much in the mess. He took his responsibility seriously. When he did say something, he was apt to be pretty grim about it.

"You guys may not believe it," Manes said. "But some guys had a good time in the Service during the war." Manes grinned. "They didn't know it at the time, maybe, but they get a few years on the outside, and they remember the good stuff. Man, how they remember. And they remember it most of all when they get together and get to drinking. Then, they —"

"I *said*, 'What's that got to do with our not paying for drinks?'" Rogers said again. Rogers was not a man long on patience.

Manes grinned, enjoying being at the center of attention. "This time I remember, I was on leave. In Kansas City, it was, I'm from Kansas City," Manes explained to me. I was new in the ship and didn't yet know the guys' hometowns. "Anyway, I was home on leave," Manes said, "and I was —"

"Get on with it, Manes," Rogers butted in. "What about the drinks, for Christ's sake?" Ordinarily Rogers would not permit any of us to take the Lord's name in vain that way, but Manes provoked him. Manes did it on purpose, too, I think. Manes and Rogers had a thing going between them.

"Hell, a guy couldn't walk down the street in Kansas City without them Legion guys grabbing him by the arm and pushing booze on him. Not if he was wearing blues, he couldn't.

"That was before Repeal," Manes went on, "Everything they had was bootleg. But it was damned good bootleg. Scotch and bottled-in-bond bourbon and rum. Hell, you name it, and those guys had it. And, like I said a minute ago, the cops wouldn't touch them. Man, that was hog heaven for a white hat, and I figure this time here in Long Beach is going to be even bigger and better."

Rogers didn't say anything. But the rest of the guys did.

"Hell, you mean those old Legion guys will buy drinks for us?" one of our young guys said wonderingly.

"And not just booze," Manes went on. "That time in Kansas City, I hooked up with a bunch of old Army guys that had a room full of broads. Women come from all over the country for these Legion conventions you know. And most of them good enough for officer gear. Anyway, this old sergeant that was there took me in that room and said: 'There you are, sailor. Pick one. We got an empty room down the hall for military operations. You pick out one and take her down there'.

"Man, I never tied into anything like the redhead who grabbed my hand and pulled me into that empty room. That old gal . . ."

"That's enough, Manes," Rogers said, but his heart wasn't in it. He was an old guy, but he was as caught up in Manes' story as any of us.

"Manes is right," Henry Stinson, our other second class on the bridge, said then. "I was in Columbus one time when the Legion came to town. I never wore blues when I was home on leave before, but that time I sure as hell did. Manes is right. You couldn't buy a drink but I never saw any women."

"Yeah, I was in New York one time when the Legion was there," Neal Oliver, a third class, said. "It was the same damned thing. Most guys in the Legion was in the Army. They didn't seem to think much of soldiers, but they sure laid it on for white hats. They kept saying it was the Navy that got them overseas and back in one piece."

"Either way, it's free booze," Manes whooped. "I don't know about the rest of you guys, but, come Liberty Call, nobody's going to see my ass for the steam."

Watchstanders' liberty started at one in the afternoon. The common herd had to wait until four-thirty or five. Watchstanders were guys who stood night watches. They were given a number of minor privileges, one of which was early liberty. Sometimes it seemed the whole Navy wasn't much more than a stack of petty privileges like that. Anyway, as a signalman, I qualified.

There's nothing like a washroom in a Navy ship when white hats get ready to go ashore. With shoreside water ready to hand there are no limits on showers or hot water. The washrooms then had white tiled decks. Sometimes those decks ran ankle deep in soapy water, and mirrors over the shaving basins got all foggy. Everybody was laughing and yelling and snapping asses with their towels. According to old Navy lore, it sometimes got so crowded you had to scrub three asses before you could be sure you scrubbed your own.

Unless a guy was shacked up or married — and almost none of us was married — getting ready for a liberty had some of the atmosphere of preparing for a hunt. Guys went ashore all shaved and pressed and shining, not just because the officer of the deck wouldn't let them off the ship any other way, but because that was the way you got women. The stink of shaving lotion, hair tonic and talcum powder sometimes got pretty strong in the washroom.

One of the big advantages of watchstanders' liberty, of course, was we got to use the washrooms before they got *really* crowded and steamed up. Another advantage was that we got ashore before the peons swamped the bars and spoiled the women with their numbers. Watchstanders' liberty was nice that way.

But some guys, even watchstanders, waited until eight or nine o'clock at night to go ashore. That way they ate on the ship and didn't spend money in restaurants. Another big advantage was that the guys who went over early had the women all liquored up and the latecomers moved in with a

much smaller investment of time and money. It was all a matter
of strategy.

My lashed seabag and hammock, with my wash bucket
dangling at one end, lay unopened upon my new bunk. I had
a lot of squaring away to do. But I had been long enough in the
Navy to know it is a good idea to go along with your new
shipmates. The sooner you fit in with the gang, the better. So,
when the guys asked me to come ashore, I went along. I guess
all the talk about the Legion convention had me as steamed up
as anybody else. Anyway, the first liberty boat was full.

The first Legionnaires we saw were at the Pico Street
Landing itself. There were only a half dozen or so. They stood
self-consciously watching the busy coming and going of shore
boats with their dinging of bells and growling of motors. Don't
ask me why, but boat coxswains gave their engine orders by
bells in those days. The engine guy sat not five feet away from
the coxswain, but the engine orders were given by bells. The
coxswain held a little line in his hand and used that to ring the
bell. It was the Navy way.

The result was a merry clinking and clanking and
dinging of bells and gunning of engines as shore boats came and
went and landing officers shouted out orders to keep at least
some kind of control. The old Legionnaires watched it all with
expressions of wonder.

Most of them were in their forties, but already their
jawlines blurred behind sagging flesh, and their waists bulged
with more fat than was pretty under cheap and poorly fitted
suits. Their manner marked them as strangers to the waterfront
and their little overseas caps — blue with embroidered lettering
and dangling with medals and badges of all kinds — marked
them as Legionnaires.

Manes, who came ashore with us and assumed command
of our little raiding party, hurried us past the old guys at the
landing. "We ain't going to get anything from these guys," he
explained impatiently. "They're not drunk. We've got to get
them up closer to the hotels. After they've started drinking."

The numbers of Legionnaires increased as we came
closer to the big hotels along Ocean Avenue. Even though it

was only midafternoon, a lot of them already showed signs of drinking. They were noisier, for one thing, and they took notice of us in our liberty blues. Some of them waved opened bottles.

"Okay," Manes said importantly. "Split up into twos and threes. Nobody ain't going to buy drinks for a big bunch of us like this. Spread out."

Things went pretty much as Manes said. Almost at once, I found myself split off alone. I was new in the ship and the guys went along with the shipmates they already knew, I guess. That was all right with me. I still was not comfortable with the thought that we came ashore deliberately to cadge drinks from drunks. I didn't have much money, but I wasn't so low that I couldn't buy my own God-damned drinks. I figured to hang around for a while then catch a movie, or just go back to the ship and get my gear squared away. I didn't really mean to come ashore in the first place.

But before I could turn away, I found myself caught up in a band of fifteen or twenty ex-soldiers from a Legion Post somewhere in Oklahoma. They grabbed me by my arms and before I knew it, I was hustled into a ground floor hotel bar. They were all laughing and yelling and acting like a bunch of preachers' kids away from home. All, that is, except for one old guy — he looked older than the others anyway — who held back and smiled quietly at his buddies' antics.

He was tall, but so thin his clothes hung from his shoulders with little more shape than they would from a wire clothes hanger. His Legionnaire's cap made his head seem even more skull-like than it was. The skin of his face in the bright California sunshine was left looking empty by the flesh melted away from under it. But no more empty than his eyes which lurked, shadowed and dark under sagging lids.

He caught me looking at him and smiled. The effect was ludicrous in such wreckage of a face. Once inside the hotel bar, though, he seemed less cadaverous. At least fewer of the awful details were seen.

"What's your name, Sailor?" a big, noisy man in a poorly fitted suit and black and white shoes called out to me. Before

I could answer, he introduced himself. "Charley Blackwood here. Headquarters Company, Second Battalion and Combat Train, One Hundred and Sixtieth Field Artillery, Forty-Fifth Division, Oklahoma National Guard. We're all from the same outfit. Went overseas together. Come back together. Now, we're in California together and we got whiskey we ain't drunk yet."

The others cheered this rather long introduction, each — or most of them, anyway — holding up his own individual bottle and pressing it on me.

"What'd you say your name was?" the big man in black and white shoes said. When I told him, he took a deep pull at his own bottle and thrust it at me. "We'll drink to that," he called. "Won't we, buddies? We'll drink to the United States Navy that took us over and brought us back. And to hell with the Kaiser both ways."

I tipped one of the offered bottles to my lips, but didn't drink much. I let most of it run back into the bottle. "Thanks, Buddy," I grinned. "That's good stuff."

"Well, there's more where it come from," the big man in black and white shoes whooped. "And don't you forget it. Okay, Sailor?" All the others pressed their own bottles on me, laughing and crying out for me to drink.

Nineteen-thirty-seven was four years after Repeal. There were lots of bars in Long Beach. There are lots of bars in all Navy towns. But the Legionnaires all seemed to have their own bottles. The Depression was not long past. Buying bottles from liquor stores was cheaper than buying bar drinks, I guess.

I fended off the bottles as best I could. I let down the Navy side, I'm afraid, by not drinking as much as white hats are supposed to. But I did put the bottles to my lips and pretend to drink until the Legionnaires passed on to more cooperative sailors.

In twos and threes, other sailors found their way into bars. A lot of them wound up in the same bar I was in. It was not long until the crowd was almost equally white hats and Legionnaires. Other customers, lowly civilians and the like, prudently drifted away and left the field to us. The noise became impressive, and the evening was but hardly begun.

As I edged my way towards the door, I again saw the old skinny guy. He smiled at me once more, but, the effect was not so bad as it was outside in the sun. He was old enough to be my father, and the way he smiled was much as a father might smile to his son. Since I never knew my father, I had to guess at that. Anyway, it was a nice smile, considering what he had to work with.

There was one characteristic of Long Beach bars then that I never saw anywhere else. They were dark. Even in the daytime. Oddly, the more expensive they were, the darker. The hotel bar I found myself in that day was dark indeed — and expensive as hell.

"Too much for you, sailor?" the skinny Legionnaire smiled.

I grinned back. "Yeah. Yeah, I guess it is." I paused. "Jesus, you guys drink like that all the time?"

"Some of us don't drink like that at any time," the Legionaire smiled. "How about a cup of coffee? Somewhere it's not so noisy."

"Coffee shop just across the lobby. Or there's a drug store down at the corner. Dealer's choice."

The old guy swayed. I thought he was going to fall right there in front of me. "You all right?" I said.

"Yes. Yes, I am all right. But maybe — maybe we better take the coffee shop. Whatever's closer."

As it happened, he did not even make it that far. "Do you mind if we rest here for a minute?" he said when no more than half way across the lobby.

We sat on a long leather sofa. The old Legionnaire breathed heavily, but smiled apologetically. "Sorry. I don't get around so well anymore."

"It's okay," I said. "We're not going anywhere."

"I am Homer Owens," he said after a moment. "From Tulsa. Do you know Tulsa?"

"No," I said. "I'm from the East Coast. I come around through the Canal. I never been in the middle of the country."

"I teach there," Owens said. "History. In the college there." That is the way he talked. In little bursts without much energy. I guess he had trouble breathing.

"What kind of history?" I said. I had to say something.

"Modern, mostly. Since 1914."

"The War?"

"Yes. Yes, the War," he said.

"Were you in the War?" I asked him.

"Yes. In the Navy, as a matter of fact. In a destroyer out of Queenstown."

I had heard of Queenstown from some of the old white hats I knew who stayed in the Navy after the War. It was an Irish port which served as a base for our ships during what we called The Great War. Our Navy did not play a very big part in that war. The worst enemy it faced was the North Atlantic weather, rather than the Germans; but, for men in the old four-piper destroyers, that was enemy enough.

"Must have been rough," I said.

"Yes. Yes, it was."

Neither of us said anything for a time. I began to wonder why Owens invited me to have a coffee with him. If he was queer, I figured I didn't have much to worry about. I could fight him off pretty easy.

He seemed to have withdrawn within himself and to be thinking of something else entirely. The silence was a little heavy.

"Did you like the Navy?" I asked then.

"Yes," Owens said. He said it almost as though he were surprised. "Yes. I liked it very much. I had never seen the ocean before. I don't know why I went with the Navy in the first place. Everyone else I knew chose the Army. Or was drafted."

"You volunteered?"

"Yes. I was very young then." He smiled again in an almost bashful way. "I didn't know any better."

I smiled in return. We really hadn't said much, but I began to feel a warmth toward the old guy. "But you didn't stay in after the War? Some guys did."

"No." His face sobered then and he became pensive. "No. I was married. My wife did not . . . did not understand. Then we had children." He pulled out his wallet and showed me a picture of a pinch-faced woman and three children.

"Nice," I said.

"I finished school and got into teaching. My father-in-law subsidized me, to tell the truth. Teaching does not pay all that well."

"Did you like teaching?"

"Not really. I liked the research and the reading and all. Most students have little interest in history. It is humiliating sometimes. History really is important, but —"

"Then why did you stay with it?"

The old guy smiled pensively. "My wife liked being a professor's wife, I guess. My father-in-law thought it was a socially acceptable job. Until I got sick, I . . ."

"You're sick?"

"You didn't notice?" The old guy smiled wryly at me.

"You look like you've lost a little weight," I said.

He croaked a kind of laugh. "I am assured I will not lose much more," he said. "I am assured I will not do much of *anything* for very long now."

I did not know how to answer that. The old guy's voice held so little hope, and such an air of lost loneliness clung to him that I wanted to change the subject. "How about the Legion?" I said. "You been in the Legion long?"

"A couple of months," the old guy said. "I didn't join until I learned the convention was going to be in Long Beach this year. I knew Long Beach was a Navy town. I wanted to see the ships again." He paused and looked down as though not wanting me to see his eyes. "I wanted to — to see the ships again."

I did not know what to say to that. If he wanted to talk — and I got the impression that he very much wanted to talk — he could damned well talk. And, after a while he did.

"Of all man's follies," he began, "probably the most futile, and the hardest to resist, is the urge to recover times which are gone. And no pain more sore than the necessary facing of the inevitable return to reality."

I never knew any college professors, but I always figured that would be kind of the way they would talk.

"Is that why you joined the Legion?" I said. "To recover times which are gone?"

The old guy smiled weakly. "Maybe. That is not why the Legion was formed, of course," he said. "The Legion was formed to get bigger pensions and more money for Veterans' hospitals." He paused. "But I am not sure it is not why so many of us join. And why so many of us . . ."

Again, he paused and looked down at his bony hands. "There is so little there, you know . . . In Oklahoma and all through America, I suspect. We have our little jobs — if we are lucky enough to have a job. We have wives and children and houses and debts. But it is all for *us*. For us as individuals. I don't know a person in the world I would do the things for that I would have done without a backward glance for any one of my old shipmates.

"Does that make sense? Does any of that make any sense at all?"

I never had a wife or children or a job. I had not even had any debts, for Christ's sake. A lot of white hats had not had any of that. There were no terms of reference, but I did not want to disappoint the old guy. "Sure," I said. "Sure it does."

He smiled at me then, with a blending of gratitude and disbelief. "It was different in the ships. In the ships, everything was for the ship. Somehow, we all accepted that. No matter the cost. Everything was for the ship.

"I was always impressed by the changing of the watch. Men on watch left their stations without a backward glance. They went to their bunks in a kind of sublime trust in those who were taking over. They slept soundly, with never a care that the new watch might not prove — prove trustworthy. I always thought that was remarkable."

It was eerie, but I often thought the very same thing. I looked at the sick old man with a fresh respect. But he, as though embarrassed at revealing something personal, laughed shortly. "Now you know how you will talk when you get old."

"Well," I said, glad to be off the subject. "What do you want to do now? There's a parade tomorrow, I understand. And there's going to be a searchlight display tonight. All the ships are holding open house for you guys. You want to come aboard my ship?"

"What is it?"

"Heavy cruiser."

The old guy was not buying. "Are there any destroyers here?" he said. "Any four-pipers?"

"No. They're all in San Diego. They got hundreds of four-pipers laid up down there."

Disappointment showed plain in his thin face. "That was all I wanted to do," he said. "That's the only reason I came out here. I thought there would be destroyers here."

"Well, hell," I said. "There's no reason you can't see one. You might even find your old ship down there. Dago's only a hundred miles or so down the road. A bus'll get you there in three or four hours."

"I have no money," the old guy said bleakly. "I sold my car for money to get this far. The hotel gave us a special rate, and I have a return train ticket or I would not be able to get home. My father-in-law did not think this trip a worthy subject for his charity."

White hats are not much known for good sense. I looked at the old guy sitting there, and I said something that surprised the hell out of me. "I got money," I said. "I got enough for that anyway. Twenty dollars ought to do it. Easy."

Hope lighted the old guy's dimming eyes, and he sat almost erect. But it did not last. "I cannot take your money," he said. "I know how much you are paid. You do not owe me anything. I . . ."

"You said a while ago what you would do for a shipmate," I said. "Let's just say I'm a shipmate. Okay?" By that time I realized it was not *a* ship the old man loved — it was the idea of ships. It was what he said about changing the watch. He spent only a few months in ships, out of what were many years of sterile life, far from the sights and sounds of the sea and its ships, but it was the ships he remembered and longed to see again.

It must have galled him to think of taking money from a stranger, but he was not strong enough to resist this final chance to see his remembered ships. "I will pay you back," he said. "Give me your name and address, and I will see you get your money back. And God's blessing as well."

I don't know about God's blessing. All I know is I never got my money back. I don't even know if the old guy lived long enough to get home. I just hope he lived long enough to see his old ships. He deserved that.

Anyway, I had a dollar or two left after giving the old guy his twenty. I spent them in a sailor bar not far from the Landing. I grinned to myself. So much for Manes and his God-damned free drinks from the Legion.

ABOUT
THE AUTHOR

Born in Oklahoma, Floyd Beaver grew up in the oil and Indian country of that state, far removed from the winds and the salt air he evokes in his stories of the U.S. Navy.

He enlisted in the United States Navy in 1938 and served throughout World War II on heavy cruisers, aircraft carriers, amphibious ships and British antisubmarine vessels. He left the Navy at the end of the war as a chief petty officer to complete his studies at the University of Tulsa.

After a brief stint on that school's economics faculty, he came to the San Francisco Bay Area. He worked in retail advertising and lived with his family in Marin County within walking distance of the sailboats he kept in Sausalito.

Of his published short stories, most are Westerns, drawn from his early life in Oklahoma's ranch and Indian country.

His later work was concerned more with the sea and the ships and men he had come to know there. It is this vicarious connection with a life now long gone which proved most therapeutic in making the frustrations of corporate life bearable.

His stories have been adapted for network radio and television.

He now lives in Mill Valley, California, and continues to sail his small black sailboat out of Sausalito's Clipper Yacht Harbor.